Exile and Pilgrim

Graeme K. Talboys was born in Ham[...] between teaching in schools and museum[...] published eight works of non-fiction (on museum edu[...] tion, drama, and matters spiritual). He has also writte[...] more than a dozen novels. The first (written when he was seventeen) was lost on a train. The next two (written in his early twenties) he wishes had been. Thankfully, he's had considerably more success with writing since then. His previous jobs have included stacking shelves, pot boy and sandwich maker, and sweeping factory floors. As an adult his first job was teaching Drama and English. Some of his pupils still speak to him. You can follow him on Twitter @graemeKtalboys and visit his website: www.graemektalboys.me.uk/

Also by Graeme K. Talboys

Shadow in the Storm
Stealing into Winter

Exile and Pilgrim

GRAEME K. TALBOYS

Book Two of Shadow in the Storm

HARPER
Voyager

Harper*Voyager*
An imprint of HarperCollins*Publishers* Ltd
1 London Bridge Street
London SE1 9GF

www.harpervoyagerbooks.co.uk

This Paperback Original 2016

First published in Great Britain in ebook format by Harper*Voyager* 2016

A catalogue record for this book
is available from the British Library

ISBN: 978-0-00-815379-3

Set in Sabon by Palimpsest Book Production Limited, Falkirk, Stirlingshire

Printed and bound in Great Britain

MIX
Paper from
responsible sources
FSC® C007454

For Ivan and Heather

PART ONE

Stone

Chapter One

A soft snap. She counted. One. Two. A dull squelch.

Hanging by her fingertips in the dark, the toe of one boot still just on the crumbling corbel, the other waving in space, she considered her options. Falling was not going to be one of them.

With care, she turned her face away from the wall and peered upward into the dark in an attempt to gauge how far she was from the corner of the tower. That was when it began to rain.

There were moments when she wondered if all the risks were worth taking. But she had the sense to indulge in such reflections over mulled wine in a warm room. Hanging off a sheer face of ancient stone in the cold and rain was more a place for doing something to ensure she would, later, be in a warm room with mulled wine.

As the rain grew heavier, icy in the night, she found a new foothold on an eroded carving and crabbed along to the narrow window. Which got narrower as she tried to climb through. And narrower.

Cenau once told her that this had originally been a temple, old even before the Evanescence. She had wondered what kind of world it was in which temples needed windows designed for firing arrows. Or maybe, she was beginning to realize, it had just been designed for deterring thieves.

Part way through the thin aperture she became stuck. With a sigh, she relaxed. At least she wasn't going to fall, would be able to sip wine and reflect on the folly of it all one more time. And, she thought, as she wriggled, cut down on the sweetmeats, especially those honeyed oatcakes.

Outside, the rain had become a deluge. It was soaking through her boots, cold air was chilling her legs, and being stuck was starting to get very uncomfortable. With a strenuous kick, a twist, and an agonizing roll of the hip bone over the lintel, she slid inside and fell head first in a heap on the floor.

Rain blew in after her, for which she was grateful. The puddle that was forming around her from water leaking out of her clothes wouldn't be noticed. All the same, she pulled off her boots and footwraps and slipped out of her coat, chafing her hands as she padded along the stone landing in bare feet.

By the time she had reached the next floor her hands were warm again, but it was wasted effort. In the glimmer of the candle she had risked lighting, she could see there was no way she would be able to pick the heavy locks.

It was frustrating. On one of the rare occasions she had no intention of stealing anything, unless you counted knowledge, the locks had defeated her. If there were answers to her question in the tower room, they'd have to stay there. For now.

All the same, she took some time to examine the door

4

and its frame, dancing on her toes to stop her feet from getting too cold. The hinges were hidden by a thick, carved stone surround. The locks were of a type she had not encountered before. The door itself was of ancient oak, studded with square-headed nails. With a sigh she blew out the candle and waited for her eyes to adjust.

'Are you going to get up, or can I have your breakfast?'

Jeniche pulled the blanket off her face and half opened one eye onto daylight. 'Mmm? What?'

'Breakfast.'

'Get out, Cenau.'

He grinned, closing the door before wandering off into the corridor.

'And stay away from my breakfast,' she called after him.

Despite the physical side of her work, and the occasional nocturnal climbing on her own account, she was getting soft. Her own room with glass in the window. A proper bed. A chest for her clothes. Books. Regular meals. Those soft, sweet, melt-in-the-mouth cakes. It was bliss. But there was barely a day went by when she didn't think fondly of her time in Makamba. The bit before all the trouble. The bit before the other daily memories. Of Wedol. Of Trag. Of Mowen Bey. Of all the ensuing deceit and the long, wandering exile.

She sorted out some clothes that hadn't been soaked the night before, dressed, passed through the latrines and wash house, and managed to slip into the refectory before Cenau gave in to temptation.

Her porridge was going cold but she spooned it in. It was one of the few things in this often cold, wet land she had taken to straight away. The rest had taken time, but it had begun to grow on her. Much as she had once feared mould and moss would.

The large room was almost deserted by the time she finished her food. Other late risers had bolted their breakfasts and carried their indigestion off to classes or work. Someone was scrubbing the floor by the long serving hatch. Two of the tutors, perhaps free of students, sat talking quietly over the remains of their meal. And weaving his way between the tables and benches was Cenau.

He arrived with a grin, a bowl, and their lunches wrapped in a cloth. The bowl was placed before Jeniche. 'Last of the porridge,' he said as he folded himself onto a bench opposite. Jeniche lifted an eyebrow and pushed the bowl across the table.

'You need it more than me.'

He didn't need telling twice. A spoon appeared and he tucked in. Jeniche sat patiently, her hands on the table in front of her. She looked at the scars she had gathered. Cenau, she observed, looked at them as well whilst he ate, seemingly fascinated by the thin strong fingers and the darkness of her flesh, wondering perhaps at the stories to which the scars were an enigmatic tabulation.

She turned her hands over. 'Can you read palms as well?' she asked, looking up and smiling.

Cenau blushed. 'Sorry,' he mumbled.

'Don't be. Study. That's what you do. Just remember it doesn't only apply to books. But also remember that people can see you studying them. Learn to see without being seen.'

She felt a fraud as soon as she'd said it. It was all too profound and made her sound as if she knew what she was talking about. Perhaps she did, if surviving counted as learning.

Cenau took her seriously. Which was also worrying. 'I've tried. I just end up looking even more obvious.'

'That's because studying is all you do.'

He looked at her with that baffled expression he often got when she talked with him. She had watched him with his tutors and he always seemed to understand them. But maybe that's because they were all part of the same world whereas she was an outsider. Maybe it was because she still didn't properly understand the language.

'You're like Cynfelyn,' he said. 'He says things like that. Makes you work.'

'You actually sound like you miss that.'

'What? The work?'

'Yes. And stop trying to change the subject.'

He grinned. 'Exactly like Cynfelyn.'

'Come on,' she said, getting up from the table. 'You can explain what I meant on the way up to the ring.'

Cenau untangled his legs from his robe, grabbed up the bag of food, and followed Jeniche out into the open. A faint dampness hung in the air after the night's rain, but the sky was clearing and promised sunshine.

The university on the island of Pengaver was unique in her experience. She had travelled widely since running from the Land of Winter and come across many places of learning where she had found respite from her wandering. In no other had they offered such a breadth of education as here in the very heart of the land of Ynysvron. The Derw, the intellectual caste of the Ynyswr people, offered book study enough to satisfy any scholar, but here in the extensive complex they also trained diplomats and rulers, doctors and surgeons, lawyers and advisers, smiths and joiners, weavers and artists, farmers and warriors.

They crossed the formal gardens of the main concourse and followed the path on between two of the older buildings. Most days they would go in the opposite direction, alongside the classrooms and across the grassed area into the Library. Today Cenau dragged along as they made their way uphill, through the trees, and along to the stables.

Jeniche loved it there, for all the sadness it evoked. The horses here were different from the steeds of Makamba. In the distant south they had been sleek, proud, and inclined to skittishness. These, whether they were the sturdy riding ponies or the great work horses, seemed stolid and gentle – although you still stayed well clear of the draft horses' feet if you wanted to keep walking on your own.

Beyond the stables and the exercise yards, the farriers' workshops and the saddlers', the broad path forked at a vast yew tree. Their path was to the left. Had they gone right, they would have climbed all the way to the top of the tor where the great round stone watchtower stood with its view of the whole of the Isle of Pengaver; Tirmawr, the mainland, in one direction and the Eastern Sea in the other.

Also up there was the enclave of the Sisterhood of Nine, an elite band of women warriors, smiths, and healers. Jeniche had never met any of them, seen only two from afar. She was, however, well aware of their fearsome reputation.

Out of reverence, Cenau sprinkled water on the ground by the roots of the yew from the barrel kept there for the purpose. Out of politeness, Jeniche did the same. These people had shown her great kindness.

When they continued, Cenau said, 'I still don't understand.'

Jeniche thought for a moment. 'Fidchell.' It was a game the Ynyswr played almost obsessively. 'Does learning the rules make you a good player?'

'No. Playing makes you a good player.'

'Same with people. You can read the rules, but you need to play, become involved. If you sit outside the action and watch, even if you pretend not to watch, everyone else will know.'

Cenau pulled a face. He wasn't very good at taking part unless it was study. He was only here now with Jeniche because his tutor, Cynfelyn, had sent instructions via Rhonwen, the Senior Librarian, that he learn certain skills. And even though he would do anything that Cynfelyn asked, Cenau still wasn't happy.

The ring was just that. A large circular clearing in the forest, covered in sawdust and wood chippings and surrounded by a grassy bank through which eight entrances led. It was a pleasant place in some ways. Warm, green, sheltered from the wind that often blew across the island. The only thing that spoiled it as far as Cenau was concerned was that it was invariably filled with people hitting each other.

They stood on the top of the bank a moment, watching a small group in padded jackets as they laid into each other with ash sticks. Jeniche looked at Cenau, who seemed confused by it all. She saw beyond the mayhem, however, and could appreciate the training that had gone into the moves, the swordplay, the quick thinking, and the teamwork.

Cenau groaned. 'I didn't think Aros was meant to be up here this morning.'

Jeniche watched the tall, muscular young man in the midst of the melee for a moment. He seemed to be here all the time now. She shrugged. 'Never mind Aros. Over to the small ring.'

At the far end of the ring, beyond the grass bank, was a

small close-cropped grassy area in front of a row of huts and a communal sweat-house. Cenau stripped off his outer robe and folded it neatly, placing it on a bench in front of one of the shelters. Jeniche took off her jacket and threw it on the ground out of the way, kicked off her boots, and unwound her footwraps.

'I don't know why I'm bothering,' said Cenau.

Barefoot, in trousers and tunic, thin, pale, and nervous, he looked like he had risen from his sickbed without having fully recovered from a long illness.

'It's a new day. Remember what we did last time. Slowly. Show me the move.'

She closed in on him as if wielding a knife. He changed position several times in quick succession as if he couldn't decide then reached out and grabbed the sleeve of Jeniche's tunic. It was partly right, but he had his feet the wrong way round, lost his balance and went over on his face.

Jeniche helped him up. 'Again. Put your feet the other way round. That's right. You're balanced now. Watch the direction of my attack. No. No. Other hand, that's it. Now use my momentum against me.'

Cenau caught her sleeve again, pulled, and Jeniche was the one to fall.

'That's better,' she said, brushing at her cropped hair to dislodge a twig.

They practised through the morning. More often than not, Cenau would end up on the ground in a tangle of limbs. Jeniche had learned at the outset that he hated physical conflict but was determined he would master these defensive moves, if only so he could stand up to Aros. The trouble was, the more tired he became, the more easily he lost his temper, the more easily he went down.

10

'Playing mud pies?'

Cenau looked up from where he lay; Jeniche turned. From the top of the bank, where Aros and the others stood, came a roar of laughter. Cenau climbed to his feet and shuffled across to the bench where his robe lay.

If Jeniche knew one thing it was that a true warrior should not mock a non-combatant. Such behaviour reduces them to the status of bully. And whilst she had never met any of the Sisterhood, she had learned enough about Ynyswr culture and the value they placed on hospitality and courtesy to realize these trainee warriors would have been taught this. It was clear they needed teaching it again.

'Is that how an Ynyswr warrior treats one of their own?' she asked in a quiet, steady voice.

Their laughter died. Aros stepped to the fore.

'Is it the place of an outsider to question—?'

'Aros!' It was Cenau who had interposed to everyone's surprise, including his own. 'Outsider? Jeniche is an honoured guest.'

Aros looked uncomfortable. Jeniche didn't know him well, but he had never shown any antagonism toward her, had never displayed any kind of bigotry. He was just normally a boisterous young man who was a bit insensitive to the effect he had on others, especially Cenau.

'I will not argue with you, Cenau,' he said formally.

'Just make fun of him when he tries something new,' said Jeniche. It was her turn to be surprised. She was not normally so reckless. And Cenau and Aros had a complicated relationship in which she really had no business becoming involved.

'Sometimes,' said Aros, 'you have to push.'

'Push a warrior, then,' replied Jeniche.

Aros shrugged and led his companions down the bank, all swagger and bonhomie, making for the hut where their clothes were. They were all big, even the three women warriors. Well-muscled, confident, just a little too full of themselves even though they had never seen real combat. Jeniche smiled. A small smile. And stood her ground.

The young warriors went brushing past her, just close enough to test her balance. At first they didn't even understand what was happening to them. Jeniche felled the first with a simple kick to the side of his leg, turned into the path of the next and threw him to his back where he lay winded. The third was flying through the air before the remaining three gathered their wits, but in turning on Jeniche they got in each other's way. Jeniche brought two heads together and suddenly Aros found himself alone facing Jeniche who now had an ash pole of her own in her hands.

'"You're tired. It wouldn't be a fair fight."' Cenau said it for the fourth time. And cackled again. He had watched bug-eyed from his bench as Jeniche had felled the warriors and then sent Aros on his way. He'd never seen anything like it. She had been teaching him the moves, but there had never been an occasion for her to demonstrate just how good she was in combat. Her years travelling through Tundur, the Black Land of Gyanag, and beyond had produced more than scars.

'Don't mention it to anyone.'

'What? Why?'

'How do you feel when Aros—' Cenau lifted his hand to signal he understood, but Jeniche thought the point should be spelled out. 'You might feel he deserves it, but that's not how you resolve a situation like this.'

12

'It was good, though.'

Jeniche grinned.

They were sitting beneath a tree eating their lunch. Cenau fished in the small pouch attached to his robe. He handed something to Jeniche. She took it and held it up to examine it. It was a thong of leather tied in a loop from which hung two keys.

'Keys.'

'Copies. So much easier to get into the tower room if you've got them.'

It was Jeniche's turn to sit bug-eyed.

Chapter Two

Aros obviously wasn't going to be taken by surprise this time. He was rested. Fed. Wearing his battle leathers rather than a padded practice jacket. And the ash pole had been swapped for a proper wooden sword. Jeniche wasn't impressed. She wore her usual light tunic and trousers, her feet in the soft boots she had 'won' several years before in Azak, her own ash sword cut to a length she found comfortable. It was two-thirds the length of the weapon wielded by Aros. But then, she was two-thirds the size of her opponent.

Several of the others had tried to talk them out of it, but Aros was determined to face Jeniche in what he had called a 'fair' fight. She had pointed out to him you don't get that on the battlefield. And the others were worried what the Sisterhood would say if they found out. They did not like interference in what they considered to be their domain.

Jeniche and Aros had listened. And ignored. Now they circled each other with slow steps on the small ring before the huts, an audience watching from the benches. Aros had been taught well, Jeniche conceded, but he had the same problem as Cenau. The scholar knew only his books and his theories. The warrior knew only his lessons and his games with his compatriots.

Aros attacked first, charging with a roar perhaps intended to intimidate. Jeniche let him bear down on her, stepped out of the way, and smacked his backside with the flat of her sword as he passed. He changed direction in an instant with impressive agility and Jeniche parried several powerful blows.

Had she tried to block them, she would probably have sprained both wrists and the fight would have been over. But Alltud had taught her well. Instilled the habit of daily practice that strengthened the muscles needed to wield a blade. And she had learned a great deal more in the years since, especially in Gyanag, where they had made an art of combat, of using your opponent's strength to your advantage.

Deflecting the blows to one side or another, she danced and twisted just inside his guard, always threatening, but never quite able to land a decisive blow. He might be an ox with muscles for brains, but Aros had stamina and Jeniche, for the second time in as many days, had to admit she was getting soft.

A fight had to be quick, especially in battle. You had to maim or kill and move on, keep going and beat your enemy before you tired. She couldn't quite beat Aros who was a lot better than she had given him credit for. She was getting tired. But she still had one advantage. She had done this for real and she knew you had to fight dirty.

Seeing she was tired, or maybe just sensing it, Aros found a second wind. He powered toward her. A heavy blow glanced off her upper arm as she rolled with it, numbing her hand. She let the practice sword drop to the ground and began to fall. She didn't hear Aros gasp with triumph any more than she heard the dismay from the others. Her only concern was to complete the roll and come up onto her feet with the sword in her left hand. Aros wasn't even looking at her when she rammed the end of it into his left kidney.

'Never take your eye off a living opponent,' she said to his surprised face as he swung round, 'otherwise they'll be wiping your giblets off their blade.'

He looked down at the sword in her left hand and then at her smile. 'Left-handed as well?'

'Just enough to stick it accurately into something vital.'

There was anger in his face. He wasn't used to being bested. Jeniche decided it was good for him. And she had been careful to ensure there was an audience.

They crowded round now, clapping them both on the back, asking questions, re-enacting moves. Through it, Jeniche and Aros watched each other warily. She could see his thoughts in his face, a succession of frowns interspersed with tiny moments of enlightenment. It gave her hope and she relaxed.

When the chatter first died, Jeniche thought nothing of it. She moved off to fetch her jacket as she was getting chilled after all the exertion. It was only when she turned to make a formal exit that she noticed the others standing back and an older woman in battle leathers walking slowly down the slope of the grassy bank.

Jeniche realized straight away that this was one of the Sisterhood. These nine female warriors lived in an enclave at the far end of the Isle of Pengaver. They were part of the Derw, the intellectual caste of the people of Ynysvron.

Royalty sent their children to the Derw to learn martial, civil, and artisanal arts. Many others found their way there as well, through merit or sheer determination. Some lasted. Some excelled. A few went on to be Derw themselves, taking their learning back out into the land for the benefit of others.

Of the warriors of Ynysvron, the Nine Sisters were considered the best. Formidable in battle. Great strategists. Smiths with legendary skills. Healers. They oversaw the training of others. Kept discipline. The one who stood there now certainly looked like she could lift an anvil without too much effort.

'Morwyn. I...' The Sister silenced Aros with a grim expression, inspected the grazes on his face and then looked across the small clearing at Jeniche. It was quick and dismissive. She turned back to Aros. 'This brawling is not seemly,' she said to him. 'Collect your things. Get those cuts attended and then visit the sweat-house.'

Aros ducked his head and made for the bench where his everyday clothes were piled.

'The rest of you. Back to your studies. Back to your work.'

She turned her back on Jeniche and began up the grassy bank, Aros following just behind her, the others dispersing.

'Will you be there on the battlefield to make sure he gets his cuts treated? Will you be there to make sure the fighting is stopped before anyone gets hurt?'

Jeniche knew it was stupid. She had been taken in by these people and treated well. It was churlish to pick an argument. But she was also angry that someone who was being trained as a warrior was treated like a child.

Morwyn stopped and turned. She certainly had the menacing look off to perfection.

17

'Do you doubt our prowess? Our valour?'

She wasn't about to insult a people known for their pride. 'No,' said Jeniche. 'But when did you last fight for your life?'

This time she did hear the gasp of dismay.

Swallows and martens hawked across the rabbit-cropped slope in the late afternoon sunlight, picking up insects as they flew. They rode the air like fish swim in water, changing speed and direction with an ease and skill that delighted Jeniche.

She sat on a comfortable bench, legs stretched out, enjoying the warmth and enjoying the view. Beyond the smooth, grassy slope that dropped down toward a stream, the southern part of the island basked in the sunlight. Patches of woodland, hedgerows, fields, orchards, dusty lanes, farm buildings, windmills with idle sails. In the distant haze was Trevisgol, the only real town, overlooking the harbour where the ferries and fishing boats came and went.

She had seen it in winter as well, when the winds screamed in from the Eastern Sea and pushed bitter fingers into every hiding place. Those and the long, grey days before spring arrived had been the hardest to bear. That first year, before she had set foot on Pengaver, the island of the Derw, she had nearly turned round and headed back south. But by the time the roads were clear, spring in these northern islands had enchanted her.

A stoneware plate hovered into view and she reached out for a chunk of bread, pulled a face, and turned to use her left hand.

'That worries me.'

Jeniche shook her head. 'It's fine. Just a bad bruise. Aros got in hard blow. I've had worse.'

18

Rhonwen merch Sioned, the Head Librarian of the Great College of the Derw narrowed her eyes. 'I would suggest you go to see our Healer...'

Honey dripped from the bread onto Jeniche's fingers. She licked it off. 'I suppose that would be Morwyn?'

'You suppose correctly.'

'It is one of my more obvious... talents. Upsetting people.'

'You certainly seem to have been upsetting the Sisterhood.'

'It didn't take much.'

'And how did it end?'

'Morwyn showed admirable restraint, considering my rudeness,' said Jeniche. 'She gave me a withering look I can still feel, and strode off into the woods.'

Rhonwen wiped her own pale fingers on a damp cloth, offered it to Jeniche as she pushed the last piece of bread in her mouth.

The Librarian was about to say something, perhaps a response to what Jeniche had said, but she changed her mind. 'Upsetting folk does not seem to have been an obvious talent until now,' she remarked instead. 'Are your feet getting restless?'

Dropping the cloth on the empty plate, Jeniche looked at her booted feet. She rocked them from side to side on her heels and then turned to look at the Librarian. Rhonwen had a dry and fierce countenance; grey hair cut as short as Jeniche's and permanently narrowed eyes from studying all those books that gave the impression of frowning disapproval. Yet she had welcomed Jeniche to the College and into the Library itself; had arranged a place for her so that she might study in return for services to the Derw.

'You've been here for just over a year. Studied hard. You

have a hunger for information, but yours isn't the scholar's temperament.'

This, thought Jeniche, sounds like it might be the start of a request to leave. And she found she wasn't surprised or hugely upset. Rhonwen was right. She wasn't a scholar like Cenau, ready to settle for a life amongst the books. She wanted to know, but she wanted to use what she knew, she wanted to see how that worked in the world.

'I sense you were cloistered once before.'

Jeniche sat upright. 'Yes.'

Rhonwen waited, but Jeniche did not want to talk about it. 'A long time ago,' was all she would concede.

The Librarian looked at her and Jeniche shivered. It was one of those looks that Teague had given her in the tower in Makamba when they sat at night watching the stars. A look that saw things in her she could never hope to fathom for herself.

'How long have you been in Ynysvron?'

'Not a full year before I came here.'

'And before that?'

Jeniche frowned. 'You know all this.'

'But how much do you know?'

'I don't understand.'

'You have read every book we have on the Evanescence and the world that existed before the collapse.' Jeniche said nothing, was conscious of the weight of the keys in the pocket of her jacket. 'You carry out your duties. And thank you for trying to teach Cenau to stand up to Aros. Aros is not deliberately malicious, I think. He just doesn't understand scholars and their... sensitivities. When they were schooled together they got on well. Since fourteen, when they began to specialize, the things they had in common have perhaps been overwhelmed by the things that now set them apart. These things have become your world. And it is a small world. You feel confined.'

'No. Yes. No.'

'Well, that is a scholar's answer,' laughed Rhonwen.

'I want for nothing here. Ynysvron is beautiful. I was once told it was and didn't quite believe it. All that talk of mist and rain and snow. Of winter. Of the people and their wise ones. So I wanted to see for myself.'

'Someone told you the Derw were the "wise ones" of Ynysvron?' She sounded incredulous. 'Perhaps they were being... satirical.'

Jeniche thought of Alltud. 'Or just drunk.'

Rhonwen laughed and Jeniche wondered what was so funny.

'I have been treated with courtesy. Offered shelter. And the tutors of the College have been patience itself.'

'They are learning a great deal from you in turn. The master atlas has much detail it lacked before.'

'But I'm not being challenged. And...'

They watched a bat make a first foray into the fading light. She couldn't think of a way to express how she knew what she knew. Ynysvron was a wonderful land. The people were vibrant and, for the most part, hospitable. Yet everywhere she had travelled on her way north to Pengaver, and on the island itself, she got the feeling that all was not well.

Whilst they had been welcoming, the people had also been wary. Every village had someone on watch, every tribal boundary was well patrolled, and whilst people at inns, farmsteads, or the great tribal roundhouses had been eager to hear her news and stories, they had kept their own news to themselves.

21

The undertone of unease had troubled Jeniche as she travelled. For a while after arriving at the Great College, she had felt it fade. Now it was back. Aros and his companions seemed to be spending more time practising their martial skills. The ferries in and out of Trevisgol were always busy with messengers.

As they sat in silence, the sun dropped behind the hills of Tirmawr to the west. More bats flickered in the shadows where the swallows had been. There were other shadows in the air; a different nightfall threatened.

'Who...?' said Jeniche, finally finding a way to express it. 'Who amongst the Derw is hunting in the night?'

Chapter Three

The three wagons creaked, clattered, and chimed their slow way up the long road from Trevisgol, wreathed in the distinctive singing voice of a young woman. They were vividly decorated. The canvas covers were painted with exotic scenes. Bright pennants flapped from poles dropped in either side of the footboards. Ribbons fluttered from the harness of the horses. Even the people on the seats wore flamboyant clothes and wide smiles. A general air of gaiety followed the small caravan, along with children from the town and fields. Even one or two students could be seen following in their wake, just far enough away to pretend they happened to be travelling in the same direction.

For all their brightness and show, they were sturdy wagons, well built with watertight beds so that they could be floated across rivers when there were no ferries or, just as often, when there was no fare to pay passage. This time, though, they had found the money. If they wanted to bring their show to Pengaver, they needed to cross the deep, racing waters by boat.

The island lay in the centre of the confluence of two vast tidal inlets of the Eastern Sea. One drove west for thirty miles surrounded by bleak moorland and high crags. The other headed south for half that distance, winding between equally high but far more hospitable upland. It was along this shorter channel, sheltered from the prevalent easterly gales, that the large ferries plied their trade, carrying people and goods between Trevisgol on the island and Durm perched on a rocky edge of Tirmawr.

Several smaller islands lay between Pengaver and the open sea, the outermost a fortified, rocky outcrop called Tarian. Jeniche had learned that the name meant 'shield'; it also meant 'target'. Whether she had been meant to draw a lesson from that, she was not sure. It was a lesson she had long since learned.

The Isle of Pengaver was not, itself, that large; just one of the many smaller islands that clustered around the larger landmasses that, together, formed the archipelago of Ynysvron.

It had once been a single landmass of high hills and deep valleys. Until the Inundation. The people had reverted to the old tribal ways, clinging to life and slowly rebuilding, forging alliances, squabbling, evolving their culture from ways that had been ancient long before the Evanescence and the floodwaters. Now the Ynyswr had been at peace, more or less, for a long time.

Their society was roughly divided into three castes, with people moving freely between them depending on their skills and inclinations. The smallest group were the Derw, the intellectual caste. Then there were the Waltarian, the warriors whose loyalty was first to their tribe and then to the land. And finally, by far the most numerous, were the Greftwr, the artisans. No one caste was seen as more important than the others, each recognized as having an integral role in the wellbeing of the people.

The best of each caste had a responsibility to pass on their skills to others. Most took on apprentices. The very best would usually end up on Pengaver where they taught and could be consulted. Education was one of the great social bonds of Ynyswr society.

Pengaver might have been small, but it was important. And it was unusual in that it was deemed to be outside any tribal territory. The Derw were scholars and experts in their respective fields. It was from their ranks that the tribes drew their doctors and lawyers, their historians and priests, their diplomats and advisers, their poets and teachers. Most of the time it was a sober and studious place, but even the Derw liked to enjoy themselves.

Jeniche had been crossing from the refectory to the Library when she heard the singing and traced it back to the wagons. The first was being manoeuvred off the main track and onto the grassed area that was surrounded on three sides by the main buildings of the College. She slowed her pace to scrutinize the newcomers, as curious as everyone else who was pretending not to watch.

With a grin, she went on her way, astounded at the number of students who suddenly had a need to cross the concourse. And then slowed again, stopped to bend to the non-existent lacing on one of her boots. Because amidst all the waving of arms, encouraging of horses, pushing of wagons, and setting of brakes, she noticed one of the players watching the students with sharp, serious eyes. She wasn't particularly familiar with the ways of travelling players, but it didn't look to her very much like the casual assessment of a potential audience.

She straightened. Perhaps it was time to be moving on.

Students and tutors came and went, walking quietly between the galleried shelves in search of books or sitting at the long, polished work tables. A small group of visiting scholars was being shown around by a senior librarian. Copyists could be seen through the arch beneath the tower, bent over their tasks; Rhonwen at her desk, supervising with that stern look.

Despite the well-established sense of calm, Jeniche found studying was difficult. Her thoughts were unsettled, as restless as her feet. And knowing she was unable to apply herself unsettled her even more. Of course, it didn't help that by the time she got into the Library after lunch, the only workspace available was directly opposite the door that gave onto the tower stairs.

She kept looking at the studded oak, wondering if the answers to her questions really were on the other side at the top of the stairs in the locked room. Questions she would perhaps be better walking away from. If they would only let her.

By instinct, her hand went to the pendant hanging at her breast beneath her clothes. It had been a long time since she had felt it give off any warmth, a long time since she had experienced the nausea associated with ancient artefacts. A long time, that is, until she had stood outside the tower room with wet feet, knowing she could not get in, conscious of a faint tingle in the pit of her stomach.

She had learned a lot about the Evanescence since those days in the Makamba Desert, yet nowhere had she come across anything that would explain the red-gold teardrop pendant, or her body's reaction to ancient objects. Who knew if the answers were here. There had been nowhere

26

else better to look and Alltud had always gone on about how learnéd the Derw were.

Alltud. There was another question, one she had been walking away from for a long time now. She shook her head and settled her gaze on the worn carving above the door in front of her in an attempt to break her line of thought. It didn't help. Although eroded by time, the depiction of four objects was clear enough. And the sword simply brought her thoughts back to Alltud.

With a sigh, she shifted in her seat and made herself look back down at the book she had been reading. There was a short chapter on Makamba and she had been asked to write an addendum including what she knew of the city and surrounding countryside. It wasn't going well. Her notes were disorganized and, in any case, she wasn't sure a thief's perspective would be entirely appropriate. Perhaps a word with Rhonwen would help.

Before she could sort her papers into the satchel she had been given, Talfryn, one of the cartographers, sat down beside her in a recently vacated chair.

'Sorry to interrupt,' he whispered. 'Would you mind?'

Jeniche smiled and shook her head. It would be a relief.

Leaving her papers, she followed the elderly Derw. As they crossed a narrow space between shelves, she glanced through the arch to where Rhonwen sat. Someone stood by her desk, leaning forward as if talking. He wore the gaudy clothes of one of the players. Jeniche shrugged. Perhaps he was asking if there were any play scripts in the Library. When they passed another gap, she saw the man had gone.

Talfryn and Jeniche went through to the room where the maps and atlases were kept. The Derw not only studied them, but restored and copied old ones as well as creating new ones. Many were practical maps used in the administration of Ynysvron. Land deeds, tribal boundaries, records of mineral wealth, and much more were all kept here and there were often lawyers poring over the originals and comparing them with copies. Some of the other maps were works of art – as accurate as they could be made, but also richly illustrated and coloured. Jeniche had spent many hours in there.

At a large table beneath a vast window of plain glass, a wonder in itself, Talfryn pointed to a map that he was compiling from sketches. Several others were there as well, all known to Jeniche. The smile faded from her face as she saw what they were working on.

'We understand you have been to Tundur.'

She took a deep breath. 'Yes, but I didn't see much of it.' Nor did she want to remember much, either. Not after she had been cheated like that. It was nearly five years since she had ridden away on the camel train across the vast plateau of the interior and down into Gyanag, the place the Tunduri called the Black Land. Five years since she had learned of the duplicity of that pip-squeak of a monk and that...

'Jeniche?'

'Sorry. I was thinking. Can we turn this? So north is there.'

One of the cartographers reached a hand under the lip of the table and released a catch. Slowly they swivelled the large tabletop, locking it off again when Jeniche gave the nod.

'Thanks,' she said. 'I travelled up into Tundur from Beldas. All the way up to Kodor.'

Talfryn picked up a pointer and traced a route on one of the large sketches. 'There?'

Jeniche leaned across to look. 'No. That's the main trade route. It's relatively new, crossing the gorge into Kodor.' She shook her head, the memory of the gentle nun Mowen Bey bleeding her life out in the snow. 'There is an older route...'

'Are you all right?' asked Talfryn. He frowned as Jeniche wiped a tear from her cheek.

'A... friend died there.'

The elderly Derw put a trembling hand up to his mouth. There had been generations of relative peace in Ynysvron. And the Great College was not renowned for its rowdiness.

'I'm sorry. I didn't mean—'

Jeniche touched his arm and built a shaky smile. 'There is no need to apologize. You weren't to know. And I hadn't realized it would affect me so strongly after all this time.'

'If you'd rather...'

'No.' She pulled the sketch closer and picked up a piece of charcoal. 'May I?'

Talfryn nodded and Jeniche lightly drew in the old trade road, explaining how it was now used to bring Papaver gum down from the poppy fields. She marked the waterfalls she could remember; the pre-Ev ruins they had discovered; the high meadow where the airship had crashed, although that took a lot of explaining, which wasn't easy, as she didn't understand the principles herself. She put Kodor in its position on the edge of the gorge and explained about the bridge. After that, she tried to sketch the route they had taken over the mountains and down onto the central plateau, but gave up. There wasn't much of that part of the journey she remembered and it had snowed most of the time.

She hadn't spoken of her adventures like this before. What had opened the gates she did not know, perhaps the memory of Mowen Bey and her distraught sister. Even so, there was a lot she didn't mention: the vast city beneath the desert, her dear friend Trag, the fights. Learning to kill. The betrayal.

Lanterns glowed inside the wagons parked on the central concourse. They had been drawn together to form an open-sided square with a small, low stage set up between them. Jeniche sat outside the Library in the dusk, watching the shadows of the players lurch as they moved about inside, wondering if her feeling about them from earlier had been well founded. Probably not.

She sighed. Cenau was taking his time. She had seen him working at one of the tables in the civil law section. Perhaps he had fallen asleep. Just as she was about get up and go inside to see, Rhonwen emerged with a man in the traditional grey robes of a senior Derw. Jeniche didn't recognize him, heard only murmuring until they stopped close to where she sat in the dusky shadows.

'You are right, of course,' said the man. 'I'll get the message off to Cynfelyn straight away.'

Jeniche would have thought no more of it, but in watching the stranger stride off toward the main gate, she noticed the familiar folding of a robe over a sword.

Cenau emerged then, yawning in the early evening air and stretching his wiry frame. Jeniche turned away from following the progress of the stranger, although she thought she heard a horse.

'I want a word with you,' said Jeniche.

'Oh. Sounds ominous. I hear you got into trouble.'

'You heard wrong. And don't try to change the subject.'

Cenau grinned. 'Can we eat first?'

It was Jeniche's turn to grin. 'I don't know where you

put it all. Muscles the size of a sparrow's ankles and if you turn sideways, you disappear.'

They crossed toward the refectory, passing close to the wagons. They were dark now and silent. 'Have you seen them?' asked Cenau, lowering his voice. 'They say one of them is very beautiful.'

Jeniche stopped in her tracks and laughed. 'Cenau?'

'Sshhh!'

'Oh dear. "They" probably have poor eyesight. These are players, Cenau. It is their profession to seem something other than they are.' Thoughts of Gyan Mi and Alltud sobered her mood. 'Come on,' she added, 'let's eat.'

They carried on across to the refectory and joined the short queue. It was late and most of the College had eaten, although many still sat at table and chattered quietly. Laughter drifted from a common room next door. Cenau nudged Jeniche and said, in a whisper, 'Near the door.'

Jeniche turned as if looking for somewhere to sit.

'Ah. I take it back. She is beautiful.'

Cenau didn't hear. He was too busy staring at the players who sat at a table eating. Rather, he was staring at one of the players. Small, delicate, with long honey-coloured hair woven into plaits. Jeniche used an elbow on Cenau who returned to the real world and shuffled along to collect his food. The girl looked up and across at Jeniche, taking her breath away with a sudden smile.

After they had eaten a distracted meal, they wandered out into the late-summer dark along a path toward the garden on the far side of the Library. When Jeniche was happy no one was near, she said: 'The keys.'

Cenau glanced round. 'What about them?'

'How did you know I was interested in the tower room?'

31

'It's your subject. You probably know more about pre-Ev culture than anyone in the College. You must have heard about the room and what it is supposed to contain. And I've seen you looking at the tower door in the Library enough times.'

'So what is it supposed to contain?' she asked, touching her fingertips briefly to where her pendant lay beneath her tunic.

'Well. Artefacts. Books. Genuine things. From before the Evanescence.'

'And what makes you think I have tried to get in?'

Cenau grinned. 'I saw you.'

Jeniche swore. Half a dozen colourful epithets in four different languages. She really was losing her touch.

'I was on night watch in the Library. It's possibly the most boring duty ever devised. You make sure all the candles and lanterns are extinguished and then you make regular rounds to make sure there are no fires, especially in the winter when the stoves are kept lit to keep the damp out. Anyway, I heard a noise as I was going through the arch into the copy room. It sounded like something had fallen off the tower. I went up the stairs to look out of the window and heard something fall onto the landing.'

'Me.'

'You. And I thought the keys would be a good way of saying thank you for teaching me to defend myself.'

Jeniche nodded. 'Thank you. And thank you for not mentioning anything to anyone else.' She didn't say any more, but she still wanted to know how someone as timid as Cenau had become brave enough or recklessness enough to steal the keys, presumably from Rhonwen, have them copied without word getting back to her, and return the originals without being discovered or dissolving into a nervous heap; or how he managed to hold his curiosity in check. There was clearly a lot more to the boy than met the eye. Or more to something else.

Chapter Four

'Alive? Still alive? And Maelduin dead. My patience has ebbed with his life's blood. Fire-eyed fury will conduct me now. Stand forward. Maelduin waits at the ferry ready to keep you company.'

'Wretch. You are the one that came here with him. You are the one shall cross with him into the West.'

'This shall determine that.' He grasped the hilt of his sword.

The talking had finished. They circled each other warily as the others stood back to give them room. The torches flared in a sudden breeze, throwing shadows hither and yon. In the confusion of light, they drew their swords. The *shing* of steel was loud in the moment of silence. And then, with a roar, they leaped at each other, raising dust from the boards beneath their feet.

Sparks flew from their blades, curses flew from their mouths, and the sound of their battle rang across the concourse, echoing from the stone face of the buildings. Back and forth they went, hurling their blades at one another, their feet dancing nimbly across the floor. Inevitably, one weakened, made a poor move and found himself impaled on his opponent's sword.

In the sudden silence his dying breaths could be heard rasping in the night air. He looked up as he slowly collapsed to the floor, a hand reaching, imploring as his opponent's sword slipped out of him. The victor watched in disbelief before pulling the tip of his blade from the corpse.

The others drew close.

'Go! Go!' urged one. 'The guard has been roused. It is death if you stay.'

'What have I done? All is lost.'

'You must go!'

He fled.

A hand tapped Jeniche on the shoulder as other actors came on to the stage. Annoyed, she turned her head to see Morwyn looming over her. The Derw warrior beckoned and picked her way through the audience before she strode off through the dark to one of the benches by the door of the refectory. She sat in the dim light of a lantern, wrapped in a light cloak, and waited for Jeniche who was reluctant to leave the play.

As Jeniche sat beside her, Morwyn said, 'I am sorry. You were enjoying it.'

'No matter.' They were too far distant to hear the actors' words and the small, bright world they had created on the makeshift stage was a dance of colour in the dark. 'I can ask someone what happens.'

'I don't mean to keep you for long.'

Jeniche waited.

'Your parting words—'

'I'm sorry. I was...'

'Angry?'

35

'No.' She indicated the distant stage with an outstretched hand. 'The players understand that. Go into a fight because of anger or get angry during the fight and you will probably regret what happens. If you survive. It was just that… Several times that day I had seen examples of good… theoretical learning.'

'They practice hard. None more than Aros.'

'They play with their friends. It worries me.'

Morwyn nodded. 'Your question was… astute.'

'And hurtful.'

'Perhaps, but I've had far worse wounds, as you have, I'm sure. It's why I became a healer. But it is true. It has been a long time since I fought for my life. Ynysvron has been largely peaceful for generations. It is no paradise, but we generally manage to order our affairs without resort to violence.' She paused. 'Times change.'

A chill touched Jeniche. Her instincts had been true. Something was in the air.

'The Nine Sisters have discussed this. We sought counsel from others. And we have been watching you.' Morwyn managed to sound apologetic at that last revelation. 'Our decision was unanimous.' Now it was coming, thought Jeniche, the demand for her to leave. 'We would like you to teach them.'

Jeniche was taken aback. Counsel from whom? Observed her when? She did little beyond teaching Cenau the basics of self-defence and the daily exercises she had learned in Gyanag. She decided, however, that now was not the time to ask. Instead, she turned sideways to face Morwyn. 'I'm not a warrior.' I'm a thief, she added in silence. And it really is time to get into that tower, see if there are any answers, and then move on.

36

'Nonetheless, you can fight. Have fought. For your life.'

'And taken life as well. It's not something I am proud of.'

'That is good. A warrior may strive to perfect what they do, but they should never be proud of what it is used for. It is something that tends to be forgotten when peace is a given, but the first lesson of the warrior should be how to resolve a dispute without resort to violence.'

'And when peace is no longer a given?'

'What?!'

He stood in the door, his bony shoulders drooping.

'I'm sorry, Cenau, but if you want to carry on with your training you'll have to join in with the others. I can't be in two places at once and Morwyn was... convincing.' So much, she thought, for getting out. 'Besides, I'm only here because of the services I can offer.' She stopped. There was no need to explain. 'It'll be good for you.'

'So you say.'

Cenau stared at his feet.

'It won't be that bad. And you'll have the advantage.' She looked at his underfed frame and even she wasn't convinced.

'I don't suppose I have any choice. Cynfelyn insists.'

'Come on. We'll get up there early and you can have a head start.'

'All right.'

It was hardly an enthusiastic response, but it was the best Jeniche could hope for. They collected food from the refectory and set out along the path to the woods. 'And on the way, you can tell me about this Cynfelyn.'

'Cynfelyn?'

'Yes. You talk about him a lot. I was just curious.'

'He's my tutor.'

'Well, yes. I'd gathered that much. He clearly has a lot of faith in you.'

'What? Why do you say that?' She could hear a touch of pride in his voice as he asked.

'I've never seen him and I've been here just over a year.'

'Oh. Well, he has other duties. It is an honour to have such a senior Derw as a tutor. The trouble is, as you say, sometimes they have to go and do other things.'

'What sort of things?'

'Well… er… he's never said.'

'So how does he teach you?'

'I have a lot of research to do. And don't forget, I've been here since I was a child. A year without a tutor isn't such a hardship. Although I do miss him and he hasn't been here that long.'

'You've been here since you were a child? I thought…' She had never asked. Didn't like discussing people's childhood in case they asked about her own. 'How old are you? Where are your parents?'

Cenau shrugged. 'They were poor. I was given to the College.'

They were on the path through the forest that led to the training ring. Jeniche stopped.

'Given to the College?'

'Yes. Aros was as well. It's a kind of fostering. When you're seven. It's quite common in Ynysvron. It helps build inter-tribal bonds. The College fosters students every year. And I'm twenty now.'

'Do you see them? Your parents.'

'No. Not for a while now. It's difficult. They live a long

way away. Can't just leave the farm. And I haven't been off Pengaver since I arrived.'

He looked uncomfortable. Jeniche started walking again. 'So where is Cynfelyn?'

Cenau shrugged. 'I don't know. He writes me letters.' The miserable expression faded. 'But he rarely says where he is. Usually tells me about things he wants me to find out about.'

'What sort of things?'

'Oh, this and that. He has me studying the history of Ynysvron, its laws. And looking at maps a lot. I saw you in the map room the other day with Talfryn.'

'Yes.' She felt that familiar reluctance again.

'I went in. On night watch.'

The question hung in the air.

'Yes, Cenau. I have been to Tundur.'

'What's it like? I can't imagine. Are the mountains as high as they say? Do they really have snow all year round? How can they grow poppies if it always snows? How can they grow anything?'

'Well, there's your answer,' she said. Twenty years old and asking questions like a young child.

'It doesn't snow all year.'

'It does in the mountains.'

'How high are they?'

'High. So high that it is difficult to breathe.'

Jeniche continued answering Cenau's questions as best she could, glad he didn't ask about the God-King of Winter. That, like her childhood, was a painful subject she would much rather leave undisturbed. When they reached the ring, she made him spend a few minutes calming his mind, enjoying the early morning peace, the scent of woodland.

And so they began. Just Jeniche and Cenau at first. Exercises. Practice moves. And then some light combat. Then others began to arrive, watching as they stripped their outer robes. There was quiet laughter, but Jeniche could tell it was prompted by nerves. They had all been there when Jeniche had demonstrated the skills she had learned in Tundur and Gyanag. Some still had the bruises. Other young warriors arrived, uncertain, herded onto the grassy bank by Morwyn.

Nervous at first, but soon absorbed by her task, Jeniche explained how she had first seen combat; explained how an old monk had incapacitated several farm hands; described how she had learned the basics of this combat on her travels. It was clear that those who had not witnessed Jeniche in action did not quite believe what they were hearing.

The attack, when it came, caught everyone by surprise. Everyone but Jeniche. She had seen Morwyn sidle out of view and knew an assault was about to occur. And it was over before any of the onlookers had time to react. Jeniche had twisted her way out of a stranglehold from behind, caught up Morwyn's arm in a lock, been surprised when the massive warrior cartwheeled out of it, and then felled her with a numbing blow to the side of the knee that left her unable to stand for a while.

It had been a risk. If Morwyn had won, Jeniche would have left and the trainee warriors would no doubt have been lectured on the need to concentrate on the superior methods of the Sisterhood. As it was, Jeniche stood over the prone form of Morwyn and continued her impromptu lecture as if nothing had happened. The waverers were convinced.

Every morning after that, they met in the ring and they trained, members of the Sisterhood included. Cenau was a reluctant participant, but watching the warriors try and fail to begin with made him realize he was not alone. He relaxed, gained confidence, and began to improve. Even Aros stopped looking down at him from such a great height, although he could still always beat Cenau.

And then, once they were comfortable with the basics, she taught them to fight dirty. Cenau and Jeniche sat and watched as the others went through their drills with wooden swords and padded jackets. Cenau remained watching when Jeniche joined in, often peering through his fingers when they progressed to leathers and blunt metal swords. The bruises and cuts and broken fingers began to accumulate.

After a while, Jeniche had them practising ambushes and running battles through the woods. They became tired and hardened. More bruises and cuts accumulated as the powerful warriors of the Sisterhood began hunting their pupils across the island.

The first leaves were starting to turn colour when Jeniche bowed out. She was sore, weary and in need of some time to herself, happy that she had taught them enough techniques to adopt into their own style of fighting. She spent several days resting, reading, walking about the College, letting her grazes heal and bruises fade.

In those still, quiet days the joyous song of a robin establishing its winter territory was sometimes interrupted by the clash of weapons and the shouts of the warriors as they played their increasingly serious battle games. The College grounds were strictly out of bounds, but it didn't stop the rumours and the worries. When the warriors became so active and single-minded, conflict couldn't be far away.

One evening, after eating, Jeniche sat in her room with a book, a blanket over her shoulders to counter the first autumn chill. There was a knock at the door and she opened it to find Rhonwen standing there with a lantern.

'I'm sorry to disturb you, Jeniche, but Talfryn has a bit of a fever and it was his turn to take the night watch in the Library. Would you mind? It is a simple task, if somewhat tedious.'

Jeniche could not believe her luck. She folded her blanket and put on her jacket, patting the pocket to make sure the keys were there.

'You can work, if you wish. Use my desk, as the stoves are lit. All you have to do is check everything is well on a regular basis. If you come across a fire you simply ring the bell in the tower and then make sure you are safe. I'll show you where the bell rope is.'

They stepped out of the dormitory building into the dark night. Stars shone in the breaks between the clouds. The gravel of the path sounded loud beneath their feet. And another noise came to them; a creaking, clattering mingled with the sound of horses, soft distinctive singing.

Rhonwen stopped, peering into the distance. Beyond the main gates, several lighted wagons could be seen approaching.

'It looks like the players are back,' said Jeniche.

They carried on across the concourse to the Library, watching the wagons as they were driven through the main entrance of the College grounds. Rhonwen unlocked the Library door and they stepped into the dark space.

'Maura?'

'Over by the map room.'

It was strange hearing raised voices in the Library, especially in the silent dark.

'Jeniche has agreed to do the night watch.'

'Oh. Thank you, Jeniche. There's food on Rhonwen's desk.'

42

Jeniche could hear Maura getting closer.

'Doesn't she have a lantern?' asked Jeniche quietly.

Maura laughed. 'When you have been in here as long as I have, you can do it with your eyes closed, especially without all those students littering up the place.'

Rhonwen held up her lantern to reveal the approaching Maura. 'She has excellent hearing, Jeniche. And she loves the students.'

With the bell rope pointed out, they left Jeniche to it. She bolted the main door as instructed and made her way to Rhonwen's desk. She stood there for a while, wondering what was different. It was difficult to tell with all the shadow. Only when she turned did she realize that the tapestry that hung behind Rhonwen's chair had been changed. Instead of the pastoral scene was a highly stylized figure of indeterminate sex, standing in front of a great wooden chair. Much of the detail was obscured by shadow, and the tapestry itself looked old and faded, yet one thing was clear because Jeniche had seen it before. The sword that Alltud had found in Makamba.

It was the last thing she had expected and it left her confused. She stepped away from the tapestry, trying to settle her mind. She wanted to be focused when she climbed those stairs. She wanted to be ready. Not distracted by old memories best left buried. So she explored the copy room, looking at some of the manuscripts – a popular history of Ynysvron on one desk, a collection of poorly understood fragments from the pre-Evanescence on another, the pages of a book of myths laid out along a bench where they were being illustrated with bright vignettes. From there she wandered back and forth between the shelves, checking the stoves were secure. The map room still had the maps of

Tundur set out on the table with Talfryn's new composite map sketched in and ready for inking.

After that, she could contain herself no longer. With her heart beating painfully, something she was not accustomed to, Jeniche crossed the main Library to the tower door. It wasn't locked as she feared, at the last moment, it might be and she went in.

The ground floor was not large and contained little more than brooms, dusters, and pots of beeswax that filled the space with the warm scent of honey. She climbed the narrow stone stairs to the first floor. This was also a small space, completely empty. The next flight of steps led to the much larger space directly above the arch. A narrow corridor with a single door led to the next flight of stairs.

Jeniche tried the door. It opened onto a room lined with shelves that were full of paper, sheets of vellum, boxes of charcoal and other supplies for use in the Library below. She closed the door carefully and made her way up to the next floor. It was from the top of this flight that Cenau must have seen her, because there was the window through which she had squeezed.

On the floor where she had landed in a heap was a bag of tools, glass and lead stacked in the corner. Someone must have seen the puddle and decided it was time to re-glaze the opening. Careful to keep her lantern from showing, she climbed on up to the top floor and stood in front of the door, conscious again of the irritating tingle in her stomach.

It was not often she had the keys to somewhere she was breaking into. And she had never seen keys like this before. Small. Heavy. Sophisticated and finely tooled. She chose one and decided on a lock to try. Then looked at the key again, holding it close to the lantern. Finely tooled and, according to Cenau, fairly recently made. Certainly never used. According to Cenau.

She examined it carefully. Then the other. Both had been used. The metal was crisp, but they had most certainly been used. It was almost as if... She put the keys in her pocket and went back down a flight, risking light at the window to examine the remains of the casement. It had been exposed to the weather, but not for very long. Because the floor would also be stained if it had been open to the elements for a long period. And there was no stain.

Someone wanted her to get into that room. Which made the prospect altogether different. She now had doubts. Serious doubts. Time, perhaps, to warm herself by the stove, eat some food, and have a long, hard think.

Chapter Five

A light frost on the grass had been glistening in the early morning light when Jeniche emerged from the Library. Someone had come to open the shutters and see to the stoves, sweep round and continue with the never-ending task of keeping the books and shelves dusted. Jeniche had let them in and then slunk to her room and bolted the door, tired, bewildered, and guilty.

Tired and bewildered she understood. Guilty she did not. She thought about it as she undressed and climbed into her cold bed. She had finally gone into the room at the top of the tower, but she hadn't taken anything; hadn't even touched anything. Nor could she rid herself of the idea that others had conspired to manoeuvre her into the tower room. Yet she still felt like a naughty child.

And what she had seen there had stirred up memories and filled her dreams.

At first she felt she was falling, woke with a start in a bed that was still cold, turned restlessly, drifting into unsettled visions where faint lights danced in the dark. A deep dark. From which she could not escape. A place where strange messages were carved into the walls, where markings had been daubed in paint that had run horizontally, where water trickled and she could feel the damp.

There were still tears on her cheek when she woke again, her head aching, and the pendant round her neck almost hot to the touch. A fever claimed her and she slipped back into a well of visions, watching the distant light fade as new light beckoned ahead. On and off the lights went, revealing rooms and tunnels and the many faces of the dead.

When the sun was low in the west she woke again, bathed in sweat and feeling weak. She lay for a while before rising, waiting for the tide of sleep to recede and for her thoughts to return to their rightful places in their daytime roost. Only then did she dress and, wrapped in her heavy travelling coat, shuffle across the concourse to the bath house, passing the wagons of the players on the way.

'Hello. Oh. You don't look well. Are you all right?'

Jeniche looked up to see a flap of canvas had been pushed back, revealing the girl with the honey-coloured hair who had so captivated Cenau.

'Just a slight chill. I'm off to the steam room in the bath house.'

'Here.'

The girl disappeared and Jeniche waited. Before long, she reappeared and jumped down. 'I'll walk with you.' She proffered a small hessian bag. 'Herbs. The steam will release vapours to help.'

'Thank you. You don't need—'

'Oh that's all right. We always keep a few of these handy.' After a few more steps, she added, 'My name is Caru.'

'I'm—'

'Jeniche.'

Jeniche stopped in surprise.

Caru laughed. 'I'm sorry. I asked when we were here last. You left part way through the performance of *Olwen*.' She took Jeniche by the arm and led her on toward the bath house.

At the door, Jeniche said, 'Thank you.'

Caru smiled. 'I hope you feel better soon,' she said and was walking back toward the wagons as Jeniche went into the warm entrance of the baths with yet more to think about and worry over.

The steam room was, as she had hoped, empty. The main meal of the day was serving in the refectory. Settling into a corner, the small bag of herbs by her side, she closed her eyes and let the vapour do its work.

The thing that still puzzled her most was Cenau getting the keys. The keys that were not as new as he had claimed. Which meant he took the originals. Or older copies. So why hadn't they been missed? Or if they had, why was no one making a fuss? To which questions, already asked over and over, she must add the possibility that Cenau was lying to her, or had given her the keys at someone else's bidding. But that just raised once more the bigger questions of who and why.

Everyone in the College knew she was interested in pre-Ev cultures. She had done little but read about them since she had arrived; ask others what they knew. Such was her obsession that people now came to her with their queries. It was also an open secret that the room at the top of the tower contained pre-Ev artefacts. No one ever talked about it. The Ynyswr were, on the whole, more interested in the present and the future than the past; a people who preferred to look forward. She could not even remember how she had first heard of the tower room. And she could never bring herself to ask, as that would have meant explaining everything, opening old wounds, exposing her inner self to others. Something that had always ended in pain in the past.

Open as the secret was, it was still a secret. And she could never resist any challenge like that. Which someone also knew. Perhaps.

Her head began to spin.

Then there were all the things going on in the background. The messengers rushing back and forth. The sudden interest in her martial skills. Rhonwen talking with strangers. A growing watchfulness. The repair of neglected gates. The return of the players. Caru. Did she really ask for Jeniche's name out of idle curiosity? She must have formidable eyesight if she could see past the torchlight on the stage at night whilst acting and notice a person with skin the colour of cinnamon at the back of the audience get up and leave. And what of the way the other players seemed to be watchful?

Her head span faster.

Although she had never trusted to luck, she did trust her instincts. And they had been telling her for a long time to pack up and leave. They had whispered it at first, but it was becoming increasingly difficult to shut out the nagging voice. And if she ignored it much longer, she knew events would catch up with her.

She knew why she was ignoring it. Ynysvron was some-where she felt at home. At least, she had. The College had made her more than welcome, even though she had drifted there on little more than a whim, chasing the wild geese of her feelings and desires. And notwithstanding the one Ynyswr she would knock unconscious if she ever met him again, she had become attached to the people she had met and worked with.

Cenau probably wouldn't understand her restlessness. He seemed settled and would likely spend the rest of a quiet life here on Pengaver. Which meant that despite all her unanswered questions, or maybe because of them, she had to go straight to her room, pack her things, and leave. She had been through all sorts of grief once before by getting attached to others and the last thing she wanted was to go through it all again.

There wasn't much to pack, but it took a while. She emptied the contents of her storage chest onto the bed and by the light of a lantern sorted it into two piles – the things she had brought with her or earned and those which belonged to the College. And those keys. She would have to decide what was to be done with those.

Her own pile was small. Some spare clothes, a pack, her sword, and the book in which she kept notes about what she had learned of the Evanescence. She wrapped the book with care in an oilskin cloth and placed it in the bottom of her pack. Neatly folded clothes went in after it, along with other bits and pieces like the pouch containing her flint and tinder. The lacing was done and redone, then undone so she could get out her piece of untreated wool to oil the blade of her sword. And then she packed it all again because it didn't feel comfortable on her back.

When someone pounded on the door she had long since finished and was sitting waiting for a good chance to slip quietly round to the main gates and away. Her heart leapt as she had heard no one approach, too absorbed in her own thoughts. All the same, she slid her sword from its scabbard and opened the door with it hidden from view in her left hand.

One of the junior librarians stood outside, holding a lantern up high. 'Sorry, Jeniche. I know it's late, but Rhonwen asked me to tell you you're wanted in the Library straight away.'

Chill air drifted into her room as she watched the librarian scuttle away along the corridor. This didn't sound good. Perhaps she should just slip away now. Perhaps she should have done it an hour ago when she was finally ready. She swore under her breath.

She carried on swearing to herself as she crossed the chilly concourse in the autumn night. Even the players' wagons were dark and her steaming breath could barely be seen. Promising herself she would leave straight away afterwards, she had left her sword and pack ready, covered by a blanket.

Her heavy travel coat kept the worst of the chill out, but the cold air stung her cheeks. It wasn't a good time to start an indefinite journey. But she felt she no longer had a choice. This one last meeting, perhaps to explain why she had gone into the tower and stood in that space with those artefacts and books. Such books. Such beautiful books.

The door to the Library opened as she approached, and someone emerged wrapped in a cloak with the hood up. They walked off along the path and disappeared into the night. Inside, lanterns still burned beneath the arch and over Rhonwen's desk. She closed the door.

'Come in, Jeniche,' Rhonwen called. 'Bring a chair.'

There were several others there, in shadow or with their backs to her. If it was to do with the tower, it was going to be serious. One of them stood and moved their seat to make room. Jeniche realized it was Morwyn. She hesitated a moment and then grabbed a chair. The worst that could happen would be a telling off and expulsion, and she was going to do that to herself anyway.

Heat radiated from the stove near Rhonwen's desk. Jeniche removed her coat to reveal travelling clothes. No one remarked. The others seemed well settled and Jeniche wondered how long they had been there.

Once she was seated, Rhonwen stood. 'Thank you, Jeniche. I am sorry this is so late, but there is a degree of urgency, as you will come to appreciate. To begin with, however, let me introduce you. Morwyn, Talfryn, and Cenau you know.'

Jeniche looked round and saw a hand waving from the shadow on the other side of the stove, recognized Cenau's pale grin as he leaned forward and followed up his wave with a slight shrug.

'Beside Morwyn is Enfys, also of the Sisterhood.' A pale face beneath cropped red hair nodded slowly in the direction of Jeniche, a slight smile hovering on scarred lips.

'Celydon is the messenger who brought us the news and who must report back on our deliberations.' A starved face gave a brief, impassive nod.

'Eog is a Derw of the Braddan peoples.' He looked more like a farmer, Jeniche thought; rosy of cheek and with a broad grin framed by white whiskers.

'And for those who do not know our honoured guest,' said Rhonwen, gesturing at Jeniche, 'this is Jeniche of Antar. Scholar.'

'And warrior,' added Morwyn.

'And traveller, by the look of it,' added Celydon, his expression unchanged.

It was still feeling a bit like a tribunal.

'Celydon brought news today from Cynfelyn,' Rhonwen continued. Jeniche tried not to look like she was paying undue attention. The absent Derw intrigued her. 'He has found a hoard of material of interest to the Library.'

Jeniche was now confused. She had more than half expected to be accused of breaking into the tower room and then asked to leave. Now she found she was at a Library staff meeting – albeit a staff of unusual composition.

'You look puzzled, Jeniche,' said Eog.

'Because I am.'

Rhonwen smiled. 'It will become clear, don't worry.'

'Cynfelyn,' continued Celydon, 'found a hoard of material hidden in a cave in the far north of the Braddan tribal lands.'

Eog pulled a face. 'Not exactly. If the information Celydon was given is accurate, then it is in disputed territory. The Braddan and the Rhan both claim the isthmus.'

'But can we assume the Derw have prior claim to certain sites and monuments?'

'At a push.'

'Hence the need for this to be done without attracting attention.'

Jeniche could see Eog wasn't happy about that part, but he said no more. Her own interest had certainly been aroused. 'Certain sites and monuments' sounded very much her sort of thing.

'What sort of material?' asked Jeniche.

'Books,' said Rhonwen. 'For the most part. And I can see you want to ask and the answer is "maybe". Cynfelyn doesn't know. Which is why you are here.'

Against her better judgement and her determination to carry through her plans, Jeniche felt herself being hooked. The warning voice in her head sounded increasingly faint.

'Cynfelyn has requested that a small group joins him to assess the hoard and to bring back anything of value to the Library. He will wait for them in the village of Addas.'

Eog nodded. 'I know it.'

'And is there any danger of conflict?' asked Enfys.

'No,' said Eog; 'especially if there are Derw present.'

'But it would be politic,' added Rhonwen, 'to be prepared for a dispute. May I suggest, in the case of books, we offer to protect the originals at the Library here and provide copies to both the Braddan and Rhan peoples?'

Eog smiled. 'Excellent.'

'So who shall I tell Cynfelyn to expect?' asked Celydon.

Rhonwen looked at her hands for a moment, then at Jeniche. 'Would you, Jeniche, be prepared to accompany the party? We know from what you have shared with us that you have experience of travelling far and wide in search of antiquities and you are certainly the best person in the College to identify pre-Evanescence objects.'

Her stomach fluttered and she could not help wondering if there was something more to Rhonwen's look than a simple plea.

'You won't be alone, of course. Cenau will go. Cynfelyn is his tutor, after all, and the experience will be valuable. Eog, of course, will travel with you, as he knows the way. And there will be two other librarians I have yet to choose. But times are uncertain. So I would like Enfys and Morwyn to provide someone to protect the party.'

'Aros,' said Morwyn. 'He, too, will find the experience to be valuable.'

Jeniche was sure she heard Cenau groan.

'And Maiv and Awd,' added Enfys. 'That should be sufficient.'

After her initial excitement, Jeniche was beginning to have misgivings. Travelling with comparative strangers didn't bother her. She'd done it enough times in the past and this new voyage was hardly into the back of beyond. It was something about the timing that was too convenient and something about the story that didn't feel right. She felt she was losing control of her life. And that little voice that said she should leave was once again nagging loud and clear.

'Good,' said Rhonwen. 'I have your satchel of notes here, Jeniche. Take them now as it will be an early start tomorrow. You are travelling north and winter is approaching. I'd like you all safely back here before the first snow falls.'

As the group began to disperse, the voice began to nag more loudly. The last time she had set out on a simple trip with a group of people, much had been lost along the way.

Chapter Six

The tower dissolved into the grey early morning mist as they rode in slow procession through the gates and down the road toward Trevisgol. Jeniche was saying her private farewells to the College and the good people who lived and worked there, still telling herself there were no broken promises, no deceits and no betrayals. Once she had completed this task, she would be free to make her own way south and leave behind whatever seemed now to be haunting the shadows.

Dark grey of stone faded into the nothing and then was gone. She turned in her saddle and settled herself. It was only a short ride down to the ferry, but it was a while since she had been on a horse and she knew she would have a sore backside come nightfall. Something else she had neglected.

As their horses walked down the road, Jeniche let her thoughts wander back to the room in the tower of the Library building. The interior was still vivid in her memory. Not just the artefacts, wondrous as they were, but also the cabinets that contained them; identical to those she had seen in the city beneath the desert north of Makamba.

She leaned forward and patted the horse on its neck, her thoughts now with Trag. It was a long time ago and half a world away, yet it all seemed so vivid, desert bright in the misty northern morning where dew-laden cobwebs trembled in the hedgerows and the only hint of sunrise was a pale halo in the east.

Half way to the ferry port, they caught up with the players whose clanking, creaking wagons could be heard before they were seen. Urging her mount into a trot, she caught up with Cenau.

'Do they come to Pengaver a lot?'

Cenau regarded her with an unhappy expression. She could read it as easily as a book. It was clearly far too early in the day for him. He hadn't had any breakfast, very little sleep, and was going to be in close quarters with Aros for weeks and no escape. Now the woman who had taught him how to get thrown about by all sorts of people was wearing a sword on her back and asking about the players. 'Does it matter?' he asked.

She was clearly asking the wrong person, so she pushed forward through the column to Ruad, one of the two librarians that Rhonwen had attached to the group. She didn't remember seeing him about much, if at all, but he looked affable, had held her horse as she mounted.

'The players. Do they often come to the island?'

Ruad thought about it for a moment, and then gave a shrug. 'Usually just once a year in the summer. Why?'

'Just wondered. Thanks.'

She let her horse fall back to the end of the column again. Thinking. Because this was the players' second visit this year. And they hadn't given any performances, hadn't had the time. It seemed to her an awful waste to take a ferry to an island with three wagons just to return to the mainland two days later.

Down at the harbour they could see nothing. The mist was even thicker there. It condensed on them and dripped from their hair, found its way down necks and up sleeves. Once the wagons had stopped and the horses had settled, they could hear it dripping from the eaves of nearby buildings like rain. Cenau, when Jeniche got close enough to see, looked even more miserable than he had earlier.

'This won't last,' she said, but he didn't look convinced.

Hiding a small smile, she wandered off to find out what was happening with the ferry. There were eight in their party. She had expected the messenger, Celydon, to be with them, but he must have left the island in the night. Another little stone to add to the growing weight of... she wasn't going to call it worry just yet. Perhaps it was just like a stone in her boot and the irritation would go away as soon as it was removed.

She found the ferry master deep in conversation with one of the players. She didn't recognize the actor at first. He must wear a lot of padding for his parts, she thought. He finished his negotiations and turned a calculating stare on Jeniche before breaking into a smile and moving off in the direction of his wagons. Jeniche was left watching him go, wondering where she had seen him before. Another stone in her boot.

'Will you be travelling, young sir?' asked the ferry master.

Jeniche turned. Being mistaken for a young man, she thought gratefully, was one thing she hadn't lost. 'Eight of us from the College, each with a horse.' She handed over a letter that would vouch them passage.

The ferry master took it and tucked it inside his jacket without looking at it. He was his own man, but most of his trade was with the College. 'We'll be starting as soon as this shows signs of lifting. Shouldn't be long. We'll get the wagons on board first, if you don't mind waiting.'

It wasn't really a request.

Jeniche went and rounded up the party from the College and was somewhat surprised to find everyone deferring to her. Even Aros. He did everything he could to follow her orders, probably having been instructed to do so, but without once looking at her directly or appearing to listen. He watched Maiv and Awd, the two warriors, from the corner of his eye and followed their lead. And he watched Jeniche as well. A couple of times she just caught him as he jerked his head away to stare elsewhere.

One by one, they brought their horses up to the head of the slipway and watched in the slowly lifting mists as the wagons were winched down the slope, run across the lowered loading ramp, and manhandled onto the open deck of the broad boat.

Once the wagons were in place and tied down securely, the great draft horses followed, tethered either side of a line along the centre of the deck. Cenau and Aros went next with help from Maiv and Awd, who then took their own steeds on board. Ruad and Duald, the two librarians, followed on with Eog. Jeniche brought up the rear.

The horses were allowed to settle before the ferry master let other passengers aboard – farmers for the main part, pushing handcarts piled with produce for the market in Durm where they would all disembark.

They were afloat before most of them realized, the crew pushing the barge-like vessel off from the quayside with long oars. Aros was stalking back and forth trying to take it all in. Cenau still looked miserable.

'Sailing or being off the island?' Eog asked him.

'Both.'

'You won't be away long lad, and it will be a gentle ride. As for the boat... It's safe.'

'You won't convince him. Or me,' said Jeniche. 'Just stay with your horse, Cenau, and keep it company. We'll soon be in Durm.'

She went off to get Aros who was watching the oarsmen in the bow, pulling and steering the ferry into the centre of the channel to catch the flow of an incoming tide.

'Best stay close to your horse, Aros, in case it gets spooked.'

This time he returned her gaze. For a split second, he looked like he was going to say something. Instead, he nodded, as much to himself as to Jeniche, and made his way along the deck. He had clearly come to a decision for himself rather than just following instructions. It had taken him a while, yet it demonstrated to Jeniche that he was more than just a boneheaded fighter. She followed him back to the horses. As she went, she kept a close eye on the players who seemed, in turn, to be keeping an equally close eye on the Derw.

As she passed the last wagon, she saw Caru standing by one of the large horses, talking quietly to it, rubbing its neck. But her eyes were on Cenau. Who was too miserable to notice.

When Jeniche got back to her own horse she looked at what she could see for a long time before she could accept what it was. Perhaps it was a mistake. Perhaps she hadn't tied the laces on the saddle bag properly. Perhaps. Or maybe someone on board had gone through her things.

Looking round, she peered over the back of her own mount and that of Eog beside it. She was on the end so it could have been one of the islanders. One of the crew. One of the players. Perhaps one of the Derw had been asked by Rhonwen to make sure Jeniche wasn't taking a pre-Ev souvenir off Pengaver. None of which seemed plausible. Everything she knew about the Ynyswr told her this sort of thing just didn't happen. They would already know she hadn't taken anything from the tower room. And if something was missing, they would have confronted her openly in the presence of a judge. As for there being a thief aboard, this was possibly the most stupid place to start going through someone else's belongings. She ought to know. So it was one more mystery to vex her.

With the pretence of checking her horse's saddle, she unhooked the bags. Before putting them back, she unlaced them both and checked inside. She even counted the pages of her notebook and the notes in her satchel. Nothing was missing. Nothing seemed to have been interfered with.

'Leave something behind?'

She turned to see Eog by the head of his horse looking down at her.

'Thought I had. Found it though.'

He smiled and she repacked everything, taking care to lace the bags properly.

Durm was a busy settlement of two halves. One half stretched along the narrow shore of the inlet and was a cramped shanty town of small houses, inns, warehouses, workshops, and narrow lanes, with a series of wooden piers in various states of decay either side of the stone jetty where the ferry moored. It was noisy, brash, heavy with the smell of fish, and still enveloped in chill, heavy river mist.

As some of the party weren't used to riding in crowded spaces, Jeniche had them lead their horses along the waterfront and up the steep, winding road to the other half of Durm. This was built along the top of a rocky outcrop with water on one side and a dry gorge on the other. A narrow neck of land was the only access to the uplands beyond. The long pull up the hill made her appreciate even more just how odd it was that the players wanted to spend just a couple of nights on the island without prospect of reward.

At the top, having safely herded her party to higher ground, she turned and looked back. They were above the fog now. Although thinning beneath the bright sun, it still filled the river valley and completely obscured Pengaver. It felt to Jeniche as if they had crossed from one, hidden, world into the harsh light of another where events would be less forgiving. The thought made her shiver and she went in search of the others.

The top half of the town was just as crowded and noisy as the lower half though considerably sweeter smelling. It was market day and produce from Pengaver was just a small part of what was on sale. Aros and Cenau were like kids pretending to be adults. Not having been off the island for years, they dawdled, gawped, and forgot to argue. Jeniche hoped that would continue.

By the time they had worked their way through to the causeway out of the town, three wagons stood there ready to set out.

'Where are you headed?' asked the chief player as Jeniche drew alongside his wagon.

She was reluctant to be precise. 'North.'

He smiled back broadly. 'Then we must travel together. Unless you are in a hurry?'

Even in a civilized and relatively peaceful land like Ynysvron it was sensible to travel in groups and impolite to refuse an offer of companionship, especially from someone you already knew.

'Only as far as the weather dictates,' she replied, wondering where in the north the players were headed with heavy wagons; remembering how she had been told that they headed south to the town of Gwydr for the winter.

For all of Jeniche's suspicions, the others seemed happy to have the company. Cenau's horse seemed to have hitched itself to one of the wagons, he rode so close. Jeniche smiled, seeing the honey-coloured hair of Caru as she chattered away to the almost terminally shy young Derw. She was also pleased to see Aros taking his duties seriously. He rode at the head of the column with Maiv, a sturdy warrior who had shaved off her blonde hair for the expedition. Her companion Awd, who rode at the rear of the column beside Jeniche, had done the same.

She had never seen an Ynyswr warrior in full battle dress. It was impressively professional. She had travelled round half the world and seen some unusual weaponry and bizarre armour. This was plain, well made, and designed for strength and lightness.

The battle leathers she had seen before were now covered with a shirt of light mail. Sturdy boots. Thick trousers. A plain helmet with nose guard hung from the pommel of the saddle. At their waist they wore a knife and the long sword that Ynyswr warriors favoured. The horses had a leather blanket that offered some protection to their flanks. Looped into it were spears made of ash, three on each side.

Awd turned from her scrutiny of the horizon behind them and caught Jeniche looking at the spears. She grinned, drew one in a single, fluid movement, span it with a light flick of her fingers and offered it to Jeniche butt first. Jeniche held up her hands.

'I'd only drop it. It's a good day if I can draw my sword without slicing a bit off my ear.'

Awd looked at the well-worn, oft-repaired hilt of Jeniche's sword where it jutted up from behind her right shoulder and laughed. It was an old joke, but it broke the ice. 'I'm just going to scout round.'

Jeniche watched her go and saw Maiv drop back through the column to take the rear guard.

They stopped at midday on the roadside and rested the horses whilst they ate. Jeniche kept a close eye on her own horse and an equally close eye on the players. Everyone seemed to be getting on well, but she knew what happened when you got careless and let your guard down.

The afternoon was much the same and because the roads were good they travelled a fair distance. As the sun began to set and they looked for somewhere to camp for the night, Caru beckoned to Jeniche from the back of the last wagon. She urged her horse into a trot and rode alongside.

'Gwynfor. My father,' she added when Jeniche frowned. 'The chief player.'

Jeniche nodded. The one she knew from somewhere other than the stage.

'He thinks we are being followed.'

Chapter Seven

Shouting woke her and she rolled into a crouch. Someone had run through the camp and kicked the fire apart. In the smoky darkness, sparks flew and caught on the breeze. The horses were spooked and pulled at the picket line, shadowy figures trying to calm them. Some of the players scrambled to douse the embers that were settling on the wagons. Where the warriors had gone was anyone's guess.

It only took an instant to survey the scene before Jeniche instinctively made for one of the vantage points she had noted earlier. Grabbing the saddlebag containing her book and notes, she threw it over her left shoulder and clambered up onto the nearest wagon. From there she leapt, in the darkness, to an overhanging branch of an oak. Once she had lodged the bag safely, she leaned out over the camp to try to make sense of what was going on.

More shouting, this time from the direction of the road. There was someone running through the long grass and she caught a glint of light on a drawn sword.

'Don't get split up!' she called, wasting her breath; and

decided to shift position in case anyone out there had a bow.

Climbing higher through the half-bare branches she began to see the pale, uneven ribbon of the dirt road. One shape ran across it, but she had no way of knowing who or what it might be – friend, foe, or frightened wild animal. Moments later another followed. This one was human and, judging by the spear, it was either Awd or Maiv.

Back down at the branch where her bag was lodged, she noted its position and then swung herself onto the wagon. Several pointed objects swung in her direction, reflecting light from the fire that had been revived.

'It's Jeniche,' she said, waiting until the sharp ends were pointing somewhere else before dropping down to the ground.

'Who are we missing? Is anyone hurt?'

A quick count left them with a few bruises and minor burns and four people missing. The three warriors could look to their own affairs. Cenau, on the other hand, was another matter. Jeniche was about to start giving out instructions, but realized it was redundant.

'I'm going to look round the edges of the camp, see if Cenau's fallen over in the dark.'

She found her sword under her blanket, strapped it on to her back, and then picked a hefty brand from the fire. Being a target of arrows didn't worry her so much now. If someone had been going to shoot them, they would have done it in the initial confusion and the survivors would now be counting the dead. Heading for the deep shadow beneath the trees, she kept the burning torch low and began searching.

It was Aros who found Cenau, stumbling over his prone

form in the dark as he returned to the camp. The muffled cries guided light in the right direction and they carried Cenau to the fire where he was engulfed by the female members of the players' troupe who set about cooing him into consciousness.

A little later, Awd and Maiv came back into camp and shook their heads. After warm drinks, they went back out to patrol the perimeter with Aros. Jeniche wrapped her blanket round her shoulders and sat by the fire, suddenly cold.

'I don't see the point of it.' Aros bit into a piece of the bread they had brought with them and chewed thoughtfully. 'They didn't seem to be after anything.'

Awd shrugged and yawned. 'To deprive us of sleep.'

'But why?'

'Who knows.'

Jeniche lay wrapped in her blanket still only half awake. One or two of the players had emerged. Everyone looked tired.

'And so close to Durm.'

'It's far enough,' said Jeniche without moving.

They turned to look at her.

'It was dark. Moon just past new. Lots of cloud. We couldn't risk going for help until daylight and now they've gone.'

'I still don't see why,' persisted Aros, as he cut a piece of cheese. 'What's to be gained from attacking a bunch of players and a group of Derw looking for books?'

Gwynfor joined them by the ashes of the fire. He poked them with the toe of his boot and then sat on an old bit of log.

'Do you carry much money, Gwynfor?'

He poured some small beer from a jug and drank. 'No. Not these days. When I was younger and had a single, light wagon, I tended to keep it with me, but it was never much anyway, not worth the risk of getting stuck on the end of a rusty spear for.' He drank some more. 'Times change.'

'The rest of us haven't got anything,' said Aros. 'I mean, maybe on the way back when we have the books or whatever it is. And even then…' He shrugged. There was a lot of that going on.

Jeniche propped herself on one elbow and reached for the jug. 'It's not just why,' she said as she poured the ale into her cup, 'but who.'

'Our shadow from yesterday evening, you think?' asked Gwynfor.

There had been someone following them, way back along the road just on the edge of vision. Of course, it was a fairly busy road, even at that time of year. It might just have been other travellers heading in the same direction. When they had finally camped for the night and built a fire, Gwynfor had waited by the roadside to invite the travellers to join them.

After a while, he gave up as they seemed to have vanished. There had been a long discussion over supper as to whether there had been any tracks leading away from the road that a local traveller might use. No one could properly remember. They just assumed there must have been.

'If it was them,' said Jeniche, 'they must have had a chance to look at us. When did you notice them?'

'Same time as these two,' he replied, nodding at Awd and Maiv.

'They didn't get any closer than when we saw them,' said Aros.

'But they may have watched us leave Durm.'

They all looked at Jeniche.

'Which brings us back,' said Awd, 'to Aros's question.'

'Especially,' said Jeniche, 'if you know that there are three well-trained Derw warriors in the party.'

They all looked at each other as that sank in.

'I think,' said Gwynfor after a glance at the wagon where the women of the troupe were gathered, 'we'll keep that thought to ourselves for now.'

Apart from a sickening headache, Cenau seemed none the worse for wear. In his panic at being woken in the night he had bolted into the dark and tripped over a large stone to discover the next large stone was exactly as far away as he was tall. The lump on his left temple would go through a series of spectacular colours as it subsided.

Riding in a bumpy wagon wasn't going to be the best thing for a pounding head, but it did come with the compensation of the ministrations of Caru. So he ignored the scowl from Gwynfor, the leer from Aros, and the raised eyebrow from Jeniche and lay back as everyone else got on with the work.

Everything was tidied away and the fire thoroughly doused. Jeniche climbed the oak tree and went as high as the branches would offer support. Patches of mist littered the landscape, clinging in rags to the trees growing in the small valleys that drained the upland. Other than that, it was mile upon mile of heather, rocky outcrops, and the single pale earth road winding along the tops. Nothing moved except a distant buzzard struggling to find height in the cool air.

Looking back the way they had come, the scene was equally empty. No sign of anything, not even a side track.

She climbed back down, collected her saddlebag, and dropped down to the rough grass. By the time she had saddled her horse and settled herself in her heavy coat, the others were making their way onto the road.

Maiv dropped way back behind the rest of the column. She stayed close enough to keep contact, but far enough to give good warning. Awd did the same at the front. Aros and Jeniche between them covered the flanks as best they could, although the swathes of thick heather made riding out at any distance impossible for them and anyone else. It was when the heather gave way to thin, wind-sculpted grass that they went wider.

They rested the horses at midday. Caru perched on top of one of the wagons keeping watch whilst her mother took care of Cenau. Jeniche looked in on him and he had the grace to look sheepish. The lump on the side of his forehead worried her. It had gone down noticeably, but blows to the head were unpredictable. She went back to her meal thinking that those stones in her boot were beginning to take on the character of nails sticking through from the sole – much more uncomfortable and much more difficult to cure.

In the afternoon, a low whistle from Maiv alerted them to the distant presence of their shadow. Gwynfor beckoned to Jeniche and she rode up alongside his wagon.

'By my reckoning, we are about an hour from where the road forks. The road north cuts away to the right and the road to the western highlands goes to the left. There's a big patch of woodland there on the hillside atween the fork. Poor old Cenau'll have to leave his bed, but I have an idea.'

It had all seemed very flimsy to Jeniche, and Maiv and Awd had taken some convincing, but in the end they decided to give it a try. If it didn't work as planned, it might still be used to their advantage in other ways. So Cenau had been hauled from his nice warm billet and the players had got to work without once breaking their pace. And as the plan took shape, even Maiv and Awd had begun to think it might work. Now they were about to find out.

The most difficult thing had been getting their horses up the steep slope amongst the trees to a place where they were hidden from both roads. Eog had muttered a while and a slight breeze had begun to play amongst the branches, stirring the leaves. It was not loud enough to spook the horses, but enough to mask the occasional sound they might make. Jeniche wondered whether that was simply coincidence. She had heard things about the Derw she had never seen demonstrated, found difficult to believe. Perhaps she had just been given proof. Perhaps she was falling too deeply under their charm. It had happened before.

Before long, the wagons had passed out of view along the left-hand fork. The sight of them being decked out by the players with spare costumes and bits of scenery so that, from a distance, it looked like the Derw were riding close formation with the wagons, was a marvel to behold.

They had argued with Gwynfor that whoever was following might not take kindly to such a deception. He had shrugged. 'By the time they catch up and realize,' he had said, 'we'll have tidied everything away. With any luck they won't catch on until tomorrow.'

'Just be careful.'

Gwynfor had looked at her with an appraising eye, but in the end he had said nothing. She hoped she would meet them again. For now, though, they must do their part and stand silently amidst the trees.

71

Jeniche, watching from behind the trunk of an ancient birch, saw them first. Five riders taking their time. She signalled to Awd who moved carefully and looked down toward the road. She then watched with all the stillness of a hawk, taking in the detail of the riders' clothing, their horses, and their weapons.

At the fork, the riders stopped and a quiet discussion ensued. It was clear they knew which road the wagons had taken; it was equally clear they were not local lads paid a purseful of drinking money to cause a bit of trouble. When the talking finished, one of them galloped off along the right-hand fork whilst the others waited, watching the road and the woodland with care. If it was going to go wrong, now would be the time.

After what seemed like an hour in which cold and cramp set in, the rider returned at a walk and all five made their way along the left-hand fork. Once they were well on their way, Aros climbed up along the top of the hill to the edge of the trees and watched the riders out of sight. When he returned, they led their own mounts down the far side of the hill to the right-hand road. There they mounted and set off at a gallop, slowing after a while to a canter. Jeniche would rather have galloped until nightfall and then kept going. Four of those riders were clearly from this part of the world. The fifth, with his cropped blond hair and hard pale face, had all the look of a heartless, ravaging Occassan.

Chapter Eight

The rain fell steadily, pounding on the thatch and dripping from the eaves as they sat around the fire and steamed. Eog was applying salve to Cenau's forehead. The swelling had more or less gone, but there was still bruising around his bloodshot eye, and the young scholar was desperately tired. The others were not much better.

They had kept up a strong pace for several days across the high country and then down to the west coast. Remote farms and small villages had been their only shelter against the stormy winds out of the west until now. On the coast, they had followed the road to the fishing port of Aderyn where they had stocked up on supplies. From there they had taken the road directly north, easing up on the horses as there had been no sign of pursuit since the little deception by the players.

It was pleasant country. Unlike the bleak moorland they had crossed earlier, the valleys were lush and the hills heavily wooded. Mountains caught cloud in the distance, but they kept to the well-used roads between the numerous villages.

And although it still rained there was more shelter from the winds.

Aches and pains came and went until it was the monotony of constant riding that finally began to weary them. It was Eog who lifted their spirits temporarily one damp, overcast morning. This was his country. He had been born not far away and knew the hills and valleys well. As they passed a distinctive outcrop of rock topped by several pines, he announced they would be in Addas by late afternoon. Not long afterwards it began to rain.

And now they sat steaming and despondent. They had expected a chance to rest, dry out, have at least one proper meal and one proper sleep in something approximating a proper bed. But Cynfelyn had not been there waiting for them.

When Eog had entered the inn, the innkeeper greeted him warmly, stirred the fire and had food brought through. Locals shifted away from the hearth to let the travellers get the best of the warmth and to get as far away as they could from the less-than-sweet vapours the heat was driving from their bodies and clothing. Cenau had kept looking round, watching the door that led to a small lean-to where guests slept.

It was once they were settled and had eaten that Eog passed on the news.

'Well, where is he?' asked Cenau.

'A place I know,' replied Eog quietly.

Cenau was about to protest, but Jeniche touched his arm and shook her head when he looked at her. He fell into a sullen silence. Riding about the countryside might be an education, but he had already decided he preferred books. In a library. With a stove. The walk to and from the refectory was all the exercise he craved.

The others took the news in stoic silence, although Aros looked almost as fed up as Cenau.

'The innkeeper told me that Cynfelyn left a few days ago,' said Eog, still keeping his voice low. 'No explanation. Rode off early one morning. But there haven't been any strangers about.'

'We should rest,' said Maiv. 'It's a risk, wasting time, but we need to be fresh.'

Jeniche sighed. 'I'll take first watch.'

'Should we have someone in the stables as well?' asked Aros.

Maiv nodded.

Aros looked at the others who looked at him. 'Did I just volunteer?'

It took them a while to get started in the morning, but they had been able to wash and set out with full bellies, wearing warm, dry clothes and riding fully rested horses. The cloud had lifted as well, although it was still grey.

Eog led the way. They followed the road for a while and then took a side track up into the hills. The track was narrow and they went in single file. To their left, the pine woods were dense and gloomy. To their right, a fast-flowing stream ran in a rocky channel on the far side of a grassy meadow.

As they rounded a corner, a number of riders charged directly at them out of the shadows between the trees. Immediately there was chaos. Cenau lost control of his horse and was thrown to the ground. He landed on a thick bed of pine needles and had the sense to roll out of the way.

Maiv and Awd closed in from each end of the line, but it was difficult at first in the ensuing turmoil. Jeniche was quick to draw her sword and saw Aros do the same, turning his horse to go after one of the assailants. For a moment she thought he was going to chase him on up the road, a classic trick, but Aros let him go.

Turning back from watching Aros, she saw another of the assailants charging straight at her, sword raised. She barely had time to react, raised her own sword arm to protect herself, when Ruad came thundering between them. It was a split second and he was gone as the assailant fell dead from his saddle. Again Jeniche was caught by surprise, watching as Ruad brought his bloodied spear into a vertical position, wheeled his horse like an expert, and then dropped his spear back to the horizontal, its butt tucked back under his arm.

Aware she was putting herself in danger, she urged her horse toward where she had last seen Cenau. She skirted Maiv and Duald who were side by side and nose to tail fighting off three assailants. Awd was on her feet close to the stream trading blows with another.

On the far side of the melee, Eog had sidled up to a tree and was trying to push his mount through several riderless horses that milled nervously against the tree line. He was trying to get to Cenau who, Jeniche saw with horror, was being menaced by the Occassan she had seen days before in the smaller party that had followed them and the players.

Throwing the reins of her horse to Eog, she slid off and pushed between the other beasts, dodging in amongst the trees. Someone screamed and kept screaming until the noise cut off abruptly. It didn't stop the other sounds of battle.

She cleared the trees just in time to see the Occassan rush Cenau with a long, thin-bladed knife. They were too far away for Jeniche to help, but close enough for Cenau's expression to be clear. She had never seen him angry like this before. Angry, certainly, but he always lost control. This time there was a frightening iciness in his eye.

As the Occassan lunged, Cenau stepped slightly to one side, took the man's wrist, twisted, and placed his other hand against the assailant's elbow. The Occassan looked surprised and then, as Cenau pulled on the wrist and pushed on the elbow, he howled with pain. Cenau picked up the dropped dagger and left the man where he had fallen, his arm broken at the joint.

By the time Cenau had finished throwing up at the base of a tree, the fight was over. Apart from one of the assailants who had sped away on horseback, leaving a trail of blood, the maimed Occassan was the only survivor.

Jeniche began rounding up horses, checking that her saddle bags were untouched. She improvised a picket line between two trees and once the horses were all hitched, she looked to see what else could be done.

Eog was watching the Occassan who had crawled to a tree and sat with his back to it. His right arm was twisted at a sickening angle and he was clearly in shock. Ruad and Duald were laying out the seven bodies in a way Jeniche found surprising; they were calm, efficient, and showed no sign of squeamishness. The way they had handled themselves in battle had been a revelation as well. They must have trained in a dangerous library.

Aros was collecting dropped weapons and kept looking at the corpses. His face was pale but he kept going. Maiv and Awd had ridden off in opposite directions to scout the area. The rider that had galloped away at the start had not returned and they wanted to be certain they were safe. For the time being, at least.

With nothing else to do, Jeniche went over to Cenau who was kneeling by the stream, drinking from cupped hands.

'Feeling a bit better?'

He looked round. 'Not really.'

'You did well.'

'It was horrible.'

'You are alive and the Occ—' she coughed, covering her hesitation. Was the man really an Occassan or was that just her own fears painting an extra layer of trouble? Besides, Cenau had enough to cope with for now. Bringing Occassus into the picture wouldn't help him. 'Your assailant. He got off lightly. All his companions are dead.'

She reached down and helped Cenau to his feet.

'I thought one of them rode off,' he said.

'Two. I doubt the latter will survive long. He was losing a lot of blood.'

Cenau shivered as he followed Jeniche to the horses. They passed the Occassan, but Cenau clearly couldn't bring himself to look.

'I was lucky,' he said, his voice croaking.

'You were fighting exactly as I taught you.' He still looked miserable. 'It's hard. You have lost something you'll never get back. But to be honest, I didn't think you'd be able to do it.'

'I am tired, cold, fed up, hungry, I miss my room, I miss the Library, I have a bruise over half my face...' He sighed. 'I don't even remember it. Just that awful crunch.'

Awd rode in from the path they were going to take.

'All clear, as far as I can tell.'

The warrior looked down at Cenau with narrowed eyes, the hint of a smile on her lips. She nodded.

'What are we going to do with all this?' asked Jeniche,

waving at the corpses and then at their newly acquired horses.

'Eog!' called Awd.

The Derw came trotting over, leaving the Occassan to his own little world of pain.

'The place where Cynfelyn is waiting. Could we find it without you?'

'Well... yes.' He lowered his voice so the Occassan wouldn't hear. 'Follow this track until it comes to a small bridge over the stream. The track crosses the water, but there's a sheep path that continues alongside the stream on this side. Follow that for about two miles and you'll come to a large sheepfold with a small stone hut. That's where he is.'

'When Maiv returns, would you come with me back to Addas? We'll take that cur and the horses. They can pay for fetching the dead and whatever rites they're given. I'll catch up with the others. I'd like you to get to Dun Braddan and tell your chief and elders what has happened.'

It was late by the time they set out in their respective directions. Cenau had become withdrawn and Jeniche asked Aros to ride beside him. They might not be friends, but they knew each other and she suspected Aros was also more than a little unsettled by what had happened. She hadn't seen much of what he'd done. There had been confusion and it was over quickly. But even if he hadn't engaged directly with their attackers, he had seen his first battle, witnessed the spilling of blood and the taking of lives.

In the fading light and chill air, they followed the track up into the hills, all the weariness of travel and combat hanging heavily on them. Everywhere was quiet. The horses walked on a carpet of needles at the edge of the track. There was no bird song. No one spoke. The only sound was the stream, golden with peat, a constant gurgle as it rushed over its pebbled bed.

At the bridge, they left the track and picked their way carefully along the endless, winding sheep path. Here it was even quieter. The narrow path cut away from the stream and passed up between rocks into a broad hidden valley. The sheep fold was close by. From the hut, a thin drift of smoke could just be seen in the twilight.

They dismounted and walked their horses into the fold, closing the gap with some old thorn bushes left there for the purpose. Whilst the others waited, Maiv went to the door and knocked on it with the hilt of her sword. After a moment it opened and a tall, weather-beaten man in a rough sheepskin coat emerged, a long staff of oak in his hand.

After a day of surprises, Jeniche was looking forward to some food and rest. The others dismounted and greeted the man, Cenau brightening a little. He sought out Jeniche as she slid off her horse and pulled her forward by her sleeve.

'Come and meet Cynfelyn,' he said.

Cynfelyn looked at her with an uncertain smile.

'Hello, Jeniche,' he said.

'Hello, Alltud,' she replied. And threw a fierce punch at his jaw.

Chapter Nine

'I was tired, cold, fed up, and hungry. I'd just been through a nasty skirmish in which I discovered that Ruad and Duald, the two librarians I was travelling with, are in fact no such thing.' She shot them a glance which they pretended not to see. 'There are Occassans wandering about out there. And I am feeling more and more that I have been deceived. Again.' She glared pointedly back at Cynfelyn. 'And then you open the door. What else did you expect?'

'Librarians can learn to fight,' said Cynfelyn, mildly. 'I did.'

'Is deceit on the syllabus as well?'

'I have never deceived you.'

She threw another punch. This time it made contact, her knuckles hitting his upper arm. 'Ouch! All right. Just a bit. But let me explain.'

'Oh. This will be good. You've had years to think this one up.'

She snapped the reins and her horse cantered ahead of the main body. Cynfelyn didn't try to catch up.

It had been an uncomfortable night in more ways than one. After Cynfelyn had waved down all the swords that had appeared and released Jeniche's fist from his grip, you couldn't have sliced a farrier's knife through the atmosphere in the hut. And it would only sleep half of them. As Jeniche resolutely refused to have anything to do with taking watch, the others were in and out of the door, until they all gave up. When Jeniche woke in the morning, she had the hut to herself.

Her decision to stay with the others was pragmatic. If there were bandits, Occassans, or whatever else wandering about the countryside intent on who knew what kind of mayhem, she didn't want to face them alone. All the same, she rode slightly apart and brooded. The only ones she felt sorry for were Cenau and Aros. Whatever was going on in Ynysvron, whatever Cynfelyn was up to, they clearly hadn't been let into the secret either.

When Cynfelyn did decide to catch up, it was mid morning and they were riding along a hillside, keeping below the crest so they couldn't be seen from a distance. Weak sunlight broke through high cloud and pale shafts of light rode across the sea in the west. The jagged, dark-grey shapes of a string of islands were scattered along the horizon. Ghostly flecks of white came and went as light caught the sails of ships.

'Explain.' She hadn't felt this miserable since Trag had vanished beneath the sand and she wanted comfort. Even if it was a lie.

'I don't know where to begin. How do you think you were deceived?'

'Oh. How about that whole journey from Makamba to Rasa? You remember? Trag was swallowed by the desert. Mowen Bey was shot. Tinit Sul... Who knows what happened to him. All for some kid pretending to be the God-King.'

Cynfelyn stared at her open mouthed. Surprise gave way to anguish.

'But...' He thought back to those bleak days after she disappeared. 'When did you leave the palace?'

'What does it matter?'

'A lot.'

'When the real God-King stepped forward, I slipped out the way we had come in. Helped myself to some food and cash on the way. Went down to the camel station and worked my way into Gyanag.'

He struggled a moment for breath. 'That young man who presented himself as the God-King was the head of the palace guard. The deceit was against the Occassans, not you.'

Jeniche said nothing. Her head span. All the years of wandering. All the years of anger, bewilderment. If there was any comfort, it was in knowing that Trag's life hadn't been thrown away for an act of betrayal. As comforts went it was small. But it was enough for the time being.

'We tried to find you. Searched the palace. Searched the city. Gyan Mi sent out emissaries in all directions. They found you in Gyanag eventually, had instructions to watch out for you. Oh gods, Jeniche. I'm sorry.'

'If they knew where I was, why didn't someone tell me what had happened?'

'Because nobody knew you didn't know.'

'And nobody thought to ask why I'd taken off on my own?'

'A thousand times, Jen. A thousand times.'

They rode in silence for a while. Jeniche felt her whole

world was in pieces around her and she was trying to rebuild it from the fragments, rebuild it in a way that accounted for what she had learned, rebuild it in a way that accounted for just how fragile she must have been on reaching the palace in Rasa.

'So how do you know all this?' Her voice was faint, hesitant.

'Gyan Mi sends reports. They lost sight of you not long after you went into Azak.'

She recalled the small group of Tunduri monks that had joined the company she was travelling with. It was why she had taken off on her own again, not wanting to be reminded.

'Tinit Sul recovered. He cannot use that arm for much, but he is well. Gave up thoughts of becoming an abbot and helps run the hospital at Kodor. The other monks turned up in the palace grounds after the Occassans were routed. A bit dazed, but none the worse for their ordeal. Mowen Nah returned eventually to Rasa and is set to succeed Darlit Fen as chief engineer.'

Before he could move out of range she punched him on the arm again and then rode off ahead of him so he wouldn't see her tears.

A low warble made everyone sit up straight in their saddles. Aros, who had taken point, rode back down the line past Jeniche and spoke briefly to Cynfelyn before carrying on to Maiv who was acting as rearguard. Awd had still not rejoined the group.

'Cenau,' called Jeniche. He stopped his horse and she rode up alongside him. 'Stick with me.'

'Oh gods,' he said. 'Not again.'

Cynfelyn joined them.

'Who signalled?'

'It came from the left,' he said. 'Ruad.'

'We need to find a better spot than this.'

It was stony ground with little chance to manoeuvre and virtually no cover.

'And,' she continued, 'we really need to talk about what's going on, Allt— Cynfelyn. Whoever's attacking us isn't after books.'

They didn't get a chance to do either.

An arrow went high and wide in front of Cenau, bouncing off a rock.

'Hold tight and keep low,' called Cynfelyn and smacked the rump of Cenau's horse. Jeniche took off after him, looking up to the distant hillside where the arrow had come from. She caught a glimpse of someone on horseback retrieving a spear from a corpse before they galloped out of sight over the ridge.

Other horses followed. Twisting to look over her shoulder, Jeniche saw Aros and Ruad closing up on them. The four of them galloped on up the narrow road. Aros and Jeniche had their swords drawn.

At the top of the slope they found themselves on a rough meadow. Away to their left was the sea. To their right, rockier ground.

'Straight across,' called Aros.

They hadn't gone very far when the others appeared. Maiv stood in her stirrups and waved them on. When they reached the far side, she stayed behind to keep watch.

'Was that Awd?' asked Cenau. 'Up on the hill?'

'It was,' replied Aros. 'She's been watching our flank from the heights.'

Cenau shivered and huddled into his cloak, grim faced.

Jeniche thought Aros probably felt the same, but he was quickly learning to hide it.

'So what brought you to Ynysvron, if you were...?'

Jeniche pulled her coat tighter. The overhang didn't offer much shelter. They were out of the wind, but it was still cold, as they didn't dare risk a fire. Cenau, Awd, and Ruad slept close by. Aros dozed, turning and moaning softly. Somewhere above, the others kept watch.

'I had meant to go south through Azak,' she said quietly, 'but the locals told me there are large tracts of poisoned land down that way. So I kept heading west. You used to talk about this place all the time, so I thought I'd see for myself.'

Cynfelyn chafed his hands.

'And what's with this "Cynfelyn"?' she continued. 'I thought your name was Alltud.'

'That's what Teague called me. It's the Ynyswr word for "exile". Cynfelyn is my birth name. Emrys my family name.'

'And you're Derw?'

'Yes. Since my youth. Teague was my tutor.'

'Teague?'

'Yes.'

'And you followed her to Makamba?'

'No. No. It's a long story.'

'I seem to be part of it. Perhaps I should know the rest.'

He scratched his head. 'There's a lot I don't know myself.'

'The bits you do.'

Cynfelyn was silent for a while, trying to push his thoughts and memories into something resembling a comprehensible narrative.

'You probably noticed that all is not well in the paradise of Ynysvron.'

'Was it ever a paradise?'

'No. Hundreds of islands. As many tribes. You can imagine. But we got by. The Derw managed to hold things together. Our allegiance is to Ynysvron first, then to our tribe.'

'Have the Derw never been tempted just to take over?'

'No. Not as far as I know. Although there are some who say we once did. A long time ago. There was unrest and there was raiding from countries across the Eastern Sea. A Guardian was appointed. A battle leader. The tribes agreed to put their armies under the Guardian's leadership whenever it was needed. The raids were repelled and for generations the memory of that cooperation brought peace. A new Guardian was appointed every so often, but without an active role it became ceremonial. Eventually there came a time when a new Guardian wasn't appointed and inter-tribal disputes and discussions were left to a Council of Derw.'

'But it didn't last.'

'I don't suppose it ever does. Look at Makamba. The city managed for a very long time with just a city guard. Beldas was the same. It all kept moving along for generations. And then the Occassans turned up.'

They sat in the cold dark for a while, watching as stars appeared in the breaks between the clouds, waiting for Aros to settle again.

'When did it start breaking down here?'

'It's difficult to put a timescale to it, but about twelve years ago we began to realize there was an ongoing increase in border disputes, petty conflicts, cattle raids, that sort of thing. Nothing to worry about if they were taken one by one, but everything we heard back from local Derw suggested that trouble was being stirred from outside.'

'Occassus?'

'I don't think so. Not to begin with. They seem to have their poisonous fingers in the pie now, but to begin with it was just Santach.'

'The Warlord of Gwerin?'

'The very same. He has territorial ambitions, believes Ynysvron should be his. We might speak the same language, but there is a deep-seated and ancient enmity between our lands. It goes back well before the Evanescence. But he doesn't have the strength to hold his own country and invade this one.'

'So you think he's trying to stir up trouble to weaken any resistance.'

'And when it gets to the point of civil war, ride in as our saviour and claim the Guardianship.'

'Would that work?'

'We take it as a serious threat. We didn't know about the Occassans. I suppose he could have been a mercenary.'

They looked at each other and then both shook their heads.

'And sitting in a cold cave on our way to get some... books... with librarians who moonlight as cavalry soldiers... that's part of some plan?'

'Cenau told me he thought you'd been on the point of leaving.'

Jeniche was caught out by the change of direction. 'Oh... I... He doesn't miss much, does he.'

'Were you?'

'Why do you want to know?'

'I don't want you to stay out of some feeling of obligation. Because this *is* part of some plan. And it's not much of one. So I don't want you drawn into something again.

Not after Makamba. We didn't deceive you then. I don't want that now.'

Ruad woke them at first light.

'We think those two yesterday were probably part of the troop that attacked us earlier. There's been no activity in the night and we scouted widely. But one of them got away. So they'll be able to lead anyone back to this point at least. The sooner we leave, the better.'

So with Cynfelyn's promise that it wasn't much further, they all mounted up and ate on the move.

A pale sun was struggling to light the horizon when they emerged from a gloomy avenue of thorn trees onto a high meadow between surrounding mountains. To west and east, between the peaks, there were glimpses of a steely grey sea. But nobody had eyes for that, or for the ravens that rose noisily into the air as they rode out onto the rough pasture of the gently domed hilltop.

'Maenmawr,' said Cynfelyn quietly.

Spread around the centre of the field was a vast circle of standing stones. Solid, ancient, marked with the lichen of millennia, their impact on the senses surpassed any resemblance to their physical size. Over a hundred feet across and, by a quick count, containing forty-nine stones of different sizes and states of preservation, the formation pinned the whole of history to the landscape. Within the circle, to one side, was a rectangular enclosure made of smaller stones from the same source. Jeniche felt her flesh tingle. She could tell the others felt the same.

They dismounted. The warriors led the horses to one side beneath a line of trees and tied the beasts to a low picket where there was good grass. As they split up and vanished into the landscape to watch the approaches, Cynfelyn led a reluctant Aros, Cenau, and Jeniche toward the circle. As they neared the stones, it became clear that two of the larger monoliths formed a gateway to the interior.

Chapter Ten

The short walk up to the stones passed through wiry autumn grasses, aeons of time, and many levels of reality. As they approached the ancient gate, the stones seemed to grow and the gap between them seemed to widen. Jeniche felt a familiar queasiness; saw fluttering shadows ahead of her. Silent winds chased, the skies flickered, strange colours raced in faint swirls across the meadow and between the unchanging stones. It was as if all the days that had passed since the stones were sunk like needles into the flesh of the earth were passing at once.

Jeniche looked at the others but they seemed not to notice. She struggled to stay with them, although they were never more than a few paces away from her. It was the realm of dream. Her steps were sluggish as if she was wading against a flow of water, pushing into a strong and silent wind. And the closer to the circle they came, the fiercer the winds that tugged at her, the less contact she seemed to have with their own little part of the world, their own little part of time.

Ahead of her, almost within reach yet infinitely distant,

the others stepped between the stones and into the circle. Cynfelyn began to turn. Slowly. Slowly. Almost frozen as she, in turn, crossed the threshold.

The full power of the circle slammed through her body and she staggered, thrown to her left by the immense force. Had it not been able to pass through her, she had no doubt she would have been flattened against the sunwise stone like an insect beneath a boot.

A startled look of concern began to form on Cynfelyn's face. Her left hand went up to steady herself against the stone. There was a flash and she found herself on her back on the grass looking at the sky and then at three faces peering down at her.

'What happened?' asked Aros. 'Did you trip?'

Jeniche sat up, flexing her left hand. Cynfelyn knelt beside her, searching her eyes.

'No,' she said. 'I didn't trip.'

'You look awful,' said Cenau.

'Quiet,' growled Cynfelyn. 'I've seen you like this before.'

'Did you know?'

'What's going on?' demanded Aros.

'Is that why I'm here?' she asked, ignoring Aros and Cenau.

'No.'

Her head began to throb but she waited, unmoving and tense.

'Yes. But not for that. Rhonwen said it. You know more than anyone in Ynysvron about the Evanescence, the places and artefacts that have survived. And that wasn't my doing. Or anyone else's.'

'Cynfelyn?' Cenau sounded worried.

He stood. 'You two, walk sunwise round the inside of

the stones until you get to the small enclosure. Without bickering.'

They went.

Leaning down, he took Jeniche by the arm and helped her to her feet. The queasiness was still there. Some of the dreaminess. But she felt no worse than if she had tumbled from a stationary horse.

'It was essential to have those two here,' he said, nodding toward Aros and Cenau. 'You I wanted as a trusted friend.'

She rubbed her head. 'Why them? Are they a part of the plan as well?'

'Not just a part.'

Aros and Cenau had reached the enclosure on the far side of the circle. Jeniche looked from Cynfelyn to the other two and then back again. 'The situation is really that bad?'

'We had nothing else. Aros is a descendant of the last Guardian. Cenau, if he can pull his head out of the clouds and remember his feet are on the soil, will be the best of the Derw for many generations past and yet to come.'

'I don't understand. Do they know they're so important?'

'No. And they mustn't. Not yet. They need to work it out for themselves.'

'Santach seems to know.'

Cynfelyn shook his head. 'I doubt it. That was just bad luck.'

Jeniche raised an eyebrow, but didn't press the matter. 'So this was never about finding a hoard of books.' She looked round at the stones and could not help feeling that they all looked back.

'Will you help?'

'Do I have much choice?'

'Yes. You can walk away now.'

She was tempted to punch his arm again. 'Through that,' she said, pointing at the gateway to the stones where shadows still flickered in their circular race, 'and out to where the Gwerin and Occassans are hunting.'

'I'm sorry. We were desperate.'

'Ah. Thank you.'

'You know what I mean.'

'Not really.'

'I'll explain, but we'd better get to those two.'

Flexing her left hand again to ease the pins and needles, Jeniche set off with Cynfelyn following.

'For Aros to claim the Guardianship,' he continued quietly, 'he needs to be in possession of the Four Hallows.'

'Hallows?'

'Symbols of sovereignty that are a constant reminder to the Guardian of their role. Every child learns about them. But they were lost. So long ago they're considered by many to be myths.'

'Will possession of them be enough?'

'No, but it will be essential.'

'And what are these Four Hallows?'

'Later? Please?'

Of all the disconcerting things she had experienced, Cynfelyn pleading ranked near the top. 'Later,' she conceded. 'In full.' And raised her fist with the knuckles protruding. Without thinking, he rubbed his arm, but some of the strain fell away from his face.

'Right, you two,' he called. 'We have work to do.'

'This is as far as I got.'

They stood in the cold, silent dark. None of them knew what to say. They were at the dead end of a long passage lined with slabs of stone that were clearly of the same age as those that formed the circle above. Dim light filtered from the entrance and down the steps. The only redeeming features of the tunnel were that it was dry and that they could stand upright.

It had taken half an hour and a collection of scraped knuckles to shift the slab over the entrance. Cenau was still sucking the crushed tip of his middle finger. Jeniche was still wondering how Cynfelyn had ever managed to do this on his own. But there was a lot she had never known about him.

'Well,' she said. 'It's a cold, dark, empty hole in the ground. Empty. In case you missed that bit.'

Ignoring Jeniche, Cynfelyn groped in a dark niche and produced a length of wood with rag wrapped round one end. He smelled the rag and nodded. 'Flint?'

Jeniche fished in an inner pocket of her coat and drew out a small pouch. After fiddling for a bit in the dark, she began to strike sparks onto the rag. One took and the flame found what was left of the oil. Dark smoke billowed along the ceiling, but the torch was bright enough to illuminate the slab of stone that blocked the end of the passage. Aros and Cenau gasped. Jeniche realized why she still felt queasy.

This was a stone of an altogether different pedigree. Intricate designs covered the surface, precisely incised patterns that caught the eye and drew it on a journey the mind could not cope with. It was so unlike the worn spirals and glyphs on the other surfaces that it hardly seemed possible the two cultures had any point of connection. Yet the people who had built the circle had given rise to the pre-Ev peoples.

Jeniche reached forward to touch the slab, tracing the

patterns with her fingertips. At first it was just random wonderment. She had not been this close to a substantial pre-Ev artefact since they had been buried deep beneath the desert. There had been small items in the Library tower, perhaps the cases themselves. But this... And as she ran her fingers along the grooves, she began to follow a pattern.

She couldn't see it, but her fingers felt it there amongst all the lines and shapes as if they had once been taught it and the memory still lingered, awakened by the subtle movement. It drew her hand to one side where the lines were wider. And then her forefinger seemed reluctant to move on.

'Douse the torch.'

Cynfelyn dropped it to the floor and stamped it out. They waited.

'I can still see lights in front of my eyes from the flames,' said Aros.

'Not from the flames.'

Gently moving her other fingertips, she found the pattern that gripped her hand, a pale spectral glow around the edge. She expected something to happen. The panel was warm. Another dot of light began to wink. But nothing moved. She frowned.

And then the obvious occurred to her. If it was a door, perhaps she should push.

Her hand sank into the surface yet she could still feel its hardness beneath her palm. The sensation elicited a feverish shiver. And then her hand was pulled silently to the left. Snatching it away, she became aware of a deeper darkness revealed, of a change in the air.

'What happened? What did you do?' asked Cenau.

'Better light the torch again,' said Aros.

'No,' said Cynfelyn. 'Not yet. Jeniche? Do you think it will work again?'

She pressed her right hand to her chest, the pendant hard against her flesh, warm beneath her clothes.

Taking a breath, she stepped forward through the door, her foot searching for solid ground. As soon as she crossed the threshold, a panel in the wall flickered with a dim light. Moments later another one further along gave a faint buzz and blinked into life. It, too, was dim, but it was enough to see by.

Jeniche turned. Cenau seemed to be having trouble breathing. Aros was looking back along the passage toward daylight.

'Come on, you two,' said Cynfelyn. 'I'm as scared as you are, but we have to go in.'

Aros loosened his sword in its scabbard. 'Come on, Cenau,' he said.

Jeniche and Cynfelyn exchanged glances. Aros was learning.

Reluctantly, Cenau let himself be pushed over the threshold, stepping from a passage that was built at the beginning of a culture's life into a passage that was built at its end.

They went slowly and a few paces from the door, heard it whisper back into place. Cenau let out a small whimper.

'I don't know if I'm going to be very good at closed spaces,' he gasped.

Jeniche walked back to the door, trying to show a confidence she didn't feel. It slid open. Turning back, she smiled. The others let her past and she began walking along the smooth floor. As they walked, the panels of light ahead of them flickered on, fading behind them once they had passed. One or two stayed dark.

'Different to the desert tunnels.'

'What… have you…?' Cenau was still having trouble breathing. Cynfelyn looked worried.

'Slowly,' said Aros quietly. 'He used to get like this as a boy,' he explained to Jeniche.

Cenau forced himself to slow his breathing; Cynfelyn talking through it to take his mind off things.

'A long time ago. In Makamba. Under Makamba. Beneath the edge of the desert. It's a long story. Anyway, there the passages would light up for half a mile or more.'

'Half a mile?' wailed Cenau.

'Slow breaths,' said Aros, glaring at Cynfelyn.

Whilst Aros calmed Cenau again, Jeniche pushed Cynfelyn a few steps along the passage. 'Are they down here?' she asked in a whisper.

'Just one.'

'Who put it down here? How did they do that?'

He couldn't say any more as Cenau and Aros stood looking at them expectantly. Jeniche smiled and carried on along the passage. At the far end there was another door. It opened in the same way, with Jeniche pressing against a small panel. As it slid to one side it jammed.

With a bit of brute force they managed to push it far enough to squeeze through. The third door opened all the way onto a balcony running round a broad chamber that dropped an unknown depth into shadow. Aros was the last to step through and as he put his weight onto the balcony there was a loud crack that echoed about the dark space.

Memories of the desert and Trag hit Jeniche hard. She pushed Cynfelyn along the balcony. 'Spread out. Keep close to the wall. Cynfelyn. A little help. What are we looking for? Where is it?'

'A stone. Beneath the stones.'

'That is not useful.'

'I'll know it when we see it.'

'Nor is that.'

Another loud crack shot through the darkness and the balcony shuddered.

'Spread out some more and move. Slowly. Lightly.' As if that would make any difference, she thought.

They began to edge along, keeping close to the wall. Now and then a panel would glow, but it did little more than show a small section of balcony and an infinite depth of shadow.

'We should have brought the torch,' said Jeniche.

There was a cough and she looked back at Aros waving the torch in front of a wide grin.

'Keep tight hold of it for now. When we get somewhere more stable, we'll get it lit again.'

Edging along above an uncertain drop in the dark distorted their sense of time. They hadn't gone much further, although it seemed to take forever, when Cynfelyn called out.

'There's a structure here. With stairs.'

Jeniche breathed a sigh of relief. Stairs meant strength. She hoped.

As she joined Cynfelyn, a loud hum started from somewhere above them.

'Don't like that,' murmured Cenau.

Jeniche began fishing in her pocket for her flint.

And suddenly they were blinded by light as huge overhead panels flicked on.

Blinking, they stood dazed. As their sight adjusted, the daze turned to awe. Even Jeniche and Cynfelyn, who had seen pre-Ev structures before, were impressed. It didn't match the city beneath the desert, but it came close. A vast, empty, octagonal shaft with stairs at each angle that went down ten floors.

'What is it for?'

'I have no idea, Cenau. But I think we should find what we came for and get out. The others will think we've forgotten them.'

'There!'

'What?'

'Down there. On that structure in the centre of the floor.'

They all went to the railing where Cynfelyn stood and peered down.

'Is this wise?' asked Cenau, stepping back.

'Probably not,' said Jeniche. 'Let's go down and see.'

They clattered down the metal stairs, looking at as many wonders as they could manage without falling over their own feet. By the time they reached the bottom, the space was filled with harsh echoes.

Cynfelyn crossed the floor to the structure in the centre. It was a frame of silvery material some twenty feet high. Small boxes were embedded in the base, some of which had faintly flickering lights. Above them it became an intricate tower of interwoven bars and struts.

'On the top.' He pointed to where something dark gleamed against a pale background. 'Any good at climbing, Aros?'

'I'm bet—'

Cynfelyn placed a hand on Jeniche's shoulder. 'It has to be Aros,' he said quietly.

Cenau watched this exchange with a puzzled expression. Aros took off his sword and handed it to Cenau, who

100

nearly dropped it in surprise. Aros grinned and then began to climb. It wasn't that difficult, but some of the structure had given way and he had to be careful where he put his weight. Part way up there was another loud crack. They all froze.

'That wasn't me,' called Aros.

'Don't waste any time. Quickly. Carefully.'

Aros started to climb again. The higher he went, the more difficult it became. He tried to reach the object where it perched at the top of a kind of spire, but it was just out of reach and he had run out of footholds.

'Take your boots off and throw them down,' called Jeniche. 'Use the sides of your feet and hug the spire.' She mimed the action.

A pair of boots cartwheeled down, followed by footwraps, and Cenau gathered them up. Aros began to shin up. He only needed to go a little further and he was able to reach up and free the object. As he lifted it off, Jeniche could see it was a circle of black material.

'A stone?'

Cynfelyn didn't have time to answer. Part of the top balcony fell away from its supports and crashed down onto the balcony beneath. Dust filtered down through the bright light and they watched in horror as the next level of balcony began to peel away from the wall all the way along to the stairs.

Amid the grinding and squealing of twisting metal, Aros placed the circlet on his head to leave both hands free and clambered down to the floor. He handed the artefact to Cynfelyn who tucked it away into an interior pocket. Taking his boots from Cenau, Aros pulled them back on and stuffed the wraps into a pocket. Jeniche saw blood.

More sections of balcony fell, pulling the stairs with them. Aros grabbed his sword from Cenau and they ran.

The race up the next set of stairs was agonizing. The air was full of dust and they fought for breath as their leg muscles, unused to such action, threatened to give way. At the top Cenau had to be forced toward their exit. Ten feet short they stopped. The balcony on their side of the door was sloping toward the drop.

Jeniche looked at Cynfelyn. She knew he disliked heights, but he was keeping it well hidden.

'I'll go first,' she said. 'There's a lintel up here. Use it to take some of your weight.'

She sidled along to the door, which opened as she got close. Safely in the passage, she turned, found a good hand-hold and leaned out. Cenau was already on his way. Before he could think about it, she grabbed a handful of his clothing and hauled him in through the door.

Aros came next. He was much heavier and the floor began to sag beneath him.

'Cenau,' said Jeniche. 'Grab that and give me a hand.'

Still too flustered to think, Cenau did as he was told. He took the handhold that Jeniche had been using and grabbed Aros's sleeve. Jeniche hung onto the door lintel and grabbed his collar. Between them and his own efforts, they pulled him in through the door just as the floor gave.

Climbing over Aros where he lay on the floor, Jeniche leaned out. Cynfelyn was gripping the wall like a spider, his feet on a steeply sloping section of floor. The section directly outside the door had gone, wedged at an angle ten feet below.

'You two,' called Jeniche without turning round. 'One of you grab a leg and the other grab an arm. And don't you dare let me go, whatever happens.'

As soon as she felt them grip her right leg and arm, she leaned out into space and reached out to Cynfelyn. He looked at her, terror in his eyes. She leaned further and felt the others brace themselves.

'Come on, Alltud.' She beckoned. 'You've done it before.'

He wasn't given time to decide. The floor beneath his feet gave way completely and he was pitched sideways. Jeniche caught him under one arm, her own almost wrenched from its socket, her cry of pain loud in the chamber.

Through the agony, she stuck out her left leg, made a stirrup of her foot and said through clenched teeth, 'Climb up.'

Floundering, he clambered up, one foot pushing against the wall and slipping, the other finding purchase on Jeniche's foot. Another hand appeared and grabbed the front of his tunic.

In a nightmare of scrabbling and pulling they fell into an exhausted heap on the floor of the passage, listening as more sections of balcony collapsed, pulling away sections of wall and destabilizing the whole structure.

When the floor trembled after a particularly loud crash of steel and stonework, they scrambled away from the opening and climbed to their feet. The door closed, muffling the sound and keeping out the worst of the dust.

Limping, aching, and too tired to speak, they shuffled along the passage, squeezed through the jammed door, and made their way to the exit. More of the panels had gone out and Jeniche worried that the final door might not open.

For a few heart-stopping seconds it refused to move and then slid open slowly. Once they were through, it closed with what Jeniche would have sworn was weariness. She doubted it would ever open again of its own accord.

Daylight guided them along the old tunnel to the crude stone steps at the end. By the time they started climbing, legs still trembling, Cynfelyn was smiling. He embraced an embarrassed Jeniche, reached out and ruffled Aros's and Cenau's hair as if they were small boys.

'Ah,' said Jeniche, breathing deeply. 'Fresh air. Daylight.'

They all stopped at the top, surveying the two armies drawn up at either end of the hilltop, Braddan warriors in one direction, Rhan in the other.

'Hmm,' said Cynfelyn. 'And trouble.'

Chapter Eleven

The only movement, apart from pennants flapping in the breeze and the occasional restless horse, was Eog. As soon as he saw Cynfelyn and the others emerge from the ground, he began to walk from where the Braddan warriors were lined up facing toward the circle. Rather than entering the space, he walked sunwise round the outside of the stones.

Cynfelyn urged the others to push the slab back over the entrance. While they struggled to shift the heavy stone, he moved across the inside of the circle to meet Eog.

'Is this for our benefit?'

'Partly,' replied Eog. 'I convinced Feoras of your honest intentions...' Cynfelyn bowed his head. 'But he wanted to be sure that those bandits that attacked us were cleared out. And, of course, he thought the Rhan might have caught news of all this on the wind. There has always been friction between the two tribes, especially over this piece of land. Feoras thought it wise, therefore, to send a full muster. It seems the Rhan did hear and had the same thoughts.'

'Indeed. Are Maiv, Awd and the other two safe?'

'Yes. And glad of a break from constant watching.'

'Would you mind asking them to have our horses ready? One way or another we will need them soon.'

'And the books?'

Cynfelyn shrugged and held his hands wide. 'There were no books.'

Eog cast a quick glance at Jeniche and the other two where they stood in the small enclosure, uncertain about what they should do.

'The passage our ancestors made was empty.'

'What will you do now?'

'See if I can convince the Rhan there is nothing here worth spilling blood for unless it is to drive the Gwerin out of the land.'

'Gwerin?' Eog looked startled.

'And others.'

'Others? What others?'

'Get back to Feoras and persuade him, if he needs persuading, that his loyalty lies with Ynysvron as well as Braddan.'

Eog was about to say something but decided against it. He turned and began walking back to the line of Braddan warriors. Cynfelyn also turned. As he went back to Jeniche and the others, he was sorting through a limited list of options for the least worst solution.

In the enclosure, he made sure he was hidden from the Rhan for a moment by passing behind the largest of the stones. He slipped the circlet from the inner pocket in which it was concealed and let it drop to the soft turf. Jeniche did not need telling to step forward and stand over it after Cynfelyn had passed. She kept her eyes on him as he walked out in full view of the Rhan warriors and stopped.

'I'm going to have a chat with the Rhan,' he said over his shoulder. 'See if I can convince them there is nothing here worth fighting about.' They all looked to the line of Rhan warriors, with their painted faces and their hair spiked with clay. 'Our horses are ready, so if there's trouble, run back toward the Braddan and once you are mounted head for that peak over there.' He didn't point, just turned his eyes. 'Don't wait for anyone. Aros. Keep Cenau safe. Cenau. If he has to fight, watch his back.' He unstrapped his sword and gave it to Cenau. 'Try not to trip over it,' he added with a smile.

For Jeniche there was the ghost of a wink and then he set out toward the Rhan. As they watched him approach, she picked up the circlet and concealed it in a hidden pocket of her own with an ease and swiftness even the most experienced cutpurse would have had trouble spotting.

'How do these things usually go?' she asked, helping Cenau to buckle on the sword belt.

'The Rhan like a fight,' said Aros. 'But they are good listeners.'

The silence felt unreal. Six hundred horsemen should make a noise. Six hundred horses should make a noise. But apart from the occasional flap of a pennant in the breeze, it was as if the distant raven, that sat and croaked its deep 'pruk pruk' from a treetop, had the world to itself.

As he walked, Cynfelyn unfastened his surcoat, slipped it over his arms, and let it fall to the ground. Jeniche saw the sense in that but wasn't prepared for the rest. Because next came his boots and footwraps. Then his tunic. And then his trousers. By the time he stood before the Rhan warriors he was completely naked, his arms stretched wide.

A horse stepped forward and was walked slowly round Cynfelyn. When it was back in the line where it had started, the rider dismounted and walked toward the naked Derw.

'Your name,' demanded the horseman.

'Cynfelyn ap Emrys. Derw Hyn.'

'Comyn, warrior of Rhan.'

'Well met, Comyn.'

'Are we?'

'The Braddan are not here at my behest. Nor are they here to make war on the Rhan.'

'Why does their own Derw not speak for them?'

'Where is yours?'

Comyn conceded the point with a brief nod of the head. 'Speak.'

'My party,' Cynfelyn turned his head to where Jeniche, Aros, and Cenau stood, 'were here because I thought I had found an ancient book hoard. I was wrong. On our journey here, we were attacked by bandits. Word of this reached Dun Braddan.'

'You were attacked and survived?'

'Two of our number were escorts, gifted by the Sisterhood of Nine.'

'And they defeated the bandits.'

'The Sisterhood train well.'

'I would like to meet two warriors who can defeat bandits that Feoras thinks require a whole war host.'

'The bandits were Gwerin.'

Comyn stood a while in thought.

'And this is true?'

'This is true.'

Comyn turned and went back to his horse. As soon as he had mounted he rode forward alone. Like Eog, he would

108

not pass through the circle but went to the east of the stones. A horseman from the Braddan line rode forward to meet him.

Cynfelyn waited until he was certain they were talking before he retraced his steps to the enclosure, picking up his clothes and putting them back on as he went.

'What happens now?' asked Jeniche.

'We leave. Quietly.'

From the Braddan lines, Maiv and the others came, leading two horses each. Cynfelyn took back his sword, much to the relief of Cenau.

'Are we going back to Pengaver now?' he asked.

'If we can persuade the Braddan to act as a—'

He didn't finish as a series of sharp whistles cut the air. The two warriors in the centre stopped talking and turned their horses to stand side by side. They were facing the Braddan line which was parting as quietly as three hundred horses can. Stealth was not the issue. Speed was. Because no sooner had they drawn either side of the trackway that came up through the thorn trees than a Gwerin troop of fifty horses rode up onto the hilltop at the gallop.

Jeniche didn't have time to feel sorry for them until later. They must have thought they were going to find a party of eight, easily dealt with. Instead they rode themselves into the middle of six hundred horsemen, all seasoned warriors, whose leaders had just made a treaty. That didn't stop them trying to complete what they had originally intended.

Maiv and Awd mounted and turned their horses to form a block whilst Ruad and Duald ran the other mounts into the circle. Cynfelyn and the others ran forward to meet them. Arrows struck the turf and bounced off the stones as mounted archers tried to find a target.

Awd dismounted one and Maiv went full tilt into their midst with her sword swinging and hacking.

It broke the flow of the Gwerin troop and gave the surrounding Braddan and Rhan warriors time to get to work.

Jeniche grabbed the reins of Cenau's mount which had slipped from his hands. Aros came up on his other side, Cynfelyn to the rear. Keeping the phalanx as tight as they dared, they pushed through the melee.

Horses raced back and forth, weapons swung, warriors shouted and screamed. Jeniche was glad Trag had not lived to see this, as the Gwerin were targeting horses as well as their riders.

Ruad and Maiv fought through to their side and, with the help of several Braddan warriors, they rode clear of the battle and urged their horses into a gallop. Several Gwerin broke free and gave chase. And from ahead, appearing from the trees, other warriors.

'Occassans!' called Jeniche.

Cynfelyn pulled ahead, his sword drawn. He slashed at the first, knocking him from his saddle, losing his sword as it got stuck in a strap. The rest of the Occassans gave him a wide berth and homed in on Jeniche, Cenau and Aros.

A lance took the first in the chest, Awd pushing through between the others and Cenau. Jeniche urged her horse forward, shouting, 'Keep low!'

They broke through the horses going the other way and kept galloping down the hill, across a stream and up the next slope until the horses slowed to a stop. Risking a backward look, Jeniche could see nothing close to them. In the distance, the battle seemed to be over.

Uncertain what to do, Jeniche sat watching, heard the

thunder of hooves from her left where there was a hidden declivity. She drew her sword, heart beating. Two horses suddenly appeared and were upon her before she could react. The fierce grin of Maiv flashed past and she nearly dropped her sword with relief. The other rider was Cynfelyn, brandishing his retrieved sword.

'Where are the others?' called Jeniche.

'Following on. Keep riding. The Braddan will keep our backs. But we have to move.'

'I bet,' said a trembling Cenau, 'it's not home to Pengaver.'

PART TWO

Spear

Chapter Twelve

'But why were the Hallows all hidden away in such obscure places?'

'They weren't. At least, that wasn't the intention. The places were presumably chosen for their symbolic value, but it was always meant that someone would know their location. It's just that whoever lay claim to them in the future... now... would have to strive for them.'

'Well, that part is working. What went wrong with the rest of the idea?'

'Nobody really knows for certain, but I did follow a trail that gave me some clues.'

'Is that what you've been doing since you came back?'

'A lot longer.'

She turned her head slowly to look at him, all too conscious of the way the deck moved beneath her.

'You mean Makamba?'

'That's where that particular trail led me. That and a desire to see Teague again.'

They both fell silent with their memories of the woman

in her tower gazing at the moon through her wonderful telescope. Jeniche forgot for a moment the long roll of the ship that was doing unpleasant things to her stomach.

An indistinct cry from somewhere above had them both looking around but they were wholly unprepared for the juddering blow that knocked the ship sideways and sent seawater splashing across the deck in front of their shelter.

Cenau woke, looked at them glassy eyed for a moment and then scrambled out of the bunk and crabbed across the deck. Ruad rose with a resigned look and followed him to make sure he wasn't pitched overboard into the roughening sea.

'Keep talking,' said Jeniche with some urgency.

'Sorry, I lost the thread.'

'Makamba. What took you there?'

He looked round to make sure no one had moved within earshot. 'When I started looking for where the Hallows had been hidden, I learned that the Derw who were given the task were not seen again after a particularly fierce storm at sea.'

'Great topic,' she said, pressing her left forearm against her rebellious stomach.

'There was an old entry in the *Annals of Brocel* that someone had been washed ashore alive after that... er... event. There was a lot else going on at the time so it was thought to be a good idea if I was exiled. That would get me out of Ynysvron with no one wondering where I was going or why.'

'This is all politics. Subterfuge.'

Cynfelyn sighed. 'Yes. And it cost me friends, but... I sometimes wonder... No matter.'

'How did you engineer it?'

'A stand-up row in the Derw Council with Annys, a close and trusted friend. I slapped her face. And that is about as insulting as you can get in Ynysvron. Wars were once fought for less.'

Jeniche had never seen Cynfelyn look so depressed.

'Where did you go?'

'Um? Oh. I took a ship... sorry... to Brocel. Chased an ancient rumour.'

The long roll of the ship was changing. Every now and then the prow would drop suddenly and spray would shoot into the air and speckle their faces. Cynfelyn pulled himself to his feet and peered out at Cenau.

'Get him away from the rail and find him a bucket,' he called.

Swinging back in with the movement of the ship, he settled down on the deck and wedged himself back into the corner of the shelter. Other cries could be heard and the crew could be seen performing actions that even had the fearless Jeniche sweating at the thought; hanging from the rigging with one foot looped under rope while they took in canvas, swinging out over the side and timing their leaps to the rhythm of the waves. It did nothing for her queasiness either to watch the horizon pitch up and down.

'What was this rumour?'

'About a man and a sword.'

Jeniche sat up a bit from her miserable huddle, cast a glance at Cynfelyn's blade where it lay on the deck beside him. A sword. The new picture of the world she had been rebuilding from the shattered fragments of the old was swept aside once again. She was in no condition to think of reconstruction, but certain things now made greater sense to her. That they should raise vivid memories of nearly drowning

117

in the river at Beldas did nothing to quell her rebellious stomach.

'I still have that fancy one, safely hidden,' he said, well aware of what she was thinking. 'And all the questions that go with it.'

There were many questions she could have asked, many conversations they could have had, but she wasn't ready for that yet, no matter how much Cynfelyn seemed to want it. 'Is it one of the Hallows?' she asked.

'Without a doubt.'

'In Makamba?'

He shrugged.

'But why was it taken all the way there to be hidden?'

'I don't know,' he said. 'I'd lost track of it way to the north of there; had come to Makamba to see Teague. Rather liked the place. You know all about that. I had no idea the sword was there. To be honest, I'd stopped looking.'

'Lost interest?'

'Yes. No. I don't know. Ynysvron seemed a long way away. It wasn't until... How did she know?'

'Who?'

'That woman. The one who hid us all in the cave. That's where the sword was.'

Jeniche moved her left hand to feel the pendant where it lay beneath her shirt. 'Perhaps it was luck.'

They looked at each other and shook their heads.

'I've thought about it a lot since then. Done a lot of research. These are ancient symbols of sovereignty for the Ynyswr. Each Hallow is associated with a direction. Carreg, the stone, with the north, which is where we found it; Gwyan, the spear, with the east, which is where we're headed; and Crochan, the cauldron, with the west.'

'And the sword, whatever it is called, with the south.'

'Cleddyf. Yes. That Derw seems to have been wandering, perhaps out of his wits, heading as far south as he could rather than somewhere in the south of Ynysvron. Perhaps he could remember nothing but that one imperative – take the sword south. He must have gone as far as Makamba and—'

A powerful wave struck the ship and Jeniche was rolled across the shelter onto Cynfelyn's legs.

'I'm not sure how much longer I'm going to last,' she said, gulping deep breaths of damp salty air.

'Do you want to keep talking?'

She nodded. 'And a bucket wouldn't go amiss.'

While Cynfelyn was out looking for one, she wedged herself firmly back into her corner, trying to keep her stomach calm. By the time he returned, the ship was shuddering and groaning and water was running across the deck in a continuous stream. The wind was beginning to shout.

'Everyone's safe,' he called, swaying back and forth as he tried to hand over the wooden pail.

Jeniche nodded, finally caught hold of it, and was instantly sick.

The storm grew and Cynfelyn wedged himself in beside an ever more miserable Jeniche, putting his arm round her shoulder to stop her head from banging against the wall. Even when her stomach was empty, she kept heaving, rapidly becoming weaker. She knew if the ship floundered she wouldn't have the strength to save herself and she didn't much care.

When she woke, she felt truly wretched. Every part of her ached, her clothes were damp, she smelled of vomit, and

119

her stomach felt like someone had been kicking it all night. The only inkling that things had passed their worst was that the deck beneath her was barely moving; that and the fact that the wind, which she last remembered as a screaming demon, had faded to silence.

Carefully, just in case anything decided to drop off, she rolled onto her side and regretted it once she saw what was on the deck next to her. It was the impetus she needed to push herself into a sitting position.

Beyond the shelter, the deck was strewn with canvas, ropes, and the remains of the shore boat beneath a length of splintered mast. The silence was worrying, but not her most immediate concern. That was trying to get from a sitting position to a standing position with muscles that felt torn and used up.

A hollow thump that made the deck shudder brought her to her feet, teeth clenched against the pain, and she staggered out into the open. Picking her way over the debris, she realized the deck, though blissfully still, was slightly canted to one side.

As she was concentrating on lifting her trembling legs and placing her feet down between all the bits and pieces strewn about, it was only when she reached the side rail that she realized they were in a bay. Close to the shore. Beneath cliffs.

The thump came again, followed by distant shouts from the far side of the vessel. She picked her way back across the deck to the other side and looked down to see just how close to shore they were. The prow of the vessel had been run up onto shingle and the crew were ramming timbers against the hull to prop it upright.

'Want some breakfast?' asked a cheery voice.

120

She turned slowly to see Cynfelyn standing by their shelter. 'What do you think?'

'I think a bit of this biscuit and a sip of fresh water would be good for you.'

She pulled a face, but crossed back to where he stood and took the flask he held and sipped some water, swilling it round before spitting it out into the bucket that had somehow remained upright in the corner. She was glad to be able to wash some of the foul taste from her mouth. A second sip burned her throat as she swallowed, but she kept it down. The proffered biscuit she ignored for the moment as she was more interested in inspecting her saddlebag, laced to something nautical she didn't know the name of at the back of the shelter above the bench.

'How are the others?' she asked as she undid the lacing and lifted the bag down.

'Alive. No injuries. Cenau is worse than you. Aros didn't fare well, but he's down on the beach helping out. The others are scouting the shore.'

'Where are we?' She opened the bag and checked inside. It all seemed dry.

'No idea. The captain doesn't think we came too far south, unfortunately.'

'Did we get blown ashore?'

'No. We wouldn't be here to talk about it if we had. The crew rowed us in this morning using makeshift oars. There are leaks below the waterline which is why the captain beached us.'

'And you wonder why I don't like water.'

He had the good grace to look chastened.

'What do you mean?' asked Cynfelyn.

'Exactly what I said,' answered Maiv. 'There is no way off the beach. We have been to both ends. And even with the tide out, there is no beach round either headland.'

'We're stuck?' That was Cenau, still shivering in a blanket and taking no warmth from the driftwood fire.

Without turning from her contemplation of the beached vessel, Jeniche said, 'No.'

'What do you mean?' asked Maiv.

'Some of the crew will have to go for help for their vessel. We'll go with them.'

They all looked at the stricken boat, its masts broken, sails torn, rigging in disarray, shore boat shattered to firewood.

'I expect,' she said, 'that you're all looking in the wrong direction.'

'Oh no,' said Cynfelyn, catching on first.

'I'm not going to like this, am I,' said Cenau quietly.

Jeniche stood, unsteadily, and turned. She looked up at the cliffs. 'They aren't that high. And they aren't sheer. But we will need to be rested and fed.'

She left them staring at the red sandstone of the cliffs and the wheeling gulls, the dizzying parade of racing clouds, whilst she crunched down the shingle beach to where the captain stood inspecting the hull.

He turned and smiled. 'Well. Not much of a voyage.'

She smiled in return. 'I can't say I'm not happier with dirt beneath my feet. We'll have to climb out. How many of your crew were you going to send?'

'Four. Are any of yours experienced climbers?'

'Just me. I think some of them will be all right, but there are two who I know don't like heights.'

'Well, they're welcome to stay here until we've repaired

122

her. We'll just get her in shape to tow round to a decent harbour. Shouldn't be more than a few days.'

'I'll put it to the others, but there's some urgency to our trip.'

'As you wish. I'll pick four pairs of safe hands to help you up.'

Jeniche scouted a route and climbed up and back down during the afternoon. Although tiring, it did much to calm her after recent events. It was all getting to be too much like the trek up into Tundur and the last thing she wanted was to lose more friends.

With solid ground beneath them, a blazing fire, their clothes cleaned and dry, and no chance of being attacked by Gwerin, Occassans, or wild beasts, they had slept well. Even Cenau had colour back in his face in the morning. And after they had bathed and eaten, they climbed.

Two of the sailors led, following the route that Jeniche had marked with pennants from the ship. A third sailor accompanied Cynfelyn. Jeniche climbed with Cenau. The fourth sailor, collecting the pennants, brought up the rear. They went slowly, but it was strenuous rather than dangerous. The rock was broken but firm, sloping back from the beach and covered with plenty of firmly rooted grasses and shrubs.

At the top, once they had moved far enough back from the edge to satisfy Cynfelyn, they parted company with the sailors and sat down to plan their route. The sailors headed south, keeping to the coast. Although they would also be heading in the same direction, Cynfelyn didn't want to be seen just yet so as to avoid word of their presence spreading to unwanted ears.

'We have food for a good few days,' he said. 'I suggest we head inland a way before we continue southward.'

There were no arguments. Cynfelyn was the only one who knew where they were headed. All he had to do now was work out where they were.

Chapter Thirteen

A chill breeze out of the north chased them all day, so they kept up a fast pace to keep warm. Although they were on foot, they maintained the familiar pattern with the warriors covering the points and flanks. Aros and Cenau walked together most of the day, arguing, sulking, both missing their comforts. Cynfelyn and Jeniche walked a little way behind them.

It was wild, bleak country. If there were settlements, they were tucked away in valleys or clinging to the coast. Cynfelyn seemed to have chosen a path that avoided them all. They made a goodly distance, but they all felt the emptiness seeping into them.

After a prolonged period of silence, just as the sun dropped behind the western hills, throwing the near-leafless trees into stark silhouette and filling the skies with homeward-bound rooks, Aros and Cenau began bickering again.

'What are they are arguing about now?'

Cynfelyn listened and then laughed. 'Cenau is trying to teach Aros logic.'

'Not working, I take it.'

'Logic is to Aros what swordplay is to Cenau. At least they are communicating without it coming to blows.'

'Did they used to?'

'Apparently. As kids. Friends. But always scrapping.'

They watched Cenau trying to force his point with gestures.

'Probably,' said Jeniche, 'because they are so alike in temperament.'

'You could be right. But it's a frightening prospect.'

'What?'

'To have pinned so many hopes on them.'

'Them? I thought it was Aros that was to be your Guardian.'

'Can you see him managing on his own? He will need an adviser he can trust. Someone his own age who comes from a background he can understand.'

'Is that why the Occassans have been targeting Cenau?'

Cynfelyn stopped in his tracks. Jeniche turned and stopped as well.

'Everything all right?' called Aros.

'Fine, thanks. Stone in my boot. Keep going.'

'Stone in your boot?' asked Jeniche.

Cynfelyn shrugged. 'Explain.'

'Every time we were attacked, there was a real effort to get to Cenau. I thought it was me they were after at first.'

'Ah. Yes.'

'What?'

'Never mind. What were you saying?'

'Just that. It seemed like they were after Cenau in particular.'

'Why would they want him? I wouldn't want anything

126

to happen to him, and he's a very bright lad, the best, but there are others who could fulfil his role at a pinch. There's only one descendant of the last Guardian and that's Aros.'

They walked on for a bit, feeling a distinct drop in the temperature now the sun had gone.

'Perhaps...'

'Go on.'

'Who did you spend most of your time with at the Great College?'

'Cenau.' He swore. 'That's so obvious, it's embarrassing.'

'And it means there is probably a spy on Pengaver, if not in the College itself. Did you have much contact with Aros?'

'Hardly any.'

'Well, that's something to be thankful for.'

'Not much.' He sighed. 'We knew it was a risky strategy, but I thought we could keep it secret.'

'They may not know any details, just that you and your student are trying to thwart them.'

'I hope so, because if they know the whole plan, that means someone on the Inner Council of the Derw has told them. Whatever the case, we have a lot less time than I thought. It might already be too late.'

At the edge of some scrubby woodland, they built a crude turf oven in a grassy bank not just to keep the flames hidden, but to bake some bread with the berries they had collected during the day. Not much was said. Cynfelyn was particularly quiet and the others sensed his mood. They warmed themselves as best they could, ate, and settled down to sleep.

The next morning was just as sombre, despite the sunshine and lack of wind. They scraped themselves latrines in various parts of the woods, washed in a narrow, icy stream, and erased all trace of their camp. Eating as they went, they resumed their journey through the empty landscape.

By mid morning the wilds gave way to rough pasture and then to fields walled with stone cleared from the ground. Their moods lifted. Eventually the track they were on widened and began to follow a long slope down into a broad valley. They began to see people at work on all those post-harvest tasks you wanted done before the snows came. Walls to be mended, gullies to be cleared of leaves, firewood to be fetched for stockpiling.

The air became tinged with the welcome scent of wood smoke and they could see long, pale-blue streamers of it drifting upward into the autumn sky. They could also see watchful eyes following them down into the village.

'It's a bit of a lost hope,' said Cynfelyn, speaking for the first time that morning, 'but can you lot try not to look too threatening.'

Jeniche looked at the hardened warriors in their battle leathers, swords at their waists, spears in hand. The others looked just as combative. Recent events had left their mark in subtle but recognizable ways.

'We look like an armed escort for one young Derw,' said Jeniche quietly.

Cynfelyn gave her a look and some of the lines of worry faded.

'Perhaps that's what the Gwerin thought without actually knowing who he was.'

Jeniche didn't answer. She'd rather think the worst and be prepared for it. Much like the villagers, she noticed. Each house had a stack of sharpened poles by the door and a lot of well-honed cutting implements were in evidence as well.

'Looks like they are expecting trouble,' said Aros from the side of his mouth.

'Let's hope,' replied Awd just as quietly, 'they don't decide we're it.'

Cynfelyn put on a bright smile and produced a pouch of money.

'We are looking to buy food, if you have any to spare,' he called.

An old Derw shuffled out of a small round hut, leaning on a stick and watching them with pale, sharp eyes. They met him half way.

'Don't mind them,' he said. 'These are nervous times.'

'Have you had trouble?' asked Cynfelyn.

'One of the boys watching sheep up on the moors has gone missing. And there are rumours of bandits.'

'Rumours?'

The old Derw shrugged. 'There are three villages in the valley. We all had a good harvest and no one has bothered us. Apart from Ilar disappearing, nothing is amiss. But I am their Derw. All tales eventually get told at my door. We have heard things, especially from the west. Bandits. Fighting. War?'

'Let's hope not. But your people are wise to be prepared. Tell them to be careful. It is not a handful of half-starved bandits out there, but soldiers of Gwerin that are causing the trouble. Do you have places to hide?'

'That bad, eh?'

'Possibly. I don't know. I don't want to cause panic.'

The old man looked them over and nodded. He put his fingers to his mouth and gave a shrill whistle that must have been heard miles away. An ancient dog ambled out of his hut and settled itself in a patch of sunlight. With a smile

129

the Derw leaned on his stick again. 'Used to be a shepherd.'

Before long a young girl came running.

'Yes, taid?'

'Tell your mother to see what bread, cheese and other victuals we can spare for these good folk.'

The young girl looked at them with bold eyes and then darted off like a hare.

'Take your ease while you wait. Some will come and stare but they mean no harm.'

They were led across to the old man's hut and Cenau and Jeniche sat on a small bench. Cenau made a fuss of the dog who accepted it as his due. Aros took his boots off and unwound the wraps. He asked the old man if he had any salve. The cuts were healing but still sore. Cynfelyn stood for all the world as if he owned the place and beamed on all and sundry who appeared, making pebbles appear from children's ears, but not before he'd had a quiet word with the warriors. When the old man came back, Cynfelyn had a quiet conversation with him as well. Ruad and Maiv, meanwhile, kept watch on the surrounding hills whilst Awd and Duald wandered about the village.

Once food had been gathered and money given in exchange, the warriors sat with the elders and offered some advice on defending their village, pointing out where thorn-topped hurdles would most effectively block the approaches, where to keep water barrels in case of fire, the best lines of retreat.

By the time they left, the village had lost its forbidding face and some of the villagers waved to them as they reached the top of the hill.

'It looks so vulnerable,' said Jeniche.

'The Madval are tough people,' said Maiv. 'And they can

be vicious fighters.' There was a touch of pride in her voice.

Jeniche laughed. 'If I was a betting girl, I'd risk a coin on your being of the same tribe.'

Maiv grinned. 'From the west on the far side of Tirmawr, close to the Cumran Mountains.'

Mid afternoon, as the sun slipped past the quarter and began heading for the horizon, Ruad whistled. He had been out on their right flank on the far side of a long, narrow copse of birch, willow, and rowan. They drew their swords and moved into a defensive formation.

Ruad appeared through the trees. 'Smoke.'

They followed him through to the other side where the ground sloped away to a small valley. On the far side it was woodland all the way to the horizon and, from its midst, smoke rose into the air above the treetops where it was caught by the breeze.

'That's not cooking fires,' said Awd.

'Exactly what I thought,' replied Ruad.

'Charcoal burners?' suggested Cenau.

'No, that's burning buildings.'

They all turned to Jeniche. 'I saw too much of that along the Gyanag–Azak border.'

'We should go and see,' said Aros.

'It's been alight for a while,' said Jeniche. 'There's some oil burning there, but the smoke is thin.'

Aros shrugged. 'We should help.'

Without waiting for the others, Aros started off in the direction of the fire.

'Aros!' It was Cynfelyn that called.

Aros looked over his shoulder and came to a stop. 'We have to help.' He appealed to the others with his hands, a look of bewilderment becoming one of anger as no one moved. He turned from them and continued toward the distant smoke.

Cenau took a hesitant step after him, but Cynfelyn stopped him with a touch on his arm.

'Aros! By your oath to the Sisterhood, stop!'

Jeniche knew there was a deep strength in Cynfelyn. She had learned as much in Makamba and on the long walk to Tundur. Yet even she was astonished by the power in his voice.

Aros was stopped in his tracks and sagged visibly in defeat.

Cynfelyn sighed. 'Come back, lad,' he said in his normal voice, 'and hear me out.'

'We should help,' said Aros again as he rejoined the group.

'Yes,' said Cynfelyn. 'We should. We really should. But we have to move on.'

Aros was looking stubborn again. 'Why?'

Jeniche was impressed that he was prepared to go up against Cynfelyn on this.

'Yes,' chipped in Cenau. 'Why? What is going on? Why do we not have time for a detour?'

Everyone's gaze had moved from Aros to Cenau and now settled expectantly on Cynfelyn. He pummelled his face as he tried to think of a satisfying response. In the end, though, it was Aros that spoke.

'It's not about books, is it? Old things. I'm normally happy to do as I'm told without question, it makes life easier, but some things are important. And I know that even Rhonwen would say that if it is a choice between books and people, it is people every time. And those people over there might need our help. It was our first lesson. Years ago.

Morwyn said. Everything we learn, be it books, swords, or ploughshares, is so we can place ourselves at the service of others.'

Cenau looked at Aros in astonishment. 'He's right,' he said and the others nodded.

'What Morwyn said was true,' replied Cynfelyn. 'It remains true.' He stopped for a moment, memories of his own first lesson bright in his mind. That summer day before any of his companions had been born. 'However, we cannot be everywhere at once. Service isn't fixed or absolute. Just as the loyalty of a Derw is to Ynysvron before their own tribe, so one service can, and sometimes must, take precedence over another. I don't know any of you as well as I would like.' He avoided Jeniche's eye as he spoke. 'You all know me even less. But I am Pen Derw, Head of the Council. This is not lightly earned, nor is it a fact I wish to be shared with anyone else. You were all chosen for this task because I trust you. The question is, do you trust me?'

Aros looked at Cenau. So did everyone else. The young scholar went red in the face. He nodded. Said, 'Yes.'

'Yes,' said Aros straight away.

Cenau gave Aros a strange look as everyone else nodded. Jeniche could see the burden of their trust in Cynfelyn's face, the hint of pleasure that Aros had deferred so readily to Cenau's judgement.

'I will do my utmost to honour the faith you have in me. And I must put it to the test immediately. I cannot tell you yet what we are doing; I ask only that you accept that it outweighs by far the possible needs of anyone over there who may have survived.'

And that, too, Jeniche could see, weighed heavily on

Cynfelyn. She saw it for a brief moment as he glanced at her. She wanted to say something, but wasn't sure what and knew it wasn't the moment.

Aros looked at the smoke laying across the distant tree-tops; turned back.

'And this is true?'

Cynfelyn nodded. 'This is true.'

They resumed their journey in reflective mood. There was much to consider, not least the fact that Cynfelyn had revealed he was Pen Derw, Head of the Council, and, in the absence of a Guardian, de facto ruler of Ynysvron. Jeniche couldn't help smiling to herself when Cenau explained the significance of the pronouncement to her. A while later, when no one else was looking, she stepped in Cynfelyn's path and gave a quick curtsy with the tip of her tongue poking out. Cynfelyn replied with a fierce scowl, but his step was a lot lighter afterwards.

Although their path rose and fell, they had long since been making their way down from the high moorland. The smoke amongst the trees was far behind them and Cynfelyn had them looking for paths that would take them in a westerly direction.

'There's a vast estuary ahead,' he explained to Jeniche, 'the river Cysgodion. And I don't want to waste any more time than necessary by going round. If we head inland now, we should get to the river close to its main crossing point.'

'I hope it's a bridge.'

He frowned. 'I—'

Jeniche reached across and held his wrist. 'I know.'

He looked at her and she saw the years of anguish etched in his face. It was a choice she knew she would not be

134

capable of coping with. At the time, those few extra seconds she had spent in the water as he had retrieved the sword had seemed a gross betrayal. The intervening years had endowed her with some wisdom and the fresh knowledge of the sword's worth to the people of Ynysvron had erased the scar of the long-healed wound.

Coming down off the high ground did nothing to protect them from the cold wind that had sprung up again. And there were fewer places for shelter as the land levelled out.

'There's going to be a lot more of this,' Cynfelyn said, waving his hand at the view ahead.

In the fading afternoon sun, the world before them seemed flat, empty, and even more bleak than the moorland they had left behind.

'Most of the east coast of Tirmawr south of here is like that,' he continued. 'Salt marsh on the coast, mud flats that stretch out for miles at low tide, the sea too shallow for all but the smallest boats for miles beyond that. Inland it is just as windswept, cold even in the summer. You can't grow crops or graze animals. Birds shun it. The fish taste disgusting. There are pools of poisoned water. There are quicksands. At night ghost lights wander and dance. Some say there are deformed beasts that prey on anyone stupid enough to stray too far from habitable land. Even the Vran, whose tribal land it is, stay clear.'

'And with an introduction like that,' said Jeniche, 'I just know that you're going to say that is where the next of the Hallows is hidden.'

Chapter Fourteen

'How much longer? I'm getting cramp.'

It was barely a whisper, muffled by the overgrown hedgerow at the forest's edge. Jeniche smiled, but Cenau did have a point. They had been watching the others for some time now and nothing much seemed to be happening. The Bron Forest, whose margins they had been walking through for some time, was silent in the way only an autumn forest could be on a cold afternoon.

'Perhaps they've forgotten us,' he added, flexing his left foot.

'I doubt that,' replied Jeniche.

She would swear his shoulders slumped, but maybe he was just easing tired muscles. Walking hour on hour, day after day is deeply tiring, especially for someone whose previous exertions were confined mainly to the quick run across the concourse to be at the front of the refectory queue. Considering that, she thought, he was holding up well.

Cenau turned from his scrutiny of the village, looked

round to make sure they were still alone, and then said, 'I think I've worked it out. He's looking for the Hallows, isn't he?'

It was a challenge.

'The what? Who?'

Cenau looked at her. Into her.

'Do you trust him?' she asked.

'Yes.'

'Then... trust him. He knows what he's doing.'

'Do you?'

'Trust him? We've had our differences, but yes.'

They went back to watching the village below them. Cynfelyn was standing in the middle of the group of buildings, clearly visible. One by one the others emerged, each shaking their head. Cynfelyn took one of the spears from Awd and drove it into the ground. The shaft leaned at an angle as the packed soil was hard, but it did not fall, which came as a relief to them all. It would have been a bad omen.

'Come on,' said Jeniche, because that was their signal to come out of hiding. They brushed off the cold leaves, picked up their packs, and made their way down the steep slope of rough, enclosed pasture, past the empty horse shelters, and on to the village.

'Strangest thing I've seen in a while,' said Cynfelyn as they came through the gate in the fence. 'Pre-Ev sites and objects you expect to be strange, but this?'

Aros stepped forward. 'They've packed up and taken everything they could carry or drive before them. There are no animals left. No carts or wagons. No cooked food. No implements or weapons. All the fires were extinguished and the hearths cleaned. It's eerie.'

'What happened?' asked Cenau.

'Who knows. Not disease. They weren't attacked. Perhaps they heard there was trouble and decided to go somewhere safer.'

'It would have to be a lot of trouble to make a whole village simply pack up and leave.'

Cynfelyn looked at Jeniche and shrugged. 'It is.'

Cenau gave Jeniche a knowing look. Cynfelyn saw and raised an eyebrow at Jeniche, who shook her head.

'So where would they all go? These look like they were foresters. Where do they go to make a living other than the forest?'

They looked at the trees that surrounded the village and its small fields. A light breeze rattled the dry, bronze leaves in the tall beeches. Cold sunlight lit the interior, picking out glades and withering bracken.

It was Ruad who voiced what they were all thinking: 'What frightens people who live here?'

Because the Bron Forest had grown over the centuries in the ruins of a vast pre-Evanescence city. At its core it was dense, dark, and forbidding. And the deeper you went into that uncanny heart, the stranger it and the creatures that lived there became.

In the end they decided not to risk a fire. It was not out of fear of anything otherworldly the forest might unleash. A village would not prosper as this one clearly had if it was blighted by constant dread. All the same, they kept a wary eye on the silent trees because something had frightened these people away.

They chose a small hut by the gateway; easier to keep warm and easy for a quick getaway. Borrowing abandoned blankets and furs from elsewhere, they made a snug nest and made a meal with some of their dwindling supplies.

Cynfelyn and Jeniche took the first watch, moving in the dusk to a sheltered spot just outside the fence that surrounded the settlement.

'Cenau has worked out what you are doing.'

'Good. It was only a matter of time. And Aros will catch up sooner or later.'

'He asked me outright, but I pretended not to know what he was talking about.'

Cynfelyn chuckled. 'I bet he wasn't much convinced by that.'

'No.'

'You're a rotten liar for a thief.'

'Bruises gone yet?'

He covered his upper arm. 'How did you ever get into that in the first place?'

'Stealing? It was hunger.'

'And when the hunger went?'

'A delight in relieving the wealthy of things they didn't actually need. Stuff they could only afford because they had perfected the art of legal theft.'

They sat in silence for a while, listening to the subtle sounds of the dying day, wondering what they would have heard had the village still been inhabited. Laughter? Singing? Quiet conversation?

'Was there much in the Library about Bron?' asked Cynfelyn.

'Lots of stuff about the ghosts and weird beasts that are said to haunt the heart of the forest, travellers' tales of strange lights – but you get that sort of thing everywhere. The only fragments of any real worth spoke of a great city. The language was obscure, but to me it suggested that several cities had grown and merged. Talfryn thought it meant that there had been a succession of cities. And that's it. Apart from one tiny snippet taken from a fragment that the chronicler said turned to dust as he handled it. Had we not seen that city beneath the desert, I wouldn't have believed it, but it claimed that whatever city had originally been here had been home to more than ten million people.'

Cynfelyn rubbed his forehead. 'All those people. How did they live? Where did they all go?'

'How many people in Ynysvron?'

He shook his head. 'There was a count during the time of the last Guardian to make sure taxation was fair. There were fewer than three million souls back then. Across all the islands. And nobody seems to think the population's increased much since. Ten million. In one city. It doesn't seem... credible.'

'But we've seen what they could do.'

'It wasn't enough, was it? All those wonders they built.'

'Perhaps the knowledge and power they had to build all those marvels also brought them the means to destroy it all.'

'Is that what the Occassans are after?'

'I don't know. They do seem to be part way there. Those flying machines. The moskets. Marvellous and terrible.' She shook her head. 'What I still don't understand is why they would want to invade Makamba. And what did they want with Gyan Mi?'

Cynfelyn drew in a sudden, deep breath and went very quiet. Jeniche narrowed her eyes. He let out the breath slowly.

'Yes. That's something else.'

'Something else?'

'I meant to tell you earlier, but... Well, it's been a bit... hectic.'

Jeniche restrained herself from sighing. 'This story gets better and better. Go on.'

'It wasn't Gyan Mi they chased after all the way to Tundur.'

She stared at Cynfelyn blankly for a moment as she tried to make sense of what he'd just said.

'I don't get it. Do you mean they wanted you?'

'There's no need to sound surprised. But, no. It wasn't me.'

'Well, who...?' She stared at Cynfelyn. He stared back. 'No. Oh, no.' There was a long pause in which she sought for something else to say. 'No.'

'After the Occassan... I forget his name. After he'd fallen for the deception that had tricked you as well, he said that it didn't matter, that he wasn't interested in the God-King. He was looking for a thief who had something that belonged to him.'

'But... Did he say what?'

'No. But unless it's your talent, there's only one thing I can think of.'

Despite the chill, she unlaced the top of her tunic and felt round her neck.

'They invaded a country for this?' she asked.

The small pendant gleamed in the dim light. They looked from it to each other. Jeniche tucked it away.

'You know you have questions you want to ask of the merchant's wife,' she said. 'Well, I have some too.'

They found that a light frost had decorated the edges of the thatching when they emerged at daybreak. Their breath formed faint clouds in the still air. It was not a morning to linger.

Once they had replaced the blankets and skins to the huts in which they had found them, they set out along the path through the forest. A breakfast of dry cheese and stale bread was taken on the march.

After the eerie silence of the previous afternoon, a semblance of life had woken with them. Birds sang. They startled a deer. A fox crossed their path, giving them little more than a quick glance before it sprang over a fallen tree and disappeared in the dying bracken.

Along their route they came across trees that had been felled, trimmed, and stacked ready to be pulled out of the forest. Elsewhere were neatly tied bundles of coppiced willow and hazel, stacked in piles. At one point the track went through a clearing where a turner's workshop had been set up. A row of treadle lathes stood along one side within a framework that had, presumably, once held an awning. Piles of wood shavings from recent work lay on the floor as if waiting for some apprentice to gather them up and take them away for kindling.

Everywhere there were signs of a working community that had simply decided to turn its back on a well-established way of life. It was beginning to fray everyone's nerves.

Around mid morning they stopped for a rest, sitting with their backs to a pile of recently cut logs. No sooner had they settled than Jeniche stood. Maiv and Awd were immediately alert.

'It's all right. I'm just feeling a touch queasy.'

'Pre-Ev queasy?' asked Cynfelyn.

Jeniche nodded. 'I'll just poke around a bit. I won't go out of sight. So rest,' she said to Ruad who had clambered to his feet.

Wandering off on her own, chewing on a bit of hard bread, she kicked about in the bracken on the far side of the track, peering into the underbrush. She didn't find anything and as they continued on their way the nausea faded.

It wasn't long, though, before present-day concerns made themselves known again.

Aros noticed it first, off to one side. He wandered into a stretch of long, rough grass and came back with a small, wooden doll. When Jeniche saw it her heart lurched, remembering little Shooly and her rooftop domain.

Ruad called out and held a knife aloft.

'This is not good,' said Maiv. 'It looks like a lot of people ran off the path here and in amongst the trees.'

They scouted along that side of the track, finding more personal possessions. Where the ground became rough, the shattered parts of the wheel of a handcart lay in the grass. A strange smell hung in the air.

Awd found the first corpse, an old man pinned face down to the ground with a broken lance. After that a child slaughtered by a sword stroke. And then they lay all around, with sword wounds, axe wounds, pierced by spears and arrows. They had been there for days – dead, rotting, scavenged.

Cenau stumbled back toward the track, watched over by Ruad, but by a great effort was not sick. The others wandered about in disbelief.

'They were hunted for sport,' said Maiv in quiet disgust. 'There's not a warrior amongst them.'

Jeniche could see Awd was close to tears.

They walked on in silence for a long time. The track wound in long curves through the edge of the forest. The clearings grew more frequent until they were in a borderland of rough pasture and widely separated trees, many of them young as if the forest was slowly claiming new territory. A herd of deer watched them from the distance for a while before moving slowly back into denser woodland.

The first person to speak was Cenau who said he would like to learn to use a sword. No one argued. Cynfelyn even looked a little relieved. Jeniche unbuckled her own from her back and handed it to the young Derw. He strapped it to his waist and practised drawing it as they walked. No one laughed when he fumbled or dropped it. Eventually Aros fell in beside him and showed him some basic exercises to help strengthen his wrist.

He gave up after a while, tired by the unfamiliar exertions, but the sword stayed at his waist. He had tried to give it back, but Jeniche refused.

'It's the right size for you,' she said. 'I had it from a good friend and it has served me well over the years. May it do the same for you.'

It felt odd to be travelling without a weapon on her back, but there had been nothing normal about her life since the day she was born. All those grim days of childhood in Antar. All the years of wandering. Living by theft in Makamba. More years of wandering. The pendant that hung around her neck.

Out of habit she reached up and touched it through her clothes. Is that what the Occassans wanted? Would it be any good to them without her? And were they here because of her? All this misery because of her?

She became aware of someone beside her, turned to see Cynfelyn. He did not look at her, kept walking, but she felt his hand on her shoulder for a moment.

'Whatever it is they want,' he said, 'none of it is your fault.'

Very gently, without breaking her stride, she punched him on the arm.

Chapter Fifteen

They could see it from miles away. Which was pretty much the idea. The ditch walls, lined with clay and lime washed, gleamed in the pale sunshine. The palisade of timber, seasoned by the salt air, sat atop like a coronet of silver grey. Vast pennants hung from pillars in the centre, moving slightly when a strong enough breeze caught them. And over it all, dispersing slowly in the still air, hung a grey smudge of smoke.

Their first sight of it had been as they crested a hill at the edge of the plain. Away to their left was the estuary they had come this way to avoid. The dull sheen of muddy water merged with the thin afternoon mists on the horizon. Below them, farmland and villages, roads and trackways, people. In the middle distance was the broad meandering river, the banks connected by a substantial bridge. And beyond, sitting in a vast loop of the slow-moving water, well above the flood plain, was Dunvran.

The citadel, centre of commerce, capital of the Vran tribe, didn't so much sit on the hill; it was the hill. The whole prominence, which stood apart from the ridge line beyond, had been carved with enormous rings of deep, sheer ditches and complex entrances. It was not only a testament to the personal power of the chieftains of the Vran, traditionally women, but a necessary bulwark against raiders out of the east.

'It seems to be busy,' said Jeniche as they stood and enjoyed the view.

'I've lost track of time,' said Cynfelyn, 'but it must be Savain, a time of assembly.'

'Is that where those villagers were heading?'

Cynfelyn shook his head. 'It would be unusual for a whole community to desert their village and attend. No. They were driven out by fear. And the thing they feared caught up with them before they could warn others.'

He turned and looked back the way they had come, the edge of the forest a dark line on the horizon.

'Maiv?'

She turned from where she had been watching the distance.

'How far does the forest stretch into the west?'

'Almost to the coast. There are villages along that edge, but very little in the interior. The main routes through are hardly used these days. People prefer to come this way via Dunvran and follow the coastal roads. Or they go west. But only as far as Cumran and the Poisoned Mountains.'

'So if you wanted to hide an army?'

'If you were prepared to risk crossing from Gwerin via the Cumran Sea, the Bron Forest would hold little to fear.'

'How would you feed so many?'

'There's plenty of game to be found.'

'Perhaps.'

'It's superstition as much as anything that keeps most people away. The folk who live and work in the forest have grown up with its oddities. They are used to the things that belong there. But if they saw something out of the ordinary, something that made them persuade a whole village to pack up and leave...'

'I think we should hurry ourselves to Dunvran and see if watchful eyes have been turned in the right direction.'

After so long apart from others and always on the alert, it was difficult not to feel disorientated by the presence of so many carefree people. It had been feeling crowded even before they reached the river. There were ferries further downstream and huge flat-bottomed barges sailing up and down, catching what they could of the breeze with their enormous sails. Jeniche insisted on the bridge.

Like the structure at Beldas, it was built on an ancient foundation, the causeway leading to it across the salt flats a more recent construction. Jeniche was intrigued to see it was, in fact, two bridges built side by side with traffic flowing in a single direction on each.

By the bridges a small cluster of huts housed a garrison that kept the traffic flowing and kept the bridge in good repair. As each of the wagons crossed an elderly man took a small toll and waved them on with a cheery smile, a young child holding his hand and standing half behind his legs.

On the far side, the causeway led to the base of Dunvran and round to the entrance of the citadel at its western end. The high eastern end was sheer walls topped by watchtowers with views across the estuary, the river, and all points north and south. Walking beneath the steep earthen banks was intimidating and reassuring in equal measure.

The vast earthwork complex that led up to the entrance dispensed with reassuring and traded solely on intimidating. Although the tracks were wide enough for two ox-drawn wagons to travel abreast, the walls and defensive structures looked down on them from all directions and they had to weave their way round several embankments before reaching the gate.

There they were stopped. The guards were polite, efficient, and extremely professional. Anyone armed had to have a very good reason for entering the citadel. A Derw was summoned and after a brief discussion they were allowed in.

Cynfelyn pulled them to one side, away from the main flow of visitors. 'I'm going to see if I can get an audience with the chieftain, Tymestl. Maiv and Awd, I'd like you to come with me. Tymestl was trained by the Sisterhood and she will probably be more inclined to speak with me if you are there. The rest of you, stay together and keep out of trouble. We may have to leave quickly, so stock up on food and anything else you want. If you get split up, come back here by the gates.'

They stood for a moment after Cynfelyn and the others had gone, not knowing what to do. Jeniche felt at home as she had spent much of her life in a city, albeit larger and very different in style to this one.

'Food first,' she said. 'And I think we should stick to the backstreets here. It's less crowded and the local shopkeepers will be glad of the custom.'

The others were happy with that suggestion and followed her as she wandered along the lane. There were shops on both sides. Those built against the outer wall were directly beneath the guard walk that looked out over the valley. In

149

the spaces between buildings stood large water barrels. Aros took a quick look.

'They're all full and fresh.'

'That must take some doing, keeping them all topped up,' said Cenau.

'At least someone is prepared.'

They wandered on, treating themselves to sweetmeats as they picked out supplies of bread and cheese, dried meat, fruit, flour and other bits and pieces. Their packs were soon full and heavy so they filled a sack as well, agreeing to take it in turns to lug it about.

The closer they got to the centre of the citadel the more crowded and noisy it became. People ambled about, looking at all the goods on display, visiting doctors and apothecaries, meeting old friends. The air was filled with the smell of food. Music played. People laughed.

Whilst they all enjoyed themselves, relaxing for the first time in weeks, they could none of them shed the memory of the villagers slaughtered in the forest. And when they came to a row of smithies up under the inner rampart that separated the western public space from the eastern fortress where the Great Hall of Tymestl stood, Jeniche decided to look for a new sword.

In all the years she had worn one, ever since Cynfelyn had picked it out from the crate in the wreck of the airship, she had never liked it. She had been glad of it, had taught herself how to use it with economy and ruthlessness, but she had never liked it. Now she walked without one, she felt defenceless. How times had changed.

They were beginning to get just a little bored and were wondering how much longer Cynfelyn and the other two would be when Aros touched Jeniche on the arm.

'There,' he said, pointing into the interior of a sword smith's workshop.

She looked at the bench where the smith's wares were laid out under the watchful eye of someone who almost matched Trag for size. Beautifully crafted and exquisitely decorated, they were all made to a common pattern.

'They're all too big for me,' said Jeniche. 'And a touch flashy for my taste.'

Aros laughed. 'We like to show off a bit. But it's not those I meant. On the wall behind the bench.'

The others had gathered round and heard Jeniche when she gasped. 'Where...? How...?'

'What is it?' asked Cenau.

Ruad and Duald crowded closer.

'On the wall,' said Jeniche.

They all stared at a matched pair of swords of similar length to the one she had given to Cenau. But there all similarity ended. The sword Cynfelyn had chosen for her was a workaday weapon. Functional. Well made. Dull. These...

She stepped across to where the smith watched a length of metal in his forge.

'The swords on the wall—'

'Not for sale,' he said without taking his eyes from the metal.

She waited.

The smith took a pair of tongs and slid the metal bar from the forge and turned to his anvil. He caught sight of Jeniche and hesitated a moment before picking up his hammer. After several blows, he cursed and threw the metal bar to the floor by the forge.

151

Jeniche fished in her pouch and brought out a handful of coins. She slapped them on the bench.

'For the spoiled metal,' she said.

The anger went out of the smith's eyes. 'Watch the forge,' he said to his outsized assistant, 'and see what you can do with that waste. A sickle or something.'

Whilst the assistant went to work, the smith moved in behind the bench, looking all the while at Jeniche.

'From your part of the world, are they?' he asked.

She smiled. 'How did you come by them?'

'I travelled once. Not that far east. But I saw them and traded some… most of my own wares for them. Beautifully made. Couldn't resist.'

'Are they Antari?' asked Cenau.

'No,' said Jeniche. 'They're from Tundur. The Palace Guard at Rasa wears them.'

'Thought they were from Gyanag,' said the smith.

'Oh, they have them there as well. Mostly made in Tundur.'

'You from there?'

'No,' said Jeniche, 'but I have been there, got to know some of the people very well. Better than I thought.'

'Can you handle a sword?' the smith asked.

Ruad laughed. The smith looked at him, frowned, and then took in Duald. He turned and unhooked one of the swords from the wall. The sinuous curve of the highly polished blade caught the light of the forge and let it dance along the cutting edge. He placed it on his long forefinger to demonstrate its balance and let Jeniche lift it. The others stood back.

In Gyanag, she had learned a series of training exercises known as the steel lotus for the shape the tip of the sword drew in the air. They were designed to improve balance, strength, co-ordination, and control as well as meld body and spirit with weapon. The sword sang as it whirled, cutting the air, filling the interior of the forge with flashes of reflected light. For the few minutes the short lotus took, she forgot what the weapon was for, forgot the horrors of recent days, and enjoyed the feel of a thing well made as it became part of her being.

As she went to hand it back to the smith, he took the other one down from the wall, looked at it, came to a decision, and placed it on the bench. Before Jeniche could say anything, the smith unhooked the scabbards and belt as well.

'They seem made for you,' he said, 'and a sword is not meant for decoration. Sadly. May they serve you well.'

'How much?'

He named a price that was fair but still more than she had.

'You had better hang them up for another day,' she said, gazing at the bright curves of steel.

And as she said it, Cenau put some coins on the bench beside the swords. 'It's only fair,' he said as Jeniche started to object. 'That pays for the sword you gave me.'

Aros fished inside his tunic and pulled out a pouch, matching Cenau's contribution. Ruad and Duald put down the rest.

'We'll twist Cynfelyn's arm when we see him,' said Duald. 'Don't worry.'

'I can't...'

'Can't have you without a sword,' said Aros, 'otherwise we'll have to do your share of the work.'

After listening to Jeniche, the smith sent his assistant off

153

in search of a saddler and while they waited, made a clip to hold the chapes of the scabbards together. The saddler brought a harness that she adapted to fit Jeniche and before long, the swords were strapped to her back in a V, a hilt at each shoulder. Once her pack was back on and comfortable, Jeniche turned to the smith who nodded his approval.

'Thank you,' she said. And when the others had moved off a few steps she leaned toward the smith and added, 'Dunvran may be a fortress, but there is trouble heading this way. Be sure that you and your loved ones are safe.'

She turned and took the sack from Cenau and they headed toward the central marketplace. The smith watched them go with a frown on his face before turning to his assistant.

The central market alone was bigger than many villages. There were stalls everywhere, selling every conceivable item. Domestic ware, furniture, jewellery, sweetmeats, clothing, blankets, potions and lotions, toys and games. There were food stalls, barbers' stalls, places to get your teeth pulled, each with its own crowd of onlookers. Musicians played, puppet shows entertained the children, jugglers kept all manner of objects aloft, even flaming torches.

Everywhere people talked and laughed and strolled at their ease. In small tents, scribes drew up contracts for people, wrote letters for them. In other tents Derw witnessed the contracts drawn up by the scribes, they solemnized marriages, presided over divorces, sorted out long-running arguments.

As they pushed their way past the stalls into an open space, a voice shouted, 'Jeniche!' and she suddenly found herself embraced by Caru, staggering and almost falling.

'Hello,' said Cenau, shyly.

He got an embrace as well and a kiss. His embarrassment deepened when he saw the wicked grin on Aros's face.

'We're over on the far side,' said Caru.

They all looked over the heads of the crowd and saw the tops of three wagons.

'Are you all safe?' asked Jeniche.

Caru took her arm in one of hers and grabbed Cenau with the other. 'Yes,' she said, leading them toward the stage. 'Those men caught up with us, but we'd put everything away by then and said that you'd cut across country to the south. Did they find you?'

'Yes.'

Caru stopped and looked round, worry taking the sun from her face.

'It's all right,' said Cenau. 'The others are here and safe.'

'For now,' added Jeniche, 'but we need to talk to Gwynfor.'

As she said it, she caught sight of a familiar-looking face standing in the shadow of a booth.

'And we need to talk to him now.'

Chapter Sixteen

The players had most of their stage packed away by the time Cynfelyn and the others reappeared. Gwynfor had taken very little persuading that it would be wise to leave. This was his family, after all. There would be other times and other places to make a bit of extra cash. It had been a good year for them. Winter was close. Packing early and heading south to Gwydr to avoid any unpleasantness was the most sensible thing to do.

Ruad's intervention up at the Great Hall with a message from Jeniche had helped Cynfelyn persuade Tymestl that the citadel was under imminent threat. She had already been wavering. News of the slaughtered villagers had horrified her. The Ynyswr fought, but it was their warriors that did battle – men and women who had chosen that path. To cut down ordinary folk, her tribespeople... And now these barbarian Gwerin and Occassans were within her walls, all set to betray her hospitality.

While they were still talking, she sent messengers out to neighbouring tribes, even those with which they had, of late, been in conflict. She also sent members of her guard down into the western enclave of the citadel to find and imprison any strangers who were acting suspiciously. No mercy was to be shown to any who resisted.

Cynfelyn had thought it best to say nothing of his quest. Whilst he might trust the warrior queen seated before him on her plain oak throne, he did not know who else might be in the chamber. Instead, he said only that he must get those in his charge to the south without delay. Tymestl thanked him for his counsel and promised that he and his group would have safe passage out of the citadel before the gates were closed.

Even as they were hitching the wagons, Jeniche noticed Vran warriors moving discreetly through the fair, searching the booths and stalls as they went. Her big fear was that the Occassans had somehow smuggled moskets into the citadel. She could not help thinking of the carnage in Makamba, all the good people who had seen their lives torn apart, all the good people who had died.

She sighed. Everywhere she had been, people lived in fear in the ruins of a civilization that had collapsed so profoundly it had left almost no mark behind but the vast cemeteries that were called cities. Now it seemed to be happening again, all the old certain ways collapsing into chaos because of the ambitions of those hungry for power.

'We're ready,' called Gwynfor.

The wagons began to edge their way through the crowds, some of the players walking ahead of the horses to make sure no one was hurt. People called out in disappointment to see them leaving, but Gwynfor just grinned and shrugged his shoulders, wishing behind the false bonhomie that he could take every single one of them with him.

Jeniche climbed up onto the last wagon and ducked under the canvas, watching through a gap between the flaps at the back. The others followed close behind, keeping watch all the while. It wasn't easy for Jeniche to remain unobtrusive. All the others blended in, but her dark skin, though not unheard of, was unusual. The Occassans might be on the lookout for her and would try to do something to stop them leaving if they saw her.

As they approached the end of the main market place, Jeniche saw one group of stall-holders being led off into a side street. There was little fuss. Such gatherings always attracted people prepared to chance a bit of petty theft, as she well knew, and the crowds let the guards get on with it.

When they reached the gate, the others from Pengaver jumped up onto the wagons and rode out as if they were with the players, helping with the brakes as they went down the slope. Shouts went up behind them and Jeniche scanned the crowd with anxious eyes. Scuffles were breaking out near the inner guardhouse that gave access to the ramparts. People were darting about, not knowing what was happening, men protecting women, women grabbing children, stall-holders instinctively putting arms over their wares. Archers on the overhead walkway were having trouble picking out targets in the crowds.

'Keep going,' called Jeniche and dropped from the rear of the wagon. She knew exactly what she was looking for.

The first Occassan went down without knowing what had hit him. People began panicking as she went after the next. They pushed away from the bright blades of her new swords, as Jeniche had hoped, allowing the archers a clearer shot. Several other Occassans went down, heavily pierced, pinned to the ground. But there were plenty more, appearing from nooks and crannies like the venomous creatures they were, clearly trying to take control of the ramparts and prevent the gates from being closed.

Jeniche came sideways at another who had time to fend off her first blow and turn to face her. Although she was not that skilled with her left hand, the Occassan did not know how to deal with two swords at once and soon fell, bleeding badly from a neck wound. Another took his place only to fall with a lance in his belly. Maiv pulled it from the corpse.

'Let the Vran fight this now,' she said as a group of Tymestl's warriors came pushing through the crowd from the direction of the main market.

Maiv and Jeniche ran through the gateway to catch up with the wagons as the great gates began to swing closed. They slammed behind them with a deep, solid, ground-shaking thud that dislodged dust into the late autumn air. Further heavy thuds followed as the locking bars and props were dropped into place.

Someone threw Jeniche a rag and she cleaned her blades as she walked alongside the wagons, hands trembling. She said a silent prayer of protection for the smith. The Tunduri blades had served her well. She hoped he had as much luck.

Above them, the walls were already thick with defenders, soldiers and citizenry, but as they came out of the maze of protective ramparts onto the head of the causeway and turned onto the road to the south, they all wondered if Dunvran could possibly survive.

In the clear afternoon light, they could see the broad valley on the far side of the river growing dark with Gwerin warriors. It was a pestilence flowing slowly down the hills from the forest and making its implacable way across the fields to the crossing point. Hedgerows were trampled. Animals and people ran and were engulfed.

Smoke began to rise from the bridges as members of the riverside garrison smashed jars of oil and tried to set fire to the structures. A troop of cavalry had already surged forward in anticipation, bearing down on the bridge keepers, who stood their ground.

'Gods protect them,' she heard someone mutter and realized it was herself.

On the flat, as they made their way round the western end of Dunvran, the wagons moved marginally faster. It still seemed painfully slow and they all felt particularly vulnerable. Anyone else who had left the citadel before the gates had closed had long since disappeared along the road to the south. There was nothing now between them and the approaching army.

As they began to tackle the slope up out of the valley, Caru jumped down with a set of chocks and walked beside Jeniche, looking over her shoulder.

'Father says we must each pack a bag of belongings in case we have to leave the wagons.' She was close to tears.

Jeniche took Caru's hand and held it tightly. The nearest she had ever had to a home, rather than just a place to sleep, had been that secret space in the roof of the stables in Makamba. The nearest she had ever had to family was Trag, gone beneath the desert sands. But Caru had been born in one of those wagons and lived all her life in them, surrounded by loved ones, as the world flowed around them.

'It might not happen,' Jeniche said, trying to sound as if she believed it. 'Dunvran's misfortune might save us. The Gwerin will want to take the citadel or lay siege to it to ensure the warriors within remain confined. It may give us a chance to get away without leaving anything behind.'

'But if they're all the way across here, where else is safe?'

It was a question for which Jeniche had no answer. She squeezed Caru's hand again. 'Pack only what you will most need for the winter,' Jeniche said. 'Plain, dull clothes if you have them, so you don't stand out.'

Caru nodded. She took a last look back at the sight that would feed her nightmares for years to come and then moved up by the rear wheel of the wagon in case the horses faltered on the hill.

Jeniche turned then and looked back along the road. Much of the valley was now obscured by the bulk of Dunvran, but she had no doubt that the dark tide was flowing over the bridges and spreading out on this side of the river, cutting down everything in its way, picking positions, and eyeing the prize.

Some madness must be driving the Gwerin. No one waged war in the winter, not with such a vast army. Perhaps they had thought they would be able to march into a citadel secured for them by the Occassans who had sneaked inside; re-supply themselves before moving on and leaving the local population behind to starve through the cold months to come. Now there would be bloody battles, but at least the Gwerin wouldn't have it all their own way and, perhaps, they really had bought a little more time for Cynfelyn to find the Hallows. She turned away and caught up with the others. It had better be worth it, she thought. The cost was already high.

Chapter Seventeen

It was a wonder that something so dark could look so bright. As Cynfelyn turned it slowly in his hands, the highly polished circlet of black stone reflected the cold sunlight, creating, for anyone who looked closely enough, a miniature of the world within a non-existent depth. As the small green star moved into the light, that shone as well, but with a different quality. There was a living richness there against the monochrome hardness.

He looked up as Jeniche crossed the floor of the long-deserted quarry to where he was sitting. She brought food and drink and he handed her the circlet in exchange. It was the first time she had seen it properly.

'So this is the crown of the Guardian.'

'Hardly seems worth it.'

'It's beautifully made.' She held it up. 'A perfect circle.'

'A trinket.' His anger had put a harsh edge on his voice. 'Nothing, not even a symbol, is worth a life.'

'So you're going to give up on your quest?'

'No. But it's not just about the Hallows any more.'

She twisted the circlet in her hands while he spooned up some soup. The star fascinated her. It had eight points like tiny arrows.

'I've seen this before. Is it a common symbol in Ynysvron?'

Cynfelyn shook his head, leaned forward to look at the jewel. 'No. We think of the year as divided into eight, but the only symbol for that is a wheel with eight spokes. There were, traditionally, seven kingdoms although I've never seen them named. Most other number symbols are threes or nines.'

Jeniche stared at it, trying to remember, whilst Cynfelyn ate in silence. When he had finished he took the circlet back and slipped it into the hidden pocket in his surcoat. After a long moment looking at his grubby, calloused hands, he stood and smiled.

'Putting on a brave face, my mother called this. Let's hope it's enough.'

They picked their way through the long undergrowth to the back of the quarry where the wagons were hidden behind a small copse of birches. Cynfelyn handed his bowl and cup to Caru who took them off to where her mother was checking that everything was secure and as weather-tight as they could make it.

Gwynfor handed Cynfelyn a small pot from which a brush protruded.

'The paint you asked for.'

'Forgive me for this. I do not wish to desecrate the homes of those that have given us shelter or offend those that have taken us in as their own. I cannot repay your long service to the Derw or your hospitality and bravery in the way it deserves. I can, however, offer this.'

With care he painted an elaborate symbol on each of the

three wagons, murmuring quietly as he did so. When he had finished, he continued with the invocation, the others standing in silence, a kestrel hovering high overhead.

'For what it is worth, these wagons and all their contents are now under the protection of the High Council of the Derw. It will not count for much if the Gwerin find them, but it will otherwise be enough to ensure they are here and untouched when you return.'

Gwynfor was crying; his wife and daughter held tightly to him. The other players were equally distraught, saying farewell to all that was theirs.

'If things get really bad in Ynysvron, you must all make your way across the sea to Brocel.' He searched in one of the many hidden pockets in his coat and pulled out a heavy gold coin. 'That will buy you all passage.' And then a small carved token. 'That will get you the protection of Pen Derw Nuala. She is a good friend to me and will be a good friend to you. May the gods and goddesses keep you safe and bring the smiles to your faces once more.'

'Be your journey downhill all the way to a broad hearth and full table,' said Gwynfor, wiping his eyes with the back of his hand.

One by one they all embraced before the players mounted their horses and rode out onto the road south. Jeniche stood and watched them go, waving as they passed out of sight.

'It can be a complete bastard, this world,' said Cynfelyn quietly. 'But you already know that better than anyone.'

Jeniche turned to see the others emerging from the quarry. They crossed the road and scrambled through the scrub on the far side, picking their way down the slope and disappearing in amongst the trees below.

The late autumn weather was beginning to turn wintry.

As Jeniche and Cynfelyn crossed the road to join the others, a cold gust swithered along, blowing branches this way and that, picking at the last of the leaves. Jeniche pulled her coat tighter and looked out over the tops of the trees. She shivered again.

Once they left the shelter of the woods on the scarp they were at the full mercy of the winds out of the east across the sea. And they were visible from miles away. The weather had become full winter almost overnight. Low, grey skies; cold that seeped up through their boots; a chill that cut through clothes and flesh to chill their very bones.

Cenau was the first to feel the cold. There was so little flesh on him that he found it hard to keep any warmth in his body. Even with struggling to keep up the fierce pace that Cynfelyn set, he felt numb. It was not just the cold, but the prospect of endless days struggling across a land forsaken by all life but the tough grasses that cut your flesh.

There were two main advantages to their situation, although Cenau would have been hard pressed to see them as that. The first was that once they were on the high marsh, they could see as far as anyone else. The second was that the people now following could clearly travel no faster than them.

Aros had spotted their pursuers first as a break in the northern skies left tiny figures silhouetted against the pale grey. They could be seen as they rode down out of the bare trees and onto rough pasture at the edge of the marsh. It was an ill-needed reminder of the Gwerin pouring out of the forest by Dunvran.

The distant figures had not remained on horseback for long. Once they had come down off the pasture to the first of the shallow, brackish pools, they would have seen that horses would slow them down. The animals were duly led back toward the hills whilst the rest of their pursuers continued on foot.

As it grew darker, Jeniche herded her companions closer together and they moved on as quickly as they could, trusting to Cynfelyn to know a route. Even then the going was not easy and they were still only on the fringes of the treacherous land.

Eventually it became too dark to travel safely and they hunkered down in a shallow dip in the ground, huddled together with Cenau in their midst. It was a restless night. The wind sang a ceaseless threnody and populated their nightmares with visions of darkness and death. Jeniche walked all night through her dreams, unable to find a way and woke at first light, stiff and exhausted. Ruad and Aros were already awake trying to see their followers without being seen.

Jeniche roused the others and, after using what little cover there was to relieve themselves, they set off again. Too tired and dispirited to talk, they kept their heads down and helped one another over the rough ground and across the narrow creeks, casting the occasional glance backwards in the growing light.

There was no sun that day, just the cloud and the wind with its voice wearing at their bodies and their spirits. All it could manage in their favour was to change direction so that by the afternoon it was flowing out of the north and onto their backs. Jeniche walked directly behind Cenau to help him if he stumbled and offer what little shelter she could.

As it began to darken on the second day, they stumbled over a length of timber trackway – single planks laid in the upper angle of crossed poles driven into the ground. It cut across their path heading out toward the lower, tidal marshes. As it offered some shelter from the wind, they clambered over and settled down in its lee to rest for the night.

'People live out here?' asked Cenau.

'They used to,' replied Cynfelyn, 'but I doubt they do any more. The world seems to be claiming itself back bit by bit.'

He looked at the others. They looked back.

'Sorry. This place is getting to me. At least I know where we are now. More or less.'

'Is that a good thing or a bad thing?' asked Maiv.

'Both.'

'Ah. The Derw gives a useful answer.' Ruad's comment was meant in jest. He was smiling. But there was an edge to his voice.

Cynfelyn held up his hands in surrender, then massaged his face. 'Good, because we are only a few days away from our goal and I have kept us to the path through the high marshes.'

'And bad?' It was Jeniche that asked.

'Because harsh as all this is, it is natural; just the sea and the land battling it out. Beyond this point it is a bit like the Forest of Bron. Out there where it is neither land nor sea, where the wind rules supreme and only the sun and stars can tell us which way is which, there are the remains of another sprawling pre-Ev city.'

Aros groaned. He was tired beyond anything he had thought possible; had seen and done things he could never have imagined. And now he was being told it was going to happen all over again. The others looked as enthusiastic.

Cenau was visibly fighting back the tears. 'I cannot go underground again,' he said quietly.

'You won't have to, lad,' said Cynfelyn. 'That is a promise.'

'How do you know?' asked Aros.

'Because no matter where we go, I will not make Cenau go underground. He has given enough. We all have. I did not know it was going to be like this. A task, yes. But I had not imagined we would be in a race against the Gwerin or the Occassans.'

Light was fading fast and tiny flecks of snow were driving past over their heads. They waited for Cynfelyn to continue. He looked old.

'I cannot ask any of you to go further. It was a foolish idea from the start.'

'What was?' asked Aros.

'We go on,' said Cenau, before Cynfelyn could reply. 'Just as long as I don't have to go underground.'

'No,' said Cynfelyn.

'Yes,' said Aros.

'Yes,' said Ruad.

'Yes,' said Maiv.

'Yes,' said Awd.

'Yes,' said Duald.

There was a pause.

'What about you, Jeniche?' asked Cynfelyn.

'I don't know,' she said, rubbing her hands together in the hope of warmth. 'I've got nothing else planned.' She grinned. 'But you'd better tell us where we're going if you're headed back inland to find somewhere with a fire and hot food.'

He punched her on the arm. Very very gently.

When they woke, there was snow drifted in against tussocks of grass and lying along the timber trackway. There was no way of knowing what time of day it was. The sky was a uniform grey and there were no shadows; the wind was still blowing from the north. Now and then a flake of snow tumbled by.

What got their stiff, frozen limbs moving was the proximity of their pursuers. Somehow they had halved the distance. They were still a long way off, well out of bowshot, but they were definitely closer.

Eating on the move again, they pressed on. Ahead of them they began to pick out other trackways, unbroken lines of snow running east to west across their path. The going was slow. Not only were they tired, but the ground was icy and they kept slipping. Ruad fell headlong from one of the trackways as they clambered over. It took long painful moments to get him back to his feet and moving again.

Behind them, the pursuers closed, seemingly unaffected by the conditions.

'Do you...' said Jeniche, drawing a second breath to finish the question, '... think they've been quickened?'

Cynfelyn cast a glance backward, able now to make out the faces of those that followed. 'Drugs? Must be.' He had no breath to spare for a longer answer.

Several of them had already clambered down the far side without noticing. The shouts of pursuit could be heard and they just wanted to move on. Cynfelyn almost did the same and then realized they had finally found what he had been looking for.

'Back!' he called. 'Back! We cross here.'

They stopped, stupefied. Aros pushed Cenau back and helped him climb up. The others struggled, slipping on the icy timbers, noticing as they did that this trackway was broader, three planks wide, and stretched much further into the distance.

'This one is supposed to go right across to the other side,' said Cynfelyn.

'But they've nearly caught up,' said Cenau.

'Then get going,' said Cynfelyn.

There seemed to be a new energy in his eyes and they trotted on along the planks. They kept to the centre as, before long, they began crossing wide pools of water crusted with thin ice. The pools grew wider, the ice thinner, the water darker and deeper.

Behind them they could hear the rhythmic pounding of pursuit.

Wasting more breath, Cynfelyn called to the others as they ran. 'When I say. Stop and help me. Heave the planks. Into the water.'

He looked over his shoulder. They were getting nearer. He listened, waiting for the sound he knew must come. But it was getting difficult to hear with that pounding behind him getting closer and closer.

And there it was. A clatter as they crossed loose planking. 'Now!'

They stopped and turned. Awd slipped on a patch of dark ice and went down heavily, but she held on to one of the uprights and was quickly back on her feet. She stayed at the back watching over the others as they bent and forced their frozen fingers to grip the icy planks.

The first one came away easily and splashed into the water below, floating slowly away. The second plank was tighter, jammed against the third. They pulled in the confined space and it sprang up suddenly, taking a layer of flesh off the back of Ruad's hand.

As they recovered themselves to attack the next plank a spear flew over their heads and caught the lead pursuer in the shoulder. He span off balance and fell into the water. His compatriots ignored him and kept coming. Closer. Closer.

The last plank came loose and lodged without falling completely.

'Back,' called Cynfelyn. 'Next section.'

They fell back as one of the pursuers jumped the eight-foot gap, bowling into their midst, knocking them aside. He tried to stand and collapsed. Jeniche pushed him off her swords with her boot. He rolled with barely a splash into the dark, icy water. She turned as another one tried to make the jump. He was met in mid air by Awd's last spear and crashed into the plank they were loosening. It went into the water with the body on it.

The other pursuers had lost momentum, but they drew their swords and started to try to climb onto the uprights, looking for ways to get across.

Another plank came loose. Then another. More organized, they split into two groups and worked methodically, backing further and further from the Gwerin, widening the gap across deep water.

The Gwerin were still making their way precariously from upright to upright, but the planks were coming away faster, and the water was getting deeper. All that splashing was causing ripples and making noise, and the thudding on the bridge was sending vibrations into the deep. And although the marshes and inlets seemed lifeless, things still lived there. Hungry things.

When the first splash came, no one saw what happened. Everyone stopped and looked; the Gwerin all out on upright poles, the others on the bridge. At first they all thought one of the Gwerin had slipped and fallen in. Huge ripples flowed out from beside the angled upright where he had been perched. But he didn't come back to the surface and the water went deadly smooth. Dark. Growing darker.

Everyone saw the next attack. Fast. Deadly. A scaly shape leaping from the water with barely a splash. Long jaws grabbing a Gwerin and pulling him off his pole and into the water before he had time to react. They could not help the Gwerin that were left, so they ran.

Chapter Eighteen

The world became unreal. From the darkening sky, more snow began to fall. Behind them was the wreck of the raised walkway, their pursuers stranded and at the mercy of a ravenous giant pike. Ahead of them, the bridge came to an abrupt end in the middle of a lake of black, still water.

Once the pounding of feet on heavy planks had gone, all that was left was the soughing of the icy wind and the pained intake of air into burning lungs. Bent over, hands on trembling knees or resting against the angled uprights of the narrow structure, they fought for breath and against despair.

'What do we do now?' asked Jeniche.

They could not swim. If the icy water did not leach the life from their exhausted bodies, the monstrous long-jawed fish would tear it out.

Cynfelyn and the others looked round with slow desperation to see if they could spot some way out of their predicament. There was no sign of the far shore. There was no way back. It did not help that night was falling.

'Cenau!'

They all turned to see the young Derw standing at the very end of the bridge. His head was on one side and as they watched, he knelt.

'Come away from the edge!'

Jeniche stepped forward, ready to grab him back, and saw his hand reach out. At first he laid it flat on the surface and then he jabbed it with a finger. Still kneeling, he turned his head, a puzzled smile on his face.

'It's… solid,' he said, as if he didn't believe it.

'Ice?' asked Aros.

'I can't see what else, but it doesn't feel like it. It's cold, but not…' he shrugged, '… icy. And it's curved.'

'What do you mean?' asked Cynfelyn, joining them at the very end of the planks.

'Kneel down.'

Cynfelyn knelt.

'Look in the distance. It's much higher than us.'

Now it was Cynfelyn's turn to put his head on one side. 'It could be an illusion. A trick of the light.'

'Light?' asked Ruad. 'At any other time that would almost be amusing.'

'Is it safe to walk on?' Maiv spoke as she joined them where the planks ended.

Whilst they were all looking out across the dark prospect, Jeniche walked back the way they had come. Leaning down and prodding with one of her swords every so often, she went as far back along the walkway as she could reach down to solid ground.

'It's all the way back here!' she called and then returned, looking down at the supports. 'The cross-beams holding the planks up are resting on the… whatever it is.'

'Glass?' suggested Aros.

'But it's vast,' replied Cenau.

Aros shrugged. 'You're the brainy one.'

Cenau pulled a face.

'Do we risk it?' Maiv wanted to know.

Awd was prodding the dark surface with the toe of her boot.

'I'll try it,' said Jeniche. 'I'm the lightest.'

'Wouldn't it make more sense for the heaviest to try?' suggested Cynfelyn.

'That would be me,' said Awd, still prodding with her toe.

'We'll hold on to you,' said Maiv, taking her arm.

Ruad grabbed Maiv, and Duald grabbed Ruad, each bracing themselves as Awd stepped out onto the smooth, dark surface.

'It didn't give at all,' said Awd. To reinforce the point, she jumped up and down. She then bent and touched the surface with her free hand.

'The surface is smooth, but it doesn't feel slippy.'

Awd nodded to Maiv, who let go of her arm, and then walked slowly away from the end of the bridge. The others waited with their breath held, but nothing seemed to happen. Maiv stepped down as well and joined her.

'Before we go anywhere,' said Cynfelyn, 'I want to be sure we can find our way back here.'

He removed his pack and took out a pale under tunic, tearing it into strips. Knotting several, he tied one end to the final upright support of the bridge. The rag flapped in the breeze.

'We should be able to see that from some distance,' he said. 'If this... whatever it is begins to give under us, try to get back here.'

One by one, they settled their packs and set off along the dark, glassy surface in the failing day. If anything, they were more exposed here and the cruel wind bit at them, the snow whipping at their flesh, snaking in ghostly spindrifts across the smooth surface.

Although it resembled glass in some respects, there was enough traction for them to walk normally. Snow and ice, however, could find no purchase. It was unnerving at first, leaving the bridge behind. They were all waiting for the dream to end with a drop through thin ice into killing water.

Tired as they were, and constantly on edge, they travelled well into the night. Putting one foot in front of another had become mechanical and they all began to feel as if they were walking in their sleep. On several occasions, Jeniche came to, uncertain if she had nodded off or just been in a trance.

Exhaustion had been passed sometime shortly after all sense of reality had disappeared. And that had been so long ago that no one could remember when it was. It came as a disorientating shock when Ruad called out.

They stumbled into each other, squinting into the dark to make each other out – dark against darkness.

'Are you all right?' Duald asked.

'No. I tripped over something.' A pause. 'Nothing broken though.'

'We stop here,' said Cynfelyn.

No one needed persuading. They found Duald and settled quickly in the scant lee of whatever he had stumbled over. Huddling together for whatever warmth they could find, they fell into a collective sleep and lay as if dead in the dark with the wind singing a lament over their bodies.

Jeniche woke first, looking into the pale eyes of a small

creature with large teeth and thick fur. She could barely move, stiff from their exertions and cold through to the bone, but she reached out a foot and prodded whoever was nearest. Aros lifted his head, eyes devoid of anything but misery.

When he saw the creature, a spark of something ignited there and he sat up. The creature turned and looked at him, brushed a whisker with a delicate paw, then sauntered off before disappearing into a small space between two rocks. It clearly had no fear of them, and as Jeniche sat up as well, she didn't need to wonder why.

They looked like they'd been washed there by the tide, draped over rocks, limp as stranded jellyfish. Cenau was a deathly white and she shuffled along the ground to sit beside him. Finding his hands, she began to chafe them. He groaned, but did not wake. Or perhaps he just pretended to be asleep. She didn't mind.

Aros was rousing the others. They didn't look much better than Cenau. Eventually they were all on their feet and trying to make sense of where they were.

The shallow trough in which they had slept was composed of blocks. It reminded Jeniche of the dry water course they had found on the edge of the desert, except here the blocks were cracked and dislodged, providing all sorts of hiding places for small furry creatures with big eyes and sharp teeth.

Climbing and standing on one side of the channel, they could see a vast expanse of dark glassy material. In what passed for daylight beneath the low cloud, detail that had been hidden from them before was now exposed. Long ripples were frozen into the surface close by, although they faded in the distance. There were colours in the surface and in places the substance was clear, allowing them to see into depths where vague shapes teased.

In the other direction was a wasteland of tumbled, broken blocks and starved grasses, the bleak landscape relieved only by drifts of thin snow. There was a new sound on the wind as well.

'The sea,' said Cynfelyn. 'It's a long way off yet, but on the far side of where we are headed this... city... sinks beneath the waves and they pound at the stones without cease.'

'We had best get going before Cenau freezes,' said Jeniche.

Cynfelyn nodded and the others fell in behind as he began to pick his way over the first jumble of stones.

'Have you been here before?' asked Jeniche.

Cynfelyn shook his head. 'No. I've seen it from off shore. There's a harbour. Was a harbour. I hope it's still there.'

He said no more but clambered up a pile of stones and onto a less-tortured surface where sand had drifted over the centuries, filling in the cracks, crevices, and dips. The wind was still cold and Jeniche was worried about Cenau's hands. The fingers were a leprous white and he was walking awkwardly. If they didn't get him warmed up soon he might not warm up at all. From Cynfelyn's frequent glances at the young Derw it was clear he had the same fears.

The one good thing about the day was the lack of snow. As they walked, the wind eased as well. But the ever-present grey skies sat over them as they stumbled their way through the ruins.

For a while they were shadowed in the distance by a creature. Having no real sense of scale, they couldn't tell if it was a kind of fox, a kind of wolf, or something even bigger. After a while it disappeared. Perhaps it was just seeing them off its territory, or maybe it realized, as Awd pointed out, there wasn't enough meat on their bones.

Not long afterwards she called out.

'Is that where we are headed?'

When everyone had caught up with her, she pointed just off to the right of their general direction. On the horizon, the ruins rose up. At this distance it was little more than a slight swelling, but Cynfelyn let out a sigh of relief.

It changed to a cry of despair as Cenau collapsed at his feet. Scooping him up, he slung the young Derw over his shoulder and began walking.

'Cynfelyn! We have to warm him,' called Aros. 'He can't carry on.'

Cynfelyn didn't stop. Instead he quickened his pace. Not knowing what to do, the others just stood.

'We have to follow,' said Jeniche. 'Trust he knows what he is doing. Saving his breath for one thing.'

Aros took off his pack and unlaced it. Grabbing the base, he upended it onto the ground. Pushing spare clothing to one side, he picked out a whetstone, his flint, and one or two other small belongings which he put in his pockets. As he began to turn the pack inside out, Ruad and Duald took their packs off as well.

'We're all going mad,' said Jeniche under her breath as they and then Maiv and Awd began to go through the same routine.

Before long they were squatting in a circle, forcing their cold fingers to undo buckles and re-fix them, re-lace bits of pack. Jeniche began to smile.

It took very little time. While they were working, she gathered all the spare bits of clothing and stuffed them into her own pack until it bulged, using a length of cord to tie over the top. It was unwieldy when she put it back on, but the others would need their hands and shoulders free for the stretcher they had just made.

They caught up with Cynfelyn and took Cenau from him. He tried to protest, but they just ignored him. Cenau was strapped in place, lifted from the ground and carried by four of them. Jeniche followed behind, counting paces. Every time she got to five thousand, she would call out and they would rotate places, with one new person carrying and one giving their shoulder a rest.

All the while, the swelling on the horizon was expanding. At first it was just a silhouette, but as they drew closer they could pick out details of light and shadow. And closer still the nuanced shades of grey that had hidden the main feature began to stand out from the cloud because, atop the hill of broken masonry, was a tower.

The structure grew and grew as they made their way across the shattered landscape, yet they seemed to come no closer. It was a while before the true scale of it all came home to their tired minds.

As they pounded forward, the rising ruins and the vast tower drew them on, a dimmed beacon guiding them through a burning darkness of spirit, feeding energy to bodies tired beyond description. And for a while they did not hear Cynfelyn. In the end he had to stand in their way to make them stop, put Cenau on the ground.

He was too tired to speak. They were too tired to understand. He kept waving, but the gesture made no sense. In the end he turned each of them away from the tower to face down the lower slopes they had already climbed. Face down to the harbour where seven sleek ships rode at anchor.

Chapter Nineteen

A quiet, hollow, wooden knocking woke Cenau. 'All right! I'm getting up.'

'No you're not, lad.'

Cenau opened his eyes in surprise and tried to sit up.

'Ow.'

He lay back down. Cynfelyn loomed over him.

'I'm not in my room.'

'Quick as ever. How do you feel?'

Now he was fully awake, the nightmare returned.

'Horrible. But warm. What happened? Where are we?'

'You collapsed. I'll tell you everything, but first I need to see your feet.'

Cenau frowned, but he ignored the pains and sat up, pulling the covers to one side. Cynfelyn took his nearest foot in his hands and felt it, flexing the joints.

'How does that feel?'

'Like I've been walking for weeks?'

Cynfelyn grinned and then pinched Cenau's big toe.

'Ouch.'

'Good.'

'Not good. That hurt.'

Cynfelyn picked up the other foot and repeated the process.

'It is good that it hurt. We thought you might have frost-bite.'

'Oh.'

'Exactly.'

'So where are we?'

'On board a warship.'

'Did we get the next of the Hallows?'

There came a soft knocking. This time it was knuckles on the door.

'Come in,' said Cynfelyn.

Jeniche backed in with a tray covered with a cloth. It was a small cabin and deliciously warm. She kicked the door closed to keep it that way. The bunk where Cenau lay filled a third of the space along one side. There were lockers beneath it and cupboards above. By the foot of the bunk was a narrow fixed table with a stool that swung out once you unlocked it. That was where Cynfelyn was perched. Above the table, open shutters revealed a panel of thick, oiled parchment set into the wall to let light into the space.

'I heard talking just now. Thought this might be appreci-ated.'

She put the tray on the end of the bed and removed the cloth to reveal several loaves, a large pie, plates, mugs, and a flagon. Cenau felt his stomach growl.

'How are your toes?' she asked as she started to share out the food.

'Fine,' replied Cenau, moving them out of pinching range.

He took a plate, but looked at Cynfelyn. 'I haven't forgotten my question,' he said.

Cynfelyn said: 'Eat.'

'What question was that?' asked Jeniche.

'Don't you start on me as well. Let me explain things in my own way.'

Jeniche and Cenau grinned at each other. It was so much easier to do when you were warm and safe.

'Do you remember the village where they had lost the shepherd boy?' Cynfelyn continued. 'I asked the Derw there to get word to Pengaver. Things were worse than I had thought and that was before Dunvran. I thought a ship might speed things up for us.'

'And they sent seven,' said Jeniche.

'Seven?'

'Seven,' confirmed Cynfelyn. 'They must have heard about Dunvran. The captain said the last he heard, it was going badly. And there are Gwerin ships abroad in the Eastern Sea as well.'

'So did we get the next of the Hallows?' Cenau asked again.

'No, lad.'

'But you're not giving up? Where are we?'

'You were in danger, so I brought you straight to the ships.'

Cenau waited. Cynfelyn said nothing.

'It is the Hallows, isn't it? That was the Carreg we found. In the north. We came east, so it must be Gwyan out there. Somewhere. Where are the ships?'

'I can see you're getting better. The ships are in a harbour on the northern edge of the waste we were crossing. Directly south of us and not too far away is a tower.'

'Then we must go.'

'Not until you have eaten and the others have rested.'

'Oh. Is everyone else all right?'

'Yes. Thank you for asking.'

'Sorry.'

Cynfelyn ruffled his hair. 'Eat. And rest. And don't breathe a word of this to Aros.'

Cenau stopped with a piece of bread half way to his mouth. He nearly dropped it as understanding dawned.

It was not nearly so warm on deck. A vicious wind had returned from the north and members of the crew were using belaying pins to knock the ice from rigging lines and pulleys. Cynfelyn and Jeniche huddled in their coats and made their way forward, grateful to get back under cover.

The forward crew quarters, where the others were staying, were far less spacious than the cabin that Cenau had been given. Palliasses had been put down for the guests beneath the crew's hammocks. But it was warm and clean, and the food was good.

Something of the exhaustion had fallen away from them. They had slept long, fed well, and been able to relax. Always looking over their shoulders and wondering whether their supplies would last had drained them as much as the walking.

'Well?' It was Aros, stretched out beneath a thick, felt blanket. 'Is he all right?'

'He'll live. And walk. I think we'd have trouble stopping him.'

There was a general nodding and murmuring of approval.

'So what happens now?' It was Ruad who asked.

'If you want to go through with this...'

Nobody said anything.

'It's late now,' Cynfelyn continued. 'We rest until first light and then we head for the tower. Once we have what we came for, we come back to the ship and they will take us round the south of the mainland.'

Even in the dim light, Cynfelyn could see the unasked questions in their faces.

'It pains me to say it to such loyal companions,' he said, 'but please trust me a little longer. I know you have questions. It will come clear. I just hope...'

'You too should rest,' said Awd. 'We will see it through. After that? Who knows. Let us worry about fording that river when we get to it.'

At first light they assembled on deck. The wind had dropped and the cloud had lifted, though the sky was still dull. The cold, however, was still there. It seemed to have taken root and there was even a hint of ice on the water in a far corner of the harbour.

All seven ships were anchored in the deepest part of the port, a vast inlet that seemed partly natural and partly man made. The walls were high and built of vast blocks of fine dressed stone that weighed many tons apiece. Other sections, particularly on the far side, were heavily silted; the shallows were dirtied as the lapping waters of the incoming tide broke against the fine mud.

The ships themselves were designed for speed and fighting. Sleek and sturdy, there was nothing there that did not need to be there. It had been a long time since raiders crossed the Eastern Sea on a regular basis, but some still did. And there were occasionally those who had fallen on hard times who had decided piracy might pay.

They had spent a day and a half on board the *Morfran*

as a guest of her captain. He joined them on the deck, a glum expression on his weathered face.

'I suspect from the state of you when you arrived on board, you have plenty of worries to keep you company. However, I cannot help but add some more. Cynfelyn will have told you that we had heard of Gwerin ships on the Eastern Sea. If that is so, we do not wish to risk being caught here. And if this cold continues, there is the danger of being iced in as well.

'The *Morgi* will be setting out soon to scout northward along the coast. If her master tells me there are Gwerin present, I must put all these ships to sea. And if the ice begins to form, I must do the same.

'We will stay here as long as we can, but I dare not risk being taken out of the fight so cheaply. May the gods and goddesses speed you.'

They thanked him for his hospitality and for the full packs they now had and when he had gone below, they turned to face the shore. It was not an encouraging scene. All the memories of crossing the waste came back in a grim, icy rush.

Even with a pale, winter sun on the horizon, visible for the first time in days, the ruins looked no better. To Jeniche, they looked worse because now she could see the scale and the detail. What chance did any of them stand, she wondered, if such a vast structure could be so comprehensively smashed down and left to decay? What must it have been like if, after all these centuries, so much of it still stood?

Inevitably, all eyes were drawn to the tower. It was a uniform grey, tapering slightly to the flat summit. Huge. Silent. Featureless.

In the end it was Cenau who spoke: 'Who built that?'

Once the question was asked it was obvious the tower

was built on top of the ruins; of similar construction, but built some time after whatever event had laid waste to hundreds of square miles of city.

'Perhaps,' suggested Cynfelyn, 'we should go and find out.'

Chapter Twenty

'Did they have warriors with them?'

The first section had been surprisingly easy. The harbour wall, inset with steps, was relatively undamaged and the slopes of rubble leading up from the waterfront had long since been smoothed over with pale, windblown sand. There was even a wide expanse of dunes further to the east, with grasses on the inland slopes; the land claiming itself back from the sea.

Here and there, where they walked, shattered blocks of masonry jutted out like bones through flesh. Weathered bones, crumbling and grey, hollow in places as if the very marrow of the dead city had been sucked out. In other places, the sand was a deep orangey brown, as if the city had died from bleeding out.

Jeniche responded: 'Why do you ask, Cenau?'

Cynfelyn grimaced. Trying to keep Cenau quiet on the subject was wasted effort. The one saving grace was that Aros seemed more intent on picking out a route than on anything Cenau had to say.

'Well, they must have come here and left the spear. And then gone on to… well… wherever it is they went. Somewhere in the south after this, I suppose.'

Jeniche and Cynfelyn exchanged a quick glance and he shook his head.

'And?'

'Well, if they had to get here… I don't know. They must have had some protection if they were carrying the Hallows.'

Jeniche was aware that some of the others were listening. They were still in sight of the ships, could hear someone calling orders, so had not yet spread out in a protective pattern. She looked back over her shoulder.

'There goes the *Morgi*,' she said.

They all stopped and watched as the vessel began to move, towed by its own shore boat. The oars rose and fell, biting the icy water. It was slow work at first, but once the ship began to move she was soon passing smoothly through the harbour entrance.

In open water, grey sails dropped and hung limply until the crew swarming in the rigging adjusted ropes. Shouts echoed across the water. The sails began to fill. As the *Morgi* began to move, the shore boat was rowed alongside and then hoisted aboard.

'Time is not on our side,' said Awd.

One by one they turned round to face the tower and the task of finding a path through the desolation before them. It was slow going. After a while, Cenau picked up the conversation.

'If they had warriors—'

'There were warriors,' cut in Cynfelyn. 'Sorry. I didn't mean that to be… Never mind. There were warriors, artisans, and Derw. Four of each. They are generally, if somewhat unoriginally, referred to as the Twelve. Other than that, we know very little. They came here and hid the spear. At least I hope it was here.'

'You hope?'

'As I said, we don't know. Anything. The party that set out to place the Four Hallows in safe keeping never came back.'

There was silence as they all digested this, crossing the last of the sandy flats before clambering up an unstable ridge of rubble. Much of it was composed of brickwork that had long since become rotten in the almost constant storm of salt air. At the top, they dusted themselves down and set out across another relatively flat area where yet more sand had drifted.

'I spent years following their every move,' said Cynfelyn eventually. There were still things he wanted Aros to work out for himself, but time was running out fast and a little help wouldn't hurt. 'I listened to stories and rumours, talked with Derw who told the tales of their village or tribe, read written accounts, learnt the history of every place to find the one thing that would tell me which path they had taken, which stream they had crossed, what ship they had boarded. Often I found I was following some other trail and had to retrace my steps to where I was certain. And I was never certain.

'What I do know is that all four of the Hallows were successfully hidden away, for they have not been seen again. The knowledge of their whereabouts was meant to be passed on as a set of clues embedded in a poem to be kept in the Library on Pengaver, but that never happened. The chronicles for that year mention a long season of fierce storms sweeping across Ynysvron after they set out. Their ship vanished without trace.'

Silence returned and they trudged on, saving their energy. It was clear there would not be much in the way of level ground after the stretch they were on. It was equally clear from the distant looming presence of the vast mound that they still had a very long way to climb.

As they approached the far side of the upper flat, their eyes were on the climb ahead, looking for ways to tackle the first slope. Only Ruad had his eyes on the ground and it was some while before the others realized he had stopped and been left behind.

'Ruad?!'

He looked up at the call from Duald and beckoned the others to join him. Cynfelyn sighed, but led the way. When they reached Ruad, they followed the direction of his pointing finger to the ground at his feet. Grinning up at them was a skull, the jaws slightly open.

'I saw some bones further back,' said Ruad. 'Thigh bones, I think. Thought they might be animal until I saw a foot.'

'How far back?' asked Jeniche.

'Quite a way.'

'Not someone who fell and died and was covered with sand, then,' said Aros.

'I thought that,' said Ruad. 'An animal could easily have scattered the bones.'

'But?' asked Cynfelyn.

Ruad pointed off to the left of where they stood.

'I don't see...' started Cenau. And then stopped. Because suddenly he did see.

Lined up in rows there were long, low mounds in the sand, many with a stone at one end. Invisible to a casual glance, once they had seen them, they kept seeing them.

191

Hundreds of them. Some were swamped by drifts. Others, like the one at their feet, had been worn away by the wind to expose first the coffin and then the contents.

'People lived here. In the ruins. Hundreds of them.'

'But not for a long while, lad. That skull is old.'

'And strange,' said Jeniche, her head on one side. She knelt beside it and carefully scraped away the sand from around it with her fingers. 'See how long it is?' She began to bury it again, scooping the cold, damp sand over it in a thin layer, patting, sculpting.

The end result was a slender face with high cheeks. Almost human, but somehow not quite.

'What is it?' whispered Maiv.

'I don't know,' said Jeniche, 'but I have seen pictures. In northern Tundur. There are mountains there that form the border with Gyanag. It's extremely isolated. The temples in that region are highly decorated and in amongst pictures of people and animals, there are these. They had eyes like the Tunduri and Gyanag.' She demonstrated, pulling the outer corners of her eyes toward her ears to elongate the shape. 'An old monk I spoke to said they were called *b'skorba*, but I heard that used elsewhere to mean pilgrim or traveller.'

'Are there others here?' asked Cenau, looking round.

'We don't have time,' said Cynfelyn. 'If you want to learn more, you must come back one day. The dead will wait for you. The living,' he flicked his eyes in the direction of the harbour, 'will not.'

They buried the skull and marked the place with a stone before moving on, Cenau walking beside Jeniche.

'Did you ever see pictures of them anywhere else?'

Jeniche shook her head. 'No. And I may be wrong about

192

that skull. People are born with deformities. It was very common after the Evanescence.'

'But you don't think so, do you.'

'No.'

The slightly unpleasant tingle deep in her stomach agreed.

They climbed. The harbour came back into view far below and far away, six ships still at anchor looking small and vulnerable. They looked for signs of the *Morgi* out to sea, but only then appreciated the significance of grey sails on a fighting ship.

The burial ground below them and the flat area beyond took on a different perspective from above. They could see their trail in the sand, knew it would not be there for long once the wind started again.

And slowly, the city grew. Each time they stopped to rest limbs or draw breath they looked back and saw more and more of the devastation laid out all around them. In some places there were hints of a pattern. Straight lines and curves, series of repeating shapes, mounds and dips, all worn away by the abrasive patience of time. The majority, though, was a chaotic mess as if a giant had kicked through an elaborate sand village, like the ones Jeniche used to watch the other Antari children make on the banks of the river by the Dhalar where she was raised.

Mid afternoon, after a steep climb, they settled in a sheltered spot to rest and eat. At this height there was a thin wind and it was good to be out of the chill. The harbour was tiny now and in the weak sunshine they could see the vast stretch of low rubble over which they had carried Cenau, the strange dark dome of glassy material sloping down into the waters and, beyond, the salt marsh stretching north into the wintry haze. And sitting on the far horizon, a distant but closing threat, were yellow, bruised clouds heavy with snow.

'It doesn't make sense.'

They stood at the base of the tower. They had been round it twice and there was no way in. Not at ground level or as high as they could clearly see in the growing dark. Cenau seemed to have lost all the strength he had gained from their rest on the ship. The others simply looked baffled.

'I could climb,' suggested Jeniche. 'It wouldn't be difficult.' She slapped the rough stonework. It was expertly constructed after an old pattern, circular, tapering slightly, though on a much larger scale than anything any of them had ever seen before, but the stone presented plenty of foot- and handholds.

'Maybe not,' said Cynfelyn, 'but it wouldn't be wise with the dark coming on and that snow approaching. And what if you got to the top and there was no way in?'

Jeniche shrugged. He was right, but they had to do something. It would be as bad stuck here in the dark and snow as anywhere else.

'We must have gone past it.'

Cynfelyn turned. 'What do you mean, Aros?'

'Well, you said the tower was built on top of this... hill. But it isn't. If you look at the gaps between the rocks. Here. See. The tower goes down. Like they built it and then piled stuff up around the base.'

Cenau groaned. 'We haven't got to go all the way back down?'

'I doubt it,' said Cynfelyn, 'but it's a good point. Somewhere on the slopes down there must be the way in.'

They stood with their backs to the curving wall and looked down the slope in the gloom.

'I don't know what it was for,' said Aros, 'but there were many people here. Living here. Dying here. Inside. Or trying to get inside. In a time of great upheaval.'

They waited as he tested the idea inside his head.

'So the entrance must be defensible.'

Even as he said it, the others began spreading out, looking down at the shape of the slope directly beneath them for something that could be easily defended. It didn't take long, even in the failing light, once they knew what they were looking for.

On the north-western slope with a view inland and of the harbour, they saw a change in the contours.

'We avoided that on the way up,' said Jeniche. 'It looked too steep.'

'Now we know why,' said Cynfelyn. He patted Aros on the arm and led the way down. Snowflakes began to drift by as if testing the air.

They made their way to where a distinct platform was visible, with a dark hole in the side of the hill behind them. The entrance wasn't big, perhaps large enough for two people on horseback to ride in side-by-side if they didn't mind scraping their knees and banging their heads, although none of them could imagine anyone getting a horse up there to begin with.

Jeniche got out her flint and they lit the first of the torches they had been given. It burned well, bright and with little smoke, but did little to illuminate the tunnel even though Maiv held it high. At first it seemed to drive the shadows before them and pile them up thickly. Once they were away from the entrance, however, they began to see more clearly.

Chapter Twenty-One

Although the pendant at her breast was warm and her stomach harboured a familiar queasiness, nothing lit up as they ventured into the passage. It was solidly built, but lacked the finesse of pre-Ev buildings. The material was rough, salvaged from the surrounding ruins and clearly constructed a long time after the downfall.

On either side of the gentle upward slope were open archways. Maiv thrust the torch into each chamber, but it was always the same – an empty rectangular room with walls of roughly dressed stone. They could have been made by anyone although it was clear they were part of the tower complex.

'Guard rooms?' suggested Awd.

'They had a lot of guards, then,' said Jeniche.

They had passed twenty of them already, arranged in pairs on either side of the passage. But they were each big enough to house a dozen people in bunks. Or store food. Or supplies. Or weapons. Or keep whatever it was that pre-Ev peoples thought needed keeping near the entrance.

All they found were small drifts of sand and long-abandoned cobwebs.

The rooms stopped just outside what was clearly the tower wall.

'How are you, Cenau?' asked Cynfelyn. They had been underground for a while, searching carefully, and he had not shown any signs of distress.

'All right so far. I think because I know the way out is open.'

It didn't stop the sudden shiver. The entrance to the tower in front of them was no bigger than an ordinary doorway and the darkness beyond was profound.

'And you, Jeniche?'

'I'm fine. There is pre-Ev stuff here, but it's not over-whelming.'

Cynfelyn turned back to Cenau.

'Do you want to carry on?'

'For now.'

'The moment you want to turn back, you say. There's no shame in it.'

Cenau nodded.

'We'd best light another torch,' said Maiv. 'This one will last a while yet, but two torches will be better.'

Awd took one from her pack and put the head to the one Maiv held. A second flame began to burn and Awd took it through the doorway into a narrower passage.

'It turns left just here,' she called, 'and slopes up a bit more steeply.'

One by one they followed up the curving passage, alone with the sound of their feet on the stone floor and their breathing in the flickering darkness. Cenau kept his hand on the wall and looked like he was trying to forget the

197

thousands of tons of rock all around him. Jeniche, just behind him, could hear his breathing shorten. She was just about to say something when they halted for a moment and then moved on again.

It soon became apparent what had stopped Awd for those few seconds. The passage levelled out and turned abruptly to the right, leading out into a vast open space. As Jeniche stepped through the opening, a panel on the far side flickered into dim and unsteady light. It was only partly visible and did little more than create a silhouette of whatever was obstructing it.

'What's that?' asked Awd. 'Someone must be there.'

'It's me,' said Jeniche. 'And this.'

She lifted the pendant out from under her clothes. It caught the light of the torches and seemed to glow.

'How does it do that?' Awd leaned closer as she spoke to look at the red-gold teardrop as it turned in the torchlight.

'I don't know. I... acquired it in Makamba. Cynfelyn has tried it but it wouldn't work for him.'

'So you've been in pre-Ev ruins before.'

She saw Cynfelyn from the corner of her eye as he tried to distract Awd.

'It's all right,' she said, hiding the pendant away. 'It's a story for a comfortable hearth and I will tell it in honour of the friend I lost. For now we need to find this spear. Do we know what it looks like? Apart from being long, thin, and pointed.'

'You'll know it when you see it,' said Cynfelyn. 'Of that I am sure.'

They spread out and moved across the floor, a torch at each end of the line held high in an attempt to illuminate the space around them. Whilst the stone floor at their feet became visible, covered in a thick layer of dust, the light from the flames reached little further. Yet they all felt the pressure of the immense space as they moved like insects crossing the floor of a great hall.

Vast as the tower had seemed from the outside, it was a large object set in a boundless landscape. And even standing right beside it, you could turn your back on it and it disappeared. Within, there was no escaping the scale of the building, the stillness of the cool air that filled the interior. They couldn't see, but it felt and sounded as if the entire tower was hollow.

Perhaps, thought Jeniche, it is just as well we cannot see. The shaft beneath the stone circle had been intimidating enough. It would have been dwarfed inside this structure.

At first there was nothing but unbroken dust. Heavy stuff. Dried silt that had blown in through cracks and tunnels and settled over the centuries. They left their mark in time's deposit and moved on.

Then came small objects – bits of broken masonry and shattered lumps of…

'Is this metal?'

They gathered round Aros who held up a short, thin length of black material he had picked off the floor. Duald produced a dagger and tapped it lightly with the hilt.

'It has the sound and feel of it.'

Awd took it from Aros's hand and felt the weight of it.

'It could be, but it's like none I've ever seen.' She held the broken end to the light. 'It's black all the way through.'

As they moved on, the scatter of debris became denser and the fragments larger until they were confronted by a tangled mass of masonry and the black metal they had discovered earlier. Much of it was a single, badly misshapen, lattice-work bowl about the size of a tribal roundhouse.

'What could have done that?' asked Cenau.

'It looks like it's fallen. That's why all the smaller bits are widely scattered.'

They all looked up, nervous, ready to run.

'It happened a long time ago, judging by the dust,' said Cynfelyn. 'And nothing seems to have come down since.'

It didn't stop any of them peering up into the dark.

'We won't find it like that. We'll search the wreckage of this… whatever it is first. Make use of that light on the other side. I can't think where else it would be.'

The first of the torches began to sputter so they lit another, leaving the dying one on the floor as a marker. As they had with the exterior of the tower, they circled the pile of rubble first, round to where the light panel flickered intermittently. It hung at an odd angle as if it had been dislodged by the falling structure.

Jeniche rubbed a hand across the surface, wiping away a thick layer of dust. The light grew brighter and they could see more clearly; not just the debris in the middle, but all the way to distant encircling walls. Ribs of stonework ran up into the darkness at regular intervals, but they were the only features in an otherwise empty space.

Aros climbed onto the wreckage with careful steps. Dust dislodged, but did little more than sift downwards. He moved all over the pile, making his way to the top by a spiral path. And came back down empty-handed.

'Nothing,' he said.

Cynfelyn swore and sat down on a length of the black metal, lowering his head into his hands. He rubbed his head for a moment and then sat upright.

200

'I was sure this was the place. So sure.'

'We'd better head back to the ships,' said Jeniche.

'A circuit of the interior perimeter, at least, especially now we have a bit more light.'

'What if there's more than one door? How will we know which is the right one?'

'Our footprints will be clear to see.'

The thought struck them all at more or less the same time.

'What are the chances?' asked Jeniche.

'There weren't any in the passage up to this chamber,' said Awd who had led the way.

'But that would get the wind. In here the dust would hardly be disturbed.'

They retraced their steps with Cynfelyn a few paces in front. As they approached the doorway by which they had entered, he slowed and the others hung back. Lowering the torch so that longer shadows would be cast across the ground, he examined the dust to either side.

At first it was just a mass of their own prints as they had stood there trying to sense how large the space was. He worked widdershins of the entrance to begin with, but found nothing. Moving to the sunward side, he was rewarded with faint dimples.

'Come up behind me and see what you think,' he called.

There is a particular sound a torch makes when it is moved quickly through the air, such as when a person at the back of a line turns because they are convinced they have heard something behind them.

'What is it, Ruad?'

He said nothing for a moment, the torch held high and

moving slowly back and forth. Shadows moved, but only those that were meant to.

'I thought I heard something.'

'Perhaps we dislodged something over in the centre and it's just slipped.'

'Perhaps. It sounded closer, but it's difficult to tell.'

After a last look, they carried on round the perimeter, close to the wall, following what they hoped were the footsteps of their predecessors.

'There are no other prints out there,' said Aros. 'If there was something else in here, we'd have seen it by now.'

'Unless it followed us in,' said Cenau, peering into the dim recesses behind them.

'There,' said Cynfelyn.

The air rang with the sound of swords being drawn.

'No. No. Sorry. Another entrance. Where the footprints lead.'

And in the silence that followed as hard stares were directed toward Cynfelyn, they all heard the light-footed scuttling of something on the move.

'Through the doorway,' said Awd quietly.

She ushered everyone through and stood with torch in one hand and sword in the other.

'We can defend this while you carry on with the search.'

'We shouldn't split up,' said Cynfelyn.

'There's little choice. Far better to give you the space to carry out your search by blocking this route here.'

'What if there are other ways up?' asked Cenau.

Cynfelyn sighed. 'It's a risk we'll have to take. Aros. Jeniche. Cenau. Would you care to join me?'

Aros and Jeniche nodded. Cenau looked beyond Cynfelyn at the narrow passage between the walls curving up into the dark. He took a deep breath and then let it out slowly.

'Oh well, a whole new set of things to be afraid of. At least it's not underground.' He was smiling as he spoke, but his hands trembled.

They counted torches and shared them out. Cynfelyn lit one and made his way up the slope with Cenau close behind, Aros next, and Jeniche to the rear. The curve was gentle but it was not long before they left behind the light of the others at their guard post.

The wall of the tower, in which they walked, was thick. Every so often, the passage levelled out and they came across small, dark, empty rooms before heading upward again. They searched each one as they passed. Jeniche also noticed small openings at regular intervals, just about big enough to insert a hand. She wondered if they had perhaps been used to attach light panels. Whenever she put a hand near one, she felt that familiar clenching of the stomach, almost as if the stone was trying to connect with her, as if her body was rejecting the touch.

It was tiring work and very soon became a waking nightmare of endless passages and no way out as the darkness closed behind them. They rested a while by one set of rooms, resuming the long upward haul knowing that whatever happened they would have to make the journey again in the opposite direction.

Their second torch was burning when they came to a different stretch. The wall to their right took on a different quality and it was some moments before they realized there was no wall there at all. There was no telling how high they were and none of them cared to venture to the edge to peer down, Cynfelyn least of all, who felt faint at the prospect.

'Why leave it open like that?' asked Aros.

'It probably wasn't, originally,' said Jeniche. 'There may have been a barrier, or a balcony. Perhaps access to that structure on the floor.'

'And perhaps we could not talk about it,' said Cynfelyn with some urgency.

Silence returned, broken once again by the sound of their boots on the passage floor and their breathing as they struggled upwards. Not long afterwards, Cynfelyn came to an abrupt stop. Cenau walked straight into him and Aros nearly did the same.

'Jeniche?'

She took off her pack and swords and squeezed past the other two to stand beside Cynfelyn as he held the torch aloft. The flames lit a chamber, fluttering in a breeze of cold, fresh air.

'We must be near the top.'

'I hope so,' she replied.

'It looks like a pre-Ev structure.'

'I can't see any panels… Shade your eyes, everyone, just in case.'

Stepping through the doorway, she wished she'd been quicker doing the same. The intensity of the light was painful, flooding the chamber with a brightness that was almost solid. She began to feel feverish and dreamy, sliding down the nearby wall until she was sitting on the floor.

'Is it… Is it here?' She wasn't sure if the words made sense. After what seemed an age she felt a hand grab the collar of her coat and pull her along the ground.

As suddenly as they had blasted out, the lights dimmed. From the passageway, she could see the chamber in the afterglow, felt herself emerging from the fever. Became aware of the narrow gallery round the edge of the chamber; of the four great arches that sloped up like bridges with steps along their tops; of the platform atop the keystone where they met at the centre; of the long, long drop into darkness where the floor of the tower lay covered with parts of shattered machinery.

Chapter Twenty-Two

'Did you see the spear, Aros? Did you see Gwyan?' she heard Cynfelyn ask.

'Up in the centre. It seemed to be floating above that platform. Should I fetch it?'

Cynfelyn said nothing. He had stepped well back from the dizzying prospect. The very thought of venturing out along one of the narrow arches to the small keystone hanging over empty space dried the flow of words in his mouth. There was a long silence. Aros stood in the doorway peering into the darkening chamber. The cool air blowing in through the large openings that had been revealed was worth savouring.

'It's meant to be me. Isn't it? Like under the stone circle.'

Jeniche looked up from where she was sitting, the awful lethargy fading. She could see Cynfelyn's look of relief, Aros's puzzlement.

'You'll need light again,' she said as she struggled to her feet. Cenau put a hand under her arm to help her.

'But why?' asked Aros.

'Get the spear,' said Cynfelyn, forcing the words out. 'We can talk about it when we are out of this nightmare.'

'Watch the steps along the top of that arch,' said Cenau. 'They're not even.'

'Hold on to her coat, Cenau, and pull her back out of the chamber as soon as it lights up. And this time, desert girl, keep your eyes closed.'

Aros stepped to the threshold. Jeniche lit another torch and handed it to him.

'And don't rush it,' added Cynfelyn. 'I want you back in one piece. If that means losing the spear, so be it.'

Aros took a deep breath and looked at Jeniche. She smiled. He nodded.

The light blasted out as before. She could feel it against her flesh, could see it through her eyelids, and felt the world dissolving about her as something tugged at her clothing. Lacking the will to resist, she allowed herself to be pulled and felt the light fading.

Turning, she leaned unsteadily against the wall and looked back into the chamber. Aros was already half way up the arch directly opposite the door, moving steadily, keeping his eyes on the steps with his torch held high directly in front of him. As the light panels began to fade, the halo of flame light around him grew stronger.

The higher he went up the arch, the narrower it became and the darker it grew. When he reached the central platform, perched over many hundreds of feet, the torch alone lit his way. At a signal from Aros, Jeniche stepped over the threshold again, to be pulled back once more by Cenau as the lights blazed out.

'The light has changed,' said Cenau quietly.

Cynfelyn still could not bring himself to look. Jeniche

207

blinked, trying to focus. It took long moments for her to realize that there was nothing wrong with her eyes. Aros stood on the small platform trying to pull the spear away from whatever force held it whilst all around him the air filled with dust.

'Aros!'

He turned at her call, hand still on the spear.

'Get off there now!'

Cynfelyn had turned at the urgency of her voice, braving the view. 'Leave the spear!'

Aros kept tugging.

'Aros!'

The lights were fading.

'Not like a warrior,' said Cynfelyn, almost to himself.

'Aros!' called Jeniche. 'Not like a warrior. Like a thief. Don't wrench at it. Pull gently. And if that doesn't work get straight back here.'

She put her hands over her ears, but it didn't block the painful, high-pitched whine that had started.

Turning to Cenau she said: 'Get Cynfelyn back down the passageway. And keep to the outer wall. This one,' she added, patting the wall that Cynfelyn was leaning against. 'Go. Now. Keep just in sight but be ready to run.'

She turned back to the chamber to see Aros raise the spear in triumph and then freeze. The look on his face told her everything. It had once been on hers in the desert when she felt the ground give beneath her feet.

'Run!'

For a long, sickening moment their eyes met across the space between them, a look of terror in his eyes. She could see them wide in his face by the dancing light of his torch. The light panels had faded almost to darkness, there was still dust in the air, and the whining was louder.

'Run!' And he ran, spear in one hand, torch in the other.

The whining stopped with an abrupt crack like thunder echoing down the length of the tower's interior and back again as a piece of stonework, after centuries of stress, shattered beneath Aros's step.

In an attempt to run faster, he missed his footing and fell headlong down the steps. He lost his grip on the torch and it went over the edge, turning over and over as it fell into the dark.

'Close your eyes!' screamed Jeniche.

She moved forward, felt the lights blaze out and, keeping her head down, ran up the steps to Aros. His nerve had gone. She could see it in his eyes, even as she fought the feverish lethargy that was sapping her. Going down onto her hands and knees in front of him, she grabbed one end of the spear and said, as calmly as she could, 'Crawl. Follow the spear.'

Inch by inch, watching Aros, watching the edges of the arch, fighting the sickness, she edged her way back down. With every step, she coaxed Aros to follow, seeing what he could not see.

Where the four arches met, the platform where the spear had been suspended was tilting as the arch they were crawling along began to collapse.

'Keep coming,' she said. 'Nearly there,' hoping it was true.

And then there was no option as the top of the arch began to fall into the depths. Letting go of the spear, she pulled her feet up under her in a crouch, grabbed the front of Aros's tunic and caught a glimpse of his startled expression as she rolled onto her back and pushed her feet into his stomach. He went flying over her and she let her momentum roll her backwards as well, uncertain if either of them were heading in the right direction, knowing it was their only chance.

The air filled with noise and more dust and in the chaos of movement she felt someone grab her arm and wrench her painfully off to one side. The floor beneath them danced and was then still. In the darkness, someone grabbed her foot and she was dragged some more along stone slabs, banging her head against a wall. Moments later came the thunderous crashing of masonry and everything around her trembled.

A tapping of stone, a flicker of light, and in the thick dust, a torch sputtered. Jeniche sat up and looked around. Cenau was helping Aros to his feet. Once there, he put his hands in the small of his back and winced, his face grazed and his lower lip bleeding.

'My doing?' she asked and began to cough as dust tickled her throat.

Aros nodded and smiled, bending to pick up the spear before dabbing at his lip with the back of his free hand.

Finding her pack amongst the others, she looked inside and found her keffiyeh, wrapping it round her mouth and nose. Then, with her swords and pack on her back, she took the torch offered by Cynfelyn and led the way back down. At first, the dust began to thin, but before long it began to thicken again.

'Keep to the outer wall,' called Jeniche.

They slowed to a crawl, passing the section that opened onto the interior of the tower. The floor was covered with grit, but seemed otherwise unscathed. And before long they were back into clearer air and could move with greater speed.

The journey down was much quicker without the need to explore each chamber they passed. It took on something of the trance-like quality of the upward journey, but they had the comforts of the ship to look forward to, provided they could get out at the bottom and provided the ships were still there.

Four figures loomed out of the growing dust, silhouetted by their sputtering torch.

'Is everyone all right?' asked Cynfelyn, peering into each face.

'A little warning would have been welcome,' said Maiv.

'We did shine a light.'

Duald laughed. 'Maiv nearly dropped her sword.'

Maiv laughed as well.

'Did you get the spear?' Ruad wanted to know.

Aros held Gwyan forward in the dim light.

'And what about you? Did you see any more of whatever was following us?'

'If there was anything,' said Awd, 'it's not likely to have survived what you sent down to us.'

She led the way out onto the floor of the tower. Shattered rubble lay everywhere, dust settling onto the destruction. The failing light panel didn't come on as Jeniche went through the entrance. It had doubtless been crushed by a block of masonry. There were deep scores on the floor slabs, and as Awd held her torch up, they could see where shrapnel had blasted the walls.

Picking their way over chunks of masonry, they followed the tower wall round to the next door. Before long they emerged into the bleak, dawn world looking forward to warmth, comfort and food. Their elation and hopes didn't survive the chill wind.

211

Bruised, battered, and covered with dust, they were all glad to be out of the stale confines of the tower. It had been vast, but even on the main floor there had been a sense of claustrophobia. Now there was a sense bordering on despair.

At first they could see no ships at all and thought they had been completely stranded. The captain had warned them, but it had not sunk in as a real possibility. It was Aros who saw the shore boat still in the harbour and even as he pointed it out, he saw three of the ships off shore just beyond the harbour mouth. And as the sun rose on a landscape transformed by an overnight fall of snow, they saw what may have been other ships on the far northern horizon.

Needing no further prompting, they scrambled down and away from the tower, choosing their footholds carefully in the snow. Everything looked different. The slope was there before them and the two relatively flat areas, one below the other, but all the other markers had disappeared. It was cold as well. The wind was not fierce, but it was now out of the north-east and smelled of the snow it had brought with it.

At the base of the long slope, on the edge of the flat area where they had found the skeletons, they dropped into a deep, soft drift. Struggling out was exhausting and Cenau's face was white and pinched by the time they had battled through to where the snow lay just a few inches deep.

Exhaustion lay just below the surface in all of them, but Cenau had little between his surface and his core. Jeniche kept close to one side of him and Aros, spear still held tightly in his hand, kept close to the other. Ruad and Duald had surged ahead in hope of getting to the shore boat before it gave up on them.

At the next slope, they more or less tumbled down into

the thick snow at the base. Aros dug Cenau out and brushed the snow from his coat before urging him on. Once they were down off the flat and stumbling across the last stretch toward the harbour, Cenau seemed to find energy. Perhaps it was the sight of Ruad and Duald waving them on.

Once they were on the top of the harbour wall they could see the shore boat was still down in the chill water, waiting for them – a dozen sailors sitting in the cold using their oars to break the ice that kept forming around them.

It was pulled in against a stair built into the wall as they climbed down the icy steps. One by one they boarded and sat. As Cynfelyn climbed aboard and settled on a bench in the centre, oars were dipping to the water and searching for purchase.

The sailors settled into a rhythm called out by their steersman and within moments, the boat was shooting along. As they reached the mouth of the harbour they had their first taste of the swell. Beyond the walls it was worse, but with three ships in sight, their sails unfurling as they watched, no one much cared.

PART THREE

Cauldron

Chapter Twenty-Three

The door banged open and Jeniche forced her head up to see who it was.

'This looks familiar,' said Cynfelyn. 'I'd ask you how you're feeling, but that would just be cruel.'

Snow blew into the cabin.

'Close the door,' she croaked. 'Cold.'

He stepped over the high threshold and closed the door behind him, settling with his back in a corner and his feet well planted.

'If it's any comfort, the others are feeling it a bit as well.'

'No. It isn't. And stop sounding so cheerful. Don't like boats. Why so many?'

Cynfelyn's smile broadened and Jeniche scowled in return as she sat up. She didn't worry about being sick. She was long past that, long past the dry retching.

'There's a clue in the name. Ynysvron. Many islands.'

'Now you tell me.'

'Ha. You speak Ketic better than some natives.'

He passed her a water bottle and she took cautious sips, pushing the stopper back in when she'd finished.

'I don't suppose there's any sign of land?'

'No.'

She took a moment to absorb the news.

'What about the Gwerin?'

'It's been three days since we last saw them.'

'Three days?'

'You've been asleep for most of it.'

'Just how far is this island of yours?'

Cynfelyn shrugged. 'I don't know. The only real clue I had was a bearing and an old tale.'

'Not much to go on. How long will we follow this trace?'

'No idea. There's no wind just now. Which is just as well, I suppose.'

'Do I want to know?'

'The snow is so heavy you can barely see a ship's length in any direction.'

Jeniche let her head droop. Seven nightmare days at sea and little more than a few sips of broth. She managed a faint laugh.

'What's funny?'

She held up a trembling, bony hand. 'I'd been thinking of leaving the Great College because I was worried I was getting soft.'

'And here you are, lazing around on a sea cruise.'

She kicked out at him from the bunk where she lay, but missed.

'Three days?'

'Like a baby.'

'I must stink.'

'Well, we didn't like to say. But it's an extreme way of getting a cabin to yourself.'

This time, the kick landed, although there was little strength in it.

She lay back and closed her eyes, grateful that the seasickness was over its worst. When she woke again, Cynfelyn was still there, sitting on the floor in the corner of the small cabin, hands folded in his lap, head bowed, snoring gently. She could not understand why, but it was a deeply comforting sight. And she was glad he was resting. He had done very little of that since they had met up again; very little for years before, by all accounts.

The door banged open and they both woke. Aros stepped over the high threshold with a basket. Snowflakes came into the small room with him, dropping to the board flooring and dissolving into small dark stains.

Aros looked pale, but he smiled and put the basket on the floor beside the bunk.

'Food,' he said, 'if you feel up to it. Don't take too long though, or Cynfelyn will eat your share.'

Jeniche was sitting up as he went back out through the door and she could see it was night, snowflakes appearing out of the darkness.

'Are we moving?'

'I shouldn't think so now,' said Cynfelyn. 'Not if it's dark. They did have the shore boats out towing, but that's backbreaking work.'

He leaned forward and lifted the cloth from the top of the basket. Apples. A round of cheese. Bread. A flask of wine. Jeniche pulled a face.

'You must have something,' said Cynfelyn. 'That's a very mild cheese. An apple, even. And we can water the wine.'

She chose an apple and pulled her knife from its sheath.

'How is Aros coping with it all?' she asked, popping a slice of the fruit into her mouth. She chewed slowly. Uncertain.

'Well, if you'll excuse the phrase, he was all at sea to begin with. Now it's just worrying him. He knows something is up, but he hasn't quite worked it out yet.'

'Will he cope?'

'Not alone.'

'Cenau?'

'I worry about him more. He has little confidence in himself, despite what he has survived. Puts it down to luck. But he's bright. Not just learned, but analytical, forward thinking. He worked it all out. He even asked if my exile had been staged.'

'What did you say?'

'I changed the subject.'

'And that worked?'

Cynfelyn shrugged, breaking off a chunk of bread to go with the cheese he had sliced from the round.

They ate slowly and in silence. It was clear from Cynfelyn's face that his thoughts were far away. Jeniche concentrated entirely on how her stomach was receiving something solid.

It was a cheer from the others that finally brought her out onto the deck of the *Morfran*. The sun shone and a fair wind was in their sails, spray flicking up occasionally as they raced along. To port and starboard the *Morgi* and the *Morlwch* kept pace.

'What's all the excitement?' she asked.

'Land,' said Cenau. 'Off that way.' He pointed off the starboard bow.

He looked like she felt, but the prospect of solid ground did no harm; and bracing winter air was fast clearing the stuffiness from her head and putting colour in his cheeks.

She looked round at the others.

'And?'

'The lookout on the *Morlwch* thinks he's seen sails directly astern.'

'Not much we can do,' said Cynfelyn, standing by the railing and looking forward, 'except have everything ready when we make landfall so we can gain as much ground as possible.'

They sat together on deck in a sheltered spot out of the way of the crew, cleaning and sharpening blades, repairing clothes and boots, talking quietly. Some of the strain went from Aros's face and he and Cenau managed to have a squabble that left them both smiling.

Cynfelyn went into the cabin where Jeniche had been sleeping and returned with the spear. He passed it to Jeniche who had not yet seen it properly. She did not like weapons. There was nothing but grief associated with them. But she knew great skill when she saw it.

'Gwyan,' said Cenau.

Aros looked up from sharpening his sword. He frowned again, watching intently as Jeniche examined the ancient weapon.

The spearhead was a simple leaf blade of highly polished metal. It gleamed in the winter sunshine as if filled with a cold light of its own. The ash shaft was long, the same height as Awd who was a head taller than any of the others. Jeniche turned it carefully and could find no flaw or kink in the grain. Simple, made with the best materials by the best smith and turner in the land; clean, bright, and true as the day it was made many centuries before. A truly potent symbol.

She laid it on the deck in their midst and Cynfelyn produced the crown from his coat, setting it down beside the spear.

'Carreg,' said Cenau.

They were transfixed. These objects were the stuff of legend, tokens of power, emblems of sovereignty. They lay at the heart of Ynysvron as a place and as an idea. Aros leaned forward a fraction. His hands were trembling and his head was shaking.

'Potent as they are,' said Cynfelyn quietly, well aware of the effect the objects were having on Aros, 'they are just symbols. The power lies in the person on whom they are bestowed and sovereignty lies in the acceptance of that person by the land and its people. Only when those work together will the symbols have true meaning and bring Ynysvron together.'

Aros began to shuffle backwards. Before he could get very far, Cenau stood and drew his sword. With clumsy movements, because he was still not used to handling it, he reversed it and offered the hilt to Aros.

It took a moment for the gesture to sink in. Aros climbed to his feet, staring at Cenau. Jeniche had seen that expression on his face before, when the platform high in the tower had moved beneath his feet. He shook his head slowly as it all began to fall into place. 'Me?'

Maiv and Awd were the next to stand, followed by Ruad and Duald.

Tears flowed down Aros's cheek. For the first time in his life, he was truly scared. 'I can't do this thing,' he said.

'Not on your own, lad. No Guardian can. But you have help already.'

222

Jeniche picked up her swords from the deck and held the hilts toward Aros.

'And you're getting more all the time.' Cynfelyn drew his own sword, a workaday weapon. Jeniche wondered where Cleddyf, which he had found in Makamba, was now hidden. 'Mine is with you as well,' he said.

'And your counsel?'

'There are wiser heads than mine, lad. Wiser heads than mine.' He looked tired again, but smiled. Jeniche wondered if anyone else saw the sadness in his eyes.

Long after the others had finished preparing and returned to their quarters to rest, Jeniche stood on the prow of the ship and for the first time enjoyed the experience. The wind was bitter on her face, but the calm seas and sunshine, the steady wind, the soothing creaks of the ship, and the liquid song of the sea against the sleek hull filled her with a sense of calm.

She should have known.

Ahead, on the horizon, land began to take on a solid form out of the mists of winter. Grey for naked rock, a deep sage green for whatever managed to grow there, tinges of white where snow had fallen. Bright specks crossed the clouds as seabirds wheeled on the wind, touching the sky with their wings.

Loud shouting and the pounding of feet broke her reverie. The captain of the *Morfran* and Cynfelyn joined her.

'Trouble,' said Cynfelyn.

'Of course,' said Jeniche.

'You're sure these islands are Inissgar?' asked the captain and then put his hands up. He'd asked several times already and knew the answer.

223

'Haul in the mains'l!' he called with a voice that must have reached the other ships.

'What's happening?' asked Jeniche.

'The Gwerin ships are closing,' said the captain, 'and there is a standing wave ahead. I'd rather meet those ships behind us, but we took the charter.'

'It's still your choice, Captain,' said Cynfelyn. 'Your ship. Your decision.'

He looked ahead again, completely still.

After a while he drew a deep breath. 'Get your people on deck, ready to disembark. Gather them below the fo'c'sle and tell them to find something solid to hold onto.'

'It's going to get rough, isn't it?' said Jeniche.

The captain smiled and then strode off, bellowing orders.

Despite losing sail, the *Morfran* didn't seem to lose speed. On either side the other ships were swarming with crew, dropping behind. Once the *Morfran* was clear ahead the other two began to turn to port, the *Morgi* passing close behind the *Morfran*'s stern.

Jeniche watched with dismay. They still had no idea how the other four ships had fared any more than they knew what had happened to the people of Dunvran. And here these two were, turning to face an enemy so that she and the others could carry on in safety.

'May the gods keep you dry,' she said and went down the steps toward her cabin.

When she came out, swords strapped to her back, everyone else had gathered and found ropes to hold onto. She hitched her pack securely to a cleat and then climbed back up to the prow.

The sea was already rougher and she staggered a little as she walked, grateful that her stomach had finally become used to the motion. What she saw didn't give her much else to be thankful for.

When the captain had mentioned a standing wave it had been a long way away and she had misjudged the distance. Now they were closer, the captain's preference to face other fighting ships became clear.

The *Morfran* had entered a narrowing channel between the two main islands of Inissgar and was being swept along by a tidal race. Waves were slapping the prow and spray splashed onto the deck and speckled her face. That, however, was nothing in comparison to what loomed directly ahead.

Much closer now, dark and sleek, with no chance to mistake the distance and size, she could see the standing wave in all its terrifying detail. The water was the colour of flint, a steep hill that poured fiercely up to a crest that was on a level with the fo'c'sle deck.

She looked back to the helm and saw several of the crew wrestling with the steering gear, turned forward to see they had edged to port where there was flat water. The sound of the sea was no longer a song beneath the hull. It had become the endless roar of the storm in the night when roofs shook and trees fell. Realizing it was too late to get safely down to the others, she grabbed the forecastle railing and hung on for her life.

Someone shouted a warning and the ship reared. The deck pushed up and made her knees buckle before it canted to the left as the vessel rode the edge of the wave. For a brief moment she felt weightless whilst the ship dropped away from beneath her and then her knees buckled again as she dropped down and the deck bounced upwards.

Losing her footing, she fell against the rail and clung on as spray raked the deck with a loud smack. Eyes stinging

225

with salt water, she stood up and looked round to try to see how the ship had fared. The *Morfran* was now moving sideways and she could see the back of the wave off to starboard as it plunged down and churned wildly in a wide vortex. If they had gone over the centre and the ship had survived that, it would surely have been pulled straight under and smashed apart.

Turning a slow circle, they were now going backwards. The captain was shouting orders and crew were swarming up the masts. The helmsman stood helpless, unable to combat the great swirling currents. Directly below Jeniche, the others stood uncertain and bruised.

The sails were set and filled out, the helmsman leaned against the steering bar and they finally began to pull away from the maelstrom, finding calmer water away from the racing tide.

Chapter Twenty-Four

Long, steep, and narrow, the carved stairway ran back and forth across the face of the sheer, granite cliff. Snow had packed into the corners of some of the steps and with successive thaws and freezings had set hard and smooth. Ruad led and hacked at the ice with a sawn-off boathook. Cynfelyn made a close study of the rock face. Everyone else took in the view, including two crew members who brought up the rear and who would stop at the top to keep a lookout over the approach.

Directly below, the *Morfran* rode at anchor in a small, rocky bay, its shallow draft allowing it close in to the shore. Although the ship had come through with its hull and masts intact, everything else had been thrown around as they had ridden the edge of the huge wave. The crew could be seen moving about on deck, checking and tidying as they went.

A flat, sloping shelf of rock made a natural landing stage for small boats in the bay. It was from there the steps rose, following faults in the cliff face. Centuries of use had worn paths across the shelf and each step they climbed sagged in the centre.

Beyond the bay to the east were the narrow tidal race and the long, inhospitable spine of rock of the other main island. The waters were calm now with no sign of the maelstrom or the standing wave, but the captain thought there must be a substantial peak of rock just beneath the surface to catch unwary vessels even at high tide. They saw none as they climbed.

'When I get to the Otherworld,' Jeniche heard Cynfelyn mutter, 'which I trust will not be for some time yet, I am going to find the Derw who hid the Hallows and words will be had. They will not be soft words.'

She smiled. Her own misery had passed for now, although she was well aware that when they had finished here they must return to Ynysvron by sea. And despite the calm weather that blessed their climb, this was the season of storms.

When they had reached the top and Cynfelyn had walked far enough away from the edge to feel safe, Cenau asked: 'Where to?'

From the sea, they had seemed like small islands. It had been a surprise to find someone had invested years of work travelling back and forth and cutting the stairway.

'This is where it got a bit vague. All I know is the ship came to this island.'

'How can you be certain it was this one?'

'Because of that down there.'

'What down there?'

'The maelstrom.'

'You knew that was there?!' said Jeniche. 'A warning would have been useful.'

'I didn't know it was that large. Everyone I spoke to about it said it was a myth or exaggerated.'

'But why come all the way out here?' asked Aros. 'And how does the maelstrom have anything to do with the...' His voice tailed off and he nodded.

'Exactly,' said Cynfelyn. 'A circlet of stone beneath a ring of stones. A spear at the top of the tallest, straightest thing they could find. And the Crochan by a natural cauldron.'

'A cauldron? We have to find a cauldron and lug it all the way down those cliffs?' asked Jeniche.

'Don't remind me,' said Cynfelyn, his face grim.

'And Cleddyf?' asked Aros.

'Let's worry about the Crochan first,' Cynfelyn replied, pretending not to see Jeniche's raised eyebrow.

'So,' said Cenau. 'Where to?'

They all looked around. There wasn't much to see. The clifftop was bleak and stony, low scrub clinging to what shelter it could find in the lee of larger rocks.

'Well, there must be something,' said Jeniche. 'You don't cut stone steps up a cliff face on a remote island for the fun of it.'

'It won't take long to look round,' said Awd.

'Just watch out for cliff edges,' said Cynfelyn with a shudder.

To keep him happy they headed inland. Before long the ground began to slope down toward a small valley where dwarf trees grew, sculpted by the prevailing wind so they all leaned to the east. Withered grass covered the slopes. Pockets of snow lingered where it had drifted deepest after the last storm. A line of stones might just have been the remains of a building. They went to see.

There were several buildings, they discovered, built of the

loose stones that must once have littered the valley. Two of them were outlines in the rough grass. A third had one wall still standing. The fourth, initially hidden behind trees, had all its walls standing to roof height. Whatever had been used for roofing had long since been torn down and burned on the hearth at one end. Next to where they found the skeletons, one with a shattered leg.

The new cairn went beside the old ones at the rear of the building, close under the yew tree that grew out of a stony bank. And when they had finished gathering stones, they gathered what little there was in the way of wood and built a fire to keep themselves warm whilst they sat and ate.

Beneath the layers of dried bracken that were crumbling to dust on the floor of the building they found two leather satchels. Something had eaten the corner of one and pulled some of the clothing from out of it. The other had been parcelled up with care in a large piece of oiled canvas. It was dry now and cracked, but seemed intact.

Cynfelyn unwrapped it, putting the old canvas to one side. The leather lacings were stiff and in the end, he cut them with a knife. Inside was another package wrapped in a finer cloth of felted wool. The lanolin had long since dried, but it had done its job and kept the damp from the book within.

They crowded as close as they could without blocking his light whilst Cynfelyn opened the cover. The pages were stiff as he turned them, but they did not tear or crumble, and the writing, though faded, was still clear. A strong hand equally skilled at sketching as at writing.

'It seems to be research. Into pre-Ev sites in Ynysvron.'

Jeniche looked closely. 'That's from Banadd Corrach's *Daearyddiaeth*. The chapter on Curiosities.'

She opened her pack and after rooting round inside, pulled out her own book. Leafing through, she found the same section that she had copied last year, not long after she had arrived. Her handwriting was smaller, so her notes took up less space, but after a quick comparison, it seemed the first half of the book they had found was identical to Jeniche's section on Ynysvron.

Cynfelyn turned the pages with care until he came to a different section.

'It's a journal,' he said. 'Kept by the Derw Eithrig. She was a noted historian and one of the group tasked with placing the Hallows in safe places.'

'No disrespect to the dead, but they got that wrong,' said Aros quietly.

'It used to be a belief that anything pre-Ev had somehow become incorruptible. But time weakens all things.'

'So presumably that was her we just buried. Who were the others?' asked Jeniche. 'Does it say what happened?'

'There were a dozen altogether. Four Derw. Four Warriors. Four Artisans. And they had a small ship.'

'All Ynyswr?'

'Of course. Why do you ask?'

She was thinking of the tower room in the Library of the Great College back on Pengaver. 'Just curious.'

'Their names are here in the front.'

'You knew them already?'

'Yes.'

He turned the book over and began working through the blank pages from the back until he came to the final entries.

'It *was* Eithrig who broke her leg. A bad fall. She couldn't

231

get down the cliff. Two of them elected to stay with her while the others went for help.'

'Where from?'

'It doesn't say.'

'Couldn't the crew of the ship have helped?'

Cynfelyn shook his head. 'I just don't know. Unless a storm was blowing up and they put to sea to ride it out. I don't know enough about sailing even to make a guess.'

They sat quietly, each making their own peace with whatever deities they held dear, knowing it could happen to any of them, giving thought to the days that Eithrig and her companions spent here. Last days. In pain. Hungry. Not knowing why they had been abandoned or what had happened to the others.

'Does it say anything in there about where the Crochan is?' asked Cenau eventually. 'There's nothing in this building resembling a cauldron, so they must have hidden it. Not underground somewhere, I hope.'

More pages were turned. The fire began to die and the last of the brushwood was thrown on, crackling faintly as the flames took. It was still light, but the sky was filling with cloud and the air had become colder.

'There's a gate, she has written here,' said Cynfelyn. 'A Shadow Gate. The Gate of Riddles. The Sieve. At the head of the valley. This valley, I suppose. I doubt there's room for another one on the island.'

He closed the book and handed it to Cenau.

'Shouldn't Jeniche have it? She's the expert,' Cenau said.

More crackling. Jeniche looked at the fire with a frown.

'Time you became one as well. For some reason, they chose pre-Ev sites to hide the Hallows. The reasons may be in here. They were clearly considered important to the sovereignty of the Guardian. And if the reasons aren't in there, then you know what you will be doing once you get back.'

Cenau took the book, felt the weight of it before stowing it in his pack. 'At least now we'll be able to find Cleddyf.'

'Yes,' said Cynfelyn, 'there won't be any trouble there.'

'But there is here,' said Jeniche. 'Listen.'

The air was populated with noise. Their own breathing, the snap of wood burning in the hearth, the sough of the wind and, in the distance, another crackle.

Cynfelyn sprang up. 'Occassans.'

'How can you tell?' asked Maiv. 'I heard nothing.'

'You heard it,' said Jeniche, 'but you don't know the sound. The Occassans have weapons they call moskets. I don't know how they work, but they cast a ball of lead faster and further than a slingshot. And they are more accurate. That crackling noise in the distance?'

Maiv nodded.

'That was moskets.'

'The *Morfran*!'

They were all on their feet by now.

'Get to this gate,' said Awd. 'Find the Crochan. Keep them safe, Aros.'

With a nod to Maiv, Ruad, and Duald, she led the way to the door of the building.

'Be careful. Those moskets have a long range.'

'We go the same way out of the door,' said Aros, 'and straight to the trees. We can work our way up the valley from there.'

The wind bit at them the moment they left the shelter of the stone walls. Following Aros, they scrambled up a stony bank beneath the stiff, leafless branches and gathered in the dark-green shade of the yew tree. After scanning all he could

233

of the surroundings, Aros moved on to the next bit of shelter, a large boulder. One by one they joined him.

Through the darkening day and growing cold, they made their way up the valley. Only once did they hear the moskets again, a brief crackling burst blown to them by the wind. There was no way of knowing where it had come from, how far it was, or what it signified.

Stumbling across the rough ground, they climbed higher and higher. The valley shrank around them. For a while they had followed the course of a narrow stream, passing a small pool that oozed peaty water. Beyond that there were no trees, no bushes, and the grass grew thin and brown.

Up there, with the distant peaks of other islands wreathed in low cloud and snowflakes dancing across the moorland, they came out onto the top of their own little world. Between them and the ocean, with its cluster of rocky outcrops already taking on a cold mantle of snow, stood two massive, upright slabs of stone holding aloft an equally massive lintel.

'I take it that's the gateway,' said Jeniche, clutching her stomach.

Beyond and through the crude stone arch they could see the clouds as they swept towards them over the ocean, dragging a heavy curtain of grey. The small, dancing snow-flakes went on their way down the valley, chased by larger flecks of white that began to fall like rain.

'Time, I think,' said Cynfelyn, 'to see where the gateway leads.'

Chapter Twenty-Five

A heaviness of head made waking difficult. The suffocating closeness of something on her face didn't help, either. Then there was the movement and the peculiar sensation of being upside down.

She moved from a muzzy half-sleep to full wakefulness and began to struggle.

'Whoa. Hold on. Keep still.'

The movement stopped and the world turned the right way up, blood flowing out of her head.

Aros grinned down at her as he put her carefully on the ground. Cynfelyn's face appeared over one of Aros's shoulders; Cenau's at the other.

'How do you feel?' asked Cenau, with a worried frown.

'She looks all right,' said Cynfelyn. 'Anything to get out of walking.'

She could see the flippancy masked concern; looked back at Aros and saw his grin was painted over nervousness.

Raising both hands, she flapped them feebly to shoo away the faces. When she tried to reinforce the gesture by saying something about a young woman and her privacy, the words would not form. Suddenly, she was frightened.

'Get out of the way, you two,' said Cynfelyn. As soon as they had stepped back, he raised a water skin to her lips. She felt a cool trickle, sought it out with the tip of her tongue.

'More,' she managed to say and felt the fear subside.

Cynfelyn obliged. Another trickle of water eased the burning in her throat and seemed to act as a lubricant to her clogged thoughts. Not that there was much to ease on its way.

She tried to sit up and Cynfelyn put a hand behind her shoulders to help her. As she reached an upright position a sick throbbing began in her left temple. It matched the nausea.

'Again?' she asked.

'Seems like it.'

He stood to one side and let her see for herself.

The scale of the scene took it beyond comprehension. She gaped. Her brain had already been struggling with reality, now it just gave up. She looked back at Cynfelyn, who shrugged, and then at Cenau and Aros, who were sitting with their backs to a wall, eating.

'How long this time?'

'Just a couple of hours.'

Her eyes strayed back to the scene beyond Cynfelyn, trying to pick out familiar details and failing.

She was determined not to ask what had happened, but the harder she thought back over events, the more her head ached. She grabbed the water skin and took another sip.

'Any food?'

Aros stood and picked up Jeniche's pack, bringing it across to her.

236

'You're starting to look a little less like a corpse,' he said.

'I see the famed Ynyswr art of flattery hasn't died.'

He grinned and went back to sit beside Cenau.

To take her mind off the tortuous conundrum that was making her eyes cross and her mind try to turn itself inside out, she went through her supplies and sliced off a bit of hard cheese and broke some bread away from one of the loaves they had been given on the *Morfran*.

'A couple of hours,' she said between mouthfuls.

'That's right.'

'And it's winter.'

'That's right.'

'So it should be pitch dark.' She thought a bit more and remembered something else. 'And freezing cold.'

'That's right.'

She picked up a piece of grit from the ground beside her and flicked it at Cynfelyn.

'I'm not going to ask.'

He smiled.

As she chewed some more on the solid bread, she had another go at making sense of their surroundings, tried at the same time to recall how they had come to be there. She gave up again on the former and, looking at the ground by her outstretched legs, decided to concentrate on the latter.

Memories assailed her in a random order as if they had been broken into fragments and scattered in all directions before making their way back to where they belonged. Some didn't even belong to her recent life, so it was safe to say that whatever had happened had been profound, inside her head if not outside.

She saw again the sandy riverbank to which she had sometimes escaped close by the Dhalar on the outskirts of

Jhilnagar, the long dark passages and empty courtyards inside the building, her own apartment, the painted room. She swept all those memories back under the carpet of later events. There were the two swords on the back wall of the sword smith's workshop. A long conversation one summer night between herself and Wedol, the baker's son in Makamba, his bright, shy face gone the way of dust. The tower room in the Library of the Great College.

'How much did you learn about the Twelve?'

The Twelve. That was another memory fitting into its place, like the picture puzzles... She shut that one out.

They eyed each other warily, but Cynfelyn said nothing.

'It must have occurred to you—'

'That one of them was like you. Yes.'

Of course it had, she realized. 'It was you, wasn't it?'

'Me, what?'

'That made sure Cenau gave me the keys to the tower room.'

Cenau kept his head down. 'Did you find whatever it was you were looking for?'

'No.'

She was still in the dark on that one. Perhaps somewhere even darker.

'I'm sorry,' said Cynfelyn. 'And I really didn't know for certain until we got to Maenmawr,' said Cynfelyn. 'Under it.'

She was too tired to get angry and her head still hurt.

'I wasn't using you,' he added, 'no matter how it seems.'

The elongated skull in the ruins below the tower. Climbing a cliff. Climbing another cliff. Eithrig's notebook.

'The Shadow Gate.' She remembered.

How they had pushed through the driving snow to reach

238

the crude doorway made of three massive slabs of stone. How they had stepped under the great slab that was the lintel, Jeniche last. How the world had vanished and with it consciousness. With a delicate touch, she searched for more. There was nothing that wanted to be found.

'The last thing I recall,' she said, 'was stepping up under that stone slab.'

'You're sure?' He looked surprised.

'I hope you're not going to tell me I climbed on a tavern table and started singing dirty songs.'

'Not exactly.'

'What, exactly.'

'I wish we knew.' He took a moment to gather his thoughts. 'The moment you joined us under the stone slab, everything went grey.'

'It was snowing.'

'No. It was like we were in a room. A proper room with flat, plastered walls. There were no windows or lanterns, none of those panels, but it was light. Half light. Like twilight when the colours fade. And there weren't any doors either. You didn't seem worried, though.'

'I was still conscious?'

'Well, you certainly weren't slumped on the floor. You walked across and stood facing one of the walls where you took out that pendant and touched it to... something. Part of the wall in front of you... Fireflies. It was a bit like fireflies, but in many different colours. They kept moving and forming patterns, then moving again. Every time the colours jumbled up, you drew on that bit of the wall with your finger and a new pattern would appear.'

Jeniche looked bemused. 'I did all that?'

'There was no one else there and it wasn't us lads.'

'Then what?'

'This.' He waved his hand over his shoulder. 'And you went out like a candle flame.'

'And you've been walking for two hours since?'

Cynfelyn nodded.

Using the wall she'd been propped against, Jeniche climbed to her feet. The nausea was still there, but the headache seemed to be fading. Taking a proper look at their surroundings threatened to bring it back.

They were on a broad, sloping road of beaten earth fifty paces wide. She counted as they crossed. Both edges were bounded with rough, dry-stone walls some four feet in height. Behind the one they had been resting against rose a sheer cliff. Beyond the other was a sheer drop. That much she could take in, even though she had never seen a road that wide before.

It was the view beyond the wall over the drop that foxed the senses simply because the scale was incomprehensible. The tower in which they had found the spear had been vast and that had been dwarfed by the ruined city in which it had been built. The city beneath the desert must also have been vast – the thought of the underground river alone was enough to make one wonder at the powers of the pre-Ev peoples. But they had all been revealed in small sections or constructed of individual buildings of graspable scale.

This was set out before them in its entirety and it was the size that made Jeniche doubt her senses. And not just the size. A city she could understand, whether it was above or below ground. The other places she had encountered, the fragments of structures, the peculiar buildings – they clearly had a function that related to people. But this...

240

'Making any sense of it?' asked Cynfelyn, standing as close to the wall as he dared.

'I can't think of an adequate word,' she said. '"Hole" just doesn't...' Her voice tailed off.

Cenau and Aros joined them and they all gazed into the crater. It was deep enough to contain small mountains with room to spare, broad enough for the far side to be dissolving in a haze, vast enough to contain in its depths a lake of milky green waters with an island at its centre. And round its sculpted sides ran the broad spiral of the road on which they stood, nothing more than a faint line in the distance.

'Did we come in at the top?' She looked up the slope.

'If there is a top, we couldn't find it, and it seemed pointless looking, as what we are after is down there.'

'But...'

'"Where's the snow? Why isn't it cold? How could this be on an island that would be dwarfed within it?" We asked all those as we were carrying you down.'

'Is it a dream?'

'And that one. But can people share a dream?'

'How can this have been missed? How can it not have been...?' Realization came. 'There were books in the tower room.'

'And if you'd had time to read them, you would have found obscure references to these places. They hid the books and maps because they wanted the Hallows to be safe. And they excelled themselves here, because there is an old tale in Ynyswr from well before the pre-Ev cultures that tells of a Spiral Castle and how a treasure lies at its heart. A treasure that will restore the world.'

She looked out across the frightening vastness. 'Does that

legend say how you get out of the castle when you have found the treasure?'

'Unfortunately, that bit seems to have been left out.'

They set off along the road, keeping to the centre. Jeniche, as the others had before, spent the first hour of their march gazing up at where there should have been a sky. The indefinable haze hurt the eyes after a while so she diverted her attention to the sheer wall on their left. It sloped back slightly and was clearly cut straight through all kinds of rock. From a distance it looked smooth, but close to one could see what looked like giant chisel marks. The only break in the uniformity was where water leaked from between layers and flowed down to culverts by the side of the road, running for a distance before disappearing beneath the ground. And when she had seen enough of that she turned her attention to the road, but by then her head was hurting again.

Eventually, like the others, she kept her gaze just ahead and fell into a steady walking rhythm, grateful that it was dry and warm enough to have her coat tied to her pack. The air was fresh but no breeze blew.

They walked thus for hours, slowly descending into the earth. Apart from the occasional fall and flow of water, there was no sound but their own booted feet. It came as a real relief when Aros spoke.

'Ahead,' he said.

In the distance, perhaps an hour's walk away, there was something on the road.

They picked up their pace, grateful for anything to relieve the monotony and the growing feeling of insignificance. The vague shape resolved itself into a solid mass – a structure that stretched the entire width of the road.

242

From that distance they thought it might be an outcrop of rock, odd as it may seem in such a neat, ordered landscape. As they drew closer, they began to understand that whatever it had originally been, it now meant trouble.

Chapter Twenty-Six

'If we keep to the far side,' said Jeniche once she had climbed back up onto the road, 'we'll stay dry. And it's an easy climb.'

'No such thing,' said Cynfelyn.

'Jeniche is right. It will save us a lot of time,' said Cenau.

Cynfelyn didn't reply. Either way, he would have to climb. Going straight down to the next turn of the spiral was by far the most sensible option. It just seemed such a long descent.

'You're sure it's safe?' he asked, keeping his eyes away from the drop.

Jeniche shrugged. 'As I can be. It all feels a lot more solid than any other ruins we've encountered.'

They looked at the long tumble of masonry. There had once been a substantial structure built right across the road and into the rock face. Some of the rooms and passages could still be seen there, high above, torn open when the structure collapsed. The sound of running water from below gave something of a clue as to its demise, as did the deep erosion gully directly in front of them.

An underground stream had undermined a broad section of the road. When it had eventually collapsed it had pulled the building down with it, blocking the route. They could have scrambled over the debris to the other side and carried on. But as Cenau had just reminded Cynfelyn, using the slope of rubble to climb down to the next layer would cut many miles from their journey and be no more arduous. Jeniche had even gone most of the way down to find a safe and easy route.

'I can only see four others,' said Cenau.

'Four what?' asked Aros, not even trying to follow Cenau's train of thought.

'The Spiral Castle is supposed to have seven gates. If this is one, there should be six others, but I can only see four.'

'This may not be the Spiral Castle.'

'Think of the legend,' said Cynfelyn, trying himself not to think of more immediate and practical matters.

Cenau looked blank.

Cynfelyn raised his eyebrows. 'Are you counting the island down there in the central lake?'

'Ah. That's six.'

'And we came in through one,' added Aros.

'Good. So if this really is the Spiral Castle, this is the gate of...'

Jeniche waited. 'Well?'

'The Gate of Water,' said a reluctant Cenau.

They all stood and listened to the song of the stream in the gully, as it splashed its way down into the carved-out depths.

'So it's not a legend,' said Jeniche.

'Perhaps,' said Cynfelyn, 'this is where the legend originates.'

245

'Or it's all a coincidence.'

'Whatever it is,' said Jeniche, 'we are wasting time. We don't know if it gets dark here and we wouldn't want to be caught on that scree if it does.'

'I thought you said it was safe.'

Jeniche shook her head. Without waiting for any more comment, she climbed back down into the water-cut gully, turning to help Cynfelyn over the edge and onto the slope.

This was where the ground was loosest, a seam of mud and gravel, but it was also the shortest section. At the bottom of the gully, where the water had once more found rock, a fast-flowing stream ran across a bed of small pebbles, washed down from the sides and long since worn smooth.

'It's always so dead.'

'What is?' asked Cynfelyn without taking his eyes off the ground directly in front of his feet. He tested a large stone with his toe and decided it would take his weight without slipping from under him. It didn't stop him keeping tight hold of Jeniche's hand.

'Whatever large pre-Ev site we've been to. No animals. No birds. No insects. Same here. Not even any lichen or slime in the water.'

'Most have been underground.'

'You get all sorts living underground.'

They came to a level slab of rock at the end of the gully, Aros and Cenau close behind. Cynfelyn let go of Jeniche and looked out across the impossible space. They had already descended a fair way, but to him it still felt like standing on the edge of the world. Jeniche stepped down onto the first tilted block of masonry, water trickling over her feet. She looked back up.

'This first bit is slippery. But we go down the other side

of this block, across that slab and then follow the edge of the scree all the way down to the road below. Take your time and concentrate on where your feet are going.'

Between them they manoeuvred Cynfelyn out of the gully and across the block. Jeniche stayed close to him all the way, guiding his boots to solid footholds. The climb down was strenuous, but presented no difficulties. There were foot- and handholds aplenty and there was no wind trying to tear them off the rock face or ice trying to detach flesh from their fingers.

Close to the bottom of the slope, Cenau let his concentration wander. He was trying to see how far it was round to the next gate rather than where his feet should go. The result was a sore backside, flesh scraped from his hands and an ankle that would be sore for days to come.

It could have been worse. He stopped his uncontrolled tumble altogether too close to the edge of the next drop. This one was sheer, the stone wall along the edge having been demolished by tumbling boulders.

'Idiot,' the other two heard Aros say as he pulled Cenau away from the edge and helped him down onto the road. 'No point in thinking about the next gate if that's going to get you killed before you get there.'

'Someone's got to do some thinking,' they heard Cenau reply, angry at his own foolishness. They waited for Aros to explode. Instead, he grinned and cuffed Cenau gently round the ear.

By the time Jeniche had Cynfelyn safely down to the road, Aros was checking Cenau's sword whilst Cenau prodded the livid flesh of his left ankle with a bloody hand.

'I hope you can walk on that,' said Cynfelyn, 'because you've used up your share of being carried; same as desert girl here.'

247

Jeniche stuck out her tongue, settled her pack, and set off down the wide, curving road.

Deeper in the earth, still crawling round the edge of the bowl of the gods, they finally came to the next gate.

'There doesn't seem any sense to it,' said Jeniche.

The building blocked the road completely. From a distance they had thought the road passed through. It was, after all, meant to be a gate. A broad arched entrance was clearly visible as they approached round the curve. But when they came close enough to see, it was to discover the road went in a hundred paces and stopped abruptly against a wall. It wasn't even made of masonry blocks, as if it had been built after the road fell out of use. The whole thing had been carved from the same rock as the road.

'I don't mind that,' Cynfelyn said in response, 'just as long as there is a safe way to walk through.'

'It's almost like they were copying something they didn't understand or couldn't see properly.'

They all looked at Cenau. He shifted uncomfortably.

'When we were at a distance, it looked like an arch with the road going through. The road goes as far back as the deep shadow. As if the person who made this didn't know what was inside or couldn't see into the shadow.'

'Except this isn't a model,' pointed out Aros.

Cenau shrugged. 'Have you seen how big this hole in the ground is?'

'So what are you getting at?'

'What if this wasn't the original? What if it was built out of... someone's dream of the Spiral Castle?'

'You've lost me,' said Aros. 'Can't see how that's possible. That's all backward.'

248

They were still trying to tease out this philosophical knot as they ventured in under the arch. Close to the rear wall, tucked behind a buttress, they found a small, open doorway. Torches were lit. They filed in.

'What were they thinking?' asked Jeniche.

'Who?'

'Your people. Hiding the Hallows away in such places.'

'I would think... Left or right?'

Jeniche looked through the left-hand arch. Her torch lit a long, narrow room with no other door. 'Right.'

'I would think,' Cynfelyn continued, 'they were setting up an adventure, a coming of age, a quest to challenge whoever had ambitions to become Guardian. I doubt they suspected it would be under such circumstances.' He lowered his voice to a whisper. 'It's certainly put those two to the test.'

'It just seems very elaborate,' she said.

'That's the Derw for you,' he replied. 'Why do it simply when you can baffle everyone else and add an extra twist?'

'How do they do it where you come from?' asked Aros from the darkness behind them.

'Do what? Hide things?'

'Govern.'

'The Makambans seem to have a very relaxed approach to government. The nineteen wealthiest merchants make up the rules, or keep the ones that have been there for centuries; but they're also supposed to pay the largest share of the costs. If you want power, you have to pay for it. Everyone else pays taxes as well. In theory. So there's a city guard, a hospital, tax collectors, things like that. That all pays for the University as well, although they make a lot of their own money by copying and selling books. As long as the docks are kept working and the merchants make money, everything else seems to roll along more or less peacefully.'

'What about Antar?'

Jeniche was silent for a while. They threaded their way through the dark passages, torchlight dancing across smooth, blank walls and smooth, blank floors.

'I left when I was young,' she said eventually. 'There's... Ahead. Something.'

Aros took the torch from Jeniche and went in front.

'There's a much larger room here,' he called back to where the others waited. 'Directly off this passage.'

'What can you see?'

'Oh...'

The others moved forward. As Jeniche expected from her increased queasiness, light panels flickered when she stepped through the doorway. Only one of them managed a steady light and even then it was pale. The rest struggled and several gave up after a few faint blinks. However, there was enough light to see the room.

'This looks familiar.'

Jeniche looked to see if Cynfelyn meant anything by the remark, but it seemed as if he was just referring to the room in the city beneath the desert which, like this one, was lined with cases. That the tower room of the Library was like this in miniature could be no coincidence, but she felt she knew Cynfelyn well enough to discern whether he was being cryptic.

Aros and Cenau didn't know where to look first, not least at Jeniche and Cynfelyn.

'You've seen this before?'

'Not this room, no,' said Cynfelyn. 'In... Beneath... I suppose it was still Makamba. Beneath the edge of the desert, there was... is a city. There was a room much like this. A whole series of rooms. We didn't explore far.'

Rows of cases with glass doors stood along the walls. Down the centre of the room were cases with glass tops. All were filled with artefacts. Only a few, by the door, looked pre-Ev.

'But different,' pointed out Jeniche. 'The one in Makamba was all pre-Ev artefacts. Hundreds of them. All locked away. A lot of this looks truly ancient.' She approached one of the cabinets and peered in, her head on one side. 'Although this looks—'

'Valuable.'

She turned. 'I wouldn't even think about that, Aros. Everything pre-Ev has a price.'

He hadn't listened, trying to pry open a door with the knife in his hand.

'Aros!'

Startled, he turned to Cynfelyn, looked at the knife in his hand with a puzzled expression.

'Put the blade away, lad.'

As it slid back into its sheath, the sound of breaking glass echoed off into the dark passages and rooms. They span to see Cenau standing with his sword out and reversed, the pommel snagged on a long shard of black glass. Torchlight glinted dangerously along the dark, vitreous edge.

Jeniche took the sword from Cenau's hand as Cynfelyn pulled him gently away from the cabinet. She unsnagged the pommel, careful to keep her fingers away from the dangerous, glassy shard.

'What? Did I just do that?'

Jeniche nodded as she slipped Cenau's sword back into its scabbard. She turned and looked at the case. 'You did. But it's... empty. What did you see in it?'

251

Cenau turned. 'A book. I saw... Why would I...?'

'It's the cabinets. We should get out. They aren't wooden cases. They're machines. The light panels aren't working, but these are.'

'Machines?'

'They... how do I know this? They make images.'

'Not a cauldron?' asked Aros.

'Not a book?' asked Cenau.

'No,' said Jeniche. 'Illusions. Nothing but illusions.'

Chapter Twenty-Seven

Jeniche did not like the way things kept reminding her of Antar. She had thought it was all left far behind, especially since she had escaped from Makamba and travelled to places where they didn't know an Antari from a hole in the ground. Recently, however, memories kept pushing their way out of the deep, dark cellar where she hoped they had been buried for good. Moods, atmospheres, feelings, thoughts, and events kept coming along to sniff them out and dig them up and throw them, half recognized, into the light of a different day.

Those hateful pre-Ev machines they had found. How did she know that they created illusions? And why did they remind her so much of the painted room? Those were just paintings. She had been in there long enough to know that, even as a child. She had touched them, examined each brushstroke, and seen all the places where the paint was flaking because the wall was damp.

She moved quietly into a more comfortable position. And then she understood. Like some of those paintings in the room, like some of the drawings in a book she'd had, like the illusions that had mesmerized Aros and Cenau, the moment you shifted perspective they all changed. Not a simple viewing from a slightly different angle, but a complete change into something else.

The one that had captivated her most as a child was the wall painted to resemble a colonnaded entrance through which could be seen an open-air terrace surrounded by a stone balustrade. Beyond was a verdant pastoral scene unlike anything in Antar, with mountains hazy in the distance. So realistic was the depiction, when she had first seen it she could not understand why she could not walk out onto the balcony, why it was always day out there. And the landscape was so enticing in itself, so captivating in being unreachable, it was a long time before she took any notice of the balusters, humble pieces of turned stone.

Why it happened, she had never known, but one day, staring at the painted wall, her perspective switched and the balusters became a series of faces in profile, facing each other in pairs. And each face was subtly different from all the others; some with high cheekbones, she now recalled, and upward-slanting eyes. Even now, looming out of the shadow of the past, the memory of that room had lost none of its power to make her flesh crawl.

In a way it was the same with the illusions to which Aros and Cenau had fallen prey. How the pre-Ev peoples had captured images that looked so real and let you view them from different angles, as if the object was there in the case, was nothing short of magic. Except there was no such thing.

But there had been another change of perspective. A subtle one. In feeling rather than in the external world. Because until that moment, she had always felt she had some control

254

over her own destiny. The Occassans may have chased her, she may have made mistakes, fallen into traps and been swept along by events caused by others, but she always felt that she was in charge of what she did. Now she no longer felt certain. And she liked that even less than all these reawakened memories.

It was the same with this place. She had seen some strange sights in her travels, not all of them left over from those cultures that had collapsed so comprehensively. This vast, symmetrical hole in the ground was, however, a wonder of a different order.

She tried to tell herself that was all it was – a big hole in the ground, devoid of life. But it was discomfiting in the extreme and she could not shake the feeling that they were being watched. That somehow they were being manipulated.

She sat up, fingering the pendant, tempted to rip it off and throw it over the wall. The impulse didn't come to much. For one thing, it would be waiting for her when they got down to that level. For another, they probably needed it to get back out. And if there was one thing she wanted, manipulated or not, reminded of Antar or not, it was to get out of this great big hole.

With no apparent night or day, they had kept going until they were exhausted, putting as much distance between themselves and the hall of illusions as they could. When they could go no further they had simply lain down in the road and slept. At least, they had tried to sleep. With no change in the light it had been difficult, tired as they were. And once they had dropped into sleep they had been restless, instinctively uncomfortable in the middle of a road with nothing at their backs, a towering cliff on one side and a sheer drop on the other.

The others were still sleeping so she practised her skills on Cenau's pack and liberated Eithrig's notebook. It told her nothing new. She returned it and wandered back uphill far enough to find some semblance of privacy. It was even more menacing on her own so she hurried back, grateful for the company even though it was somnolent. For someone who had been alone for most of her life, it was not unpleasant to find solace in the presence of her companions. She hoped they fared better than all the others to whom she had ever grown close.

'A silver penny for them?'

She turned from where she leaned on the wall, staring out over the basin.

'They're not worth it,' she said.

Cynfelyn crossed the road and came to stand beside her. He looked down to the lake of milky green. She pretended not to notice the slight nervous tremor in his hands where they rested on the top of the wall.

'It's not real, is it? The... sky. That should have given it away. But we are so used to accepting that the pre-Ev peoples were capable of great wonders, we never think what form those wonders take.'

'I think it's real in some ways. If you fell, you wouldn't survive. And we have to walk all the way round. And round. And round.'

'Not so far now. But "real" as it is, I don't think we ever left the island.'

They thought of the others. Out there in the snow, fighting off the Gwerin and Occassans. Jeniche kicked at the wall.

'Nothing we can do until we finish here,' said Cynfelyn. But he kicked the wall as well.

Jeniche had set off first to give the others a chance to make their mark on the roadside. By the time they caught up, Cenau and Aros were talking. Chastened by the ease with which they had been taken in and induced to do things so out of character, they had neither of them slept well. Dreams had twined around their memories and they were anxious to talk them out, something all Ynyswr did.

Jeniche didn't listen at first, trying to find her own rhythm in this altered world. Occasionally she heard the deeper rumble of Cynfelyn's voice as he answered a question or made a contribution to the discussion.

She smiled. The first time she had heard that voice, he had been in an alley standing over a corpse, pretending to be drunk. One day she would ask him about that corpse. She had always had a feeling it was no coincidence the two were there together in the dark as she stumbled up through the Old Town of Makamba.

She became conscious of silence and turned. The other three were watching with broad grins on their faces.

'Ah,' said Cynfelyn, 'you are still with us.'

'What? Are you being rude about me?'

'Would I ever?'

Jeniche narrowed her eyes.

'I asked you a question,' said Cenau.

'Sorry. I was just thinking about the first time I met Allt… Cynfelyn.'

'That is a tale you must tell us,' said Aros.

'Later,' cut in Cynfelyn. 'Cenau's question.'

Jeniche smiled to herself.

'We were talking about that… room,' said Cenau.

'The hall of illusions?'

'Poetic,' said Cynfelyn.

'I have been known to have my moments.' She smiled sweetly. 'What was the question, Cenau?'

'It was an observation, really. And I wondered what you thought. About the pre-Ev peoples and why they left so few books behind. It can't be because they didn't have them, surely. Can they build cities like they did, create all the wonders we know they made, without sharing the knowledge they had? And they must have told stories, kept records, sent letters to one another. Where has it all gone?'

Jeniche shook her head. 'We've only ever seen a small fraction of what they left behind, and that in itself is just a small fraction of what there was. Most of it is underwater. Like all cultures, they built most of their settlements by the sea and along rivers close to the sea. The Inundation wiped all that away.'

'But they must have built away from the sea as well; on hills and in the mountains.'

She shrugged. 'I've seen little evidence of it. And those places on high ground would have relied on the low-lying settlements where the majority lived.' She was silent a moment. More memories. 'Besides, you are assuming a book will look like a book.'

Cenau frowned. 'Like the illusion, you mean?'

'What did you see?'

'It's a bit hazy now. I thought it was a book. A valuable book. Rare. One that had all the answers.'

'Clearly an illusion. More like a dream. But did it look like a book in the Library of the Great College?'

'Well, yes.'

'Not a small, decorated wooden box?'

'No.' He looked puzzled.

'Some books in Tundur look like that. The box is the

cover. The front folds down and the lid folds back on hinges. Inside there is a pile of separate sheets of paper. You read the top of the uppermost sheet in the box and when you have finished, you turn it forward and place it on the table in front of the box and read the other side. And so on. In Gyanag, most of their documents are written on paper made from rice. It is fragile. Only important documents get written onto something more substantial.'

'But surely if they built artefacts that have survived for centuries...'

'They have made books that have survived for centuries. And you may have seen some today. Yesterday. Whenever.'

'Living pictures of books,' said Cynfelyn. 'And how can we ever know what is in them if looking at them drives you mad?'

'Perhaps they are best left unread,' said Aros. 'If they told us how to be like the pre-Ev peoples, we would surely come to the same end.'

'With that sentiment,' said Cynfelyn, 'I am inclined to agree.'

Their discussion continued, ranging widely, until they arrived at the next gate. Built of massive slabs of dark, dull rock, it presented a grim façade. An arched entrance was filled with shadow. Narrow windows looked down from every angle. The whole structure exuded an unfriendly coldness.

'So this,' said Cenau, 'would be the Gate of Joy.'

They all looked at it some more.

'Evidence of a sense of humour?'

'Or something else,' said Jeniche, lighting a torch. 'No exploring. No touching. We find our way through and keep going.'

They nodded their agreement and followed her through the main arch.

If they had expected problems they were pleasantly disappointed. The arch gave on to a passage deep in shadow that went straight through to a courtyard. They could see no doors along the way. Around the enclosure were three galleries but, as with the passage, no sign of any doors that would give access to them. At the far end was another passage that led them back out onto the road.

They kept going, none of them looking back and none of them wishing to tempt fate by voicing how easy it had been. And the silence stayed with them until they reached the next gate, closer now that the spiral was nearing its end. They were weary of the whole place, of its endless feeling of an overcast day, of its silence, of the discomfort it engendered in both body and spirit.

Here they were confronted with a structure much the same size as all the others, double doors wide open onto a great hall within. Light filtered in from high, narrow clerestory windows. If the space had ever been furnished then the benches and tables, the hearth, the wall hangings, had all been removed or long since fallen to dust.

'It's almost like they gave up trying,' said Cynfelyn.

'Or maybe we have,' said Jeniche. 'What is this place meant to be?'

'The Gate of Carousal,' said Aros. 'The Mead Hall of the Otherworld, the place where new arrivals from the world of the living are celebrated.'

'Perhaps no one told them we were coming.'

Chapter Twenty-Eight

Crossing the flat open space at the bottom of the immense crater was even more disconcerting than crawling in a spiral round its wall. Exposed as they had felt, the wall had at least offered a small amount of protection from one direction, something they could get their backs against. Out here they could be seen from all sides and there was nowhere to hide.

The road followed a spiral path all the way to the centre, with gullies either side carrying a small trickle of clear water. They didn't follow it, but cut straight across, wanting to be finished with the unreal world as soon as they could.

As they came closer to the centre, they could hear something faintly above their footfall. It was the first noise since the stream that they had not created themselves.

'What is that?' Aros had stopped to listen. 'It sounds familiar.'

The others stopped as well for a moment.

'Only one way to find out,' said Cynfelyn. 'And I suspect it could get a whole lot more interesting.'

They started walking again, jumping over gullies and crossing the road every time it swept round across their path. The familiar sound grew louder.

Jeniche kept looking at the distant walls, picking out the gateways, trying to see where it was they had entered this bizarre place. Try as she might, the top end of the road seemed to elude her, fading into the background before it reached the rim. If that was a rim. It certainly wasn't a sky beyond.

'A grindstone.' It was Aros. 'That's what it sounds like. One of those small grindstones in the Sisterhood's workshops. They hum like that.'

They walked on.

'That would be a fine place to be right now,' he added a while later, casting a look around at the dead place. 'Sitting on the bench after an hour in the sweat-house, polishing some leather, watching sparks fly from a blade being sharpened, listening to the breathing of the bellows in the forge.' His own world, the place he was comfortable, the place where he knew the rules.

'What about you, Cenau?' asked Jeniche. 'Where would you like to be right now?'

He blushed. 'On the concourse of the Great College. At night. Watching a play.'

Aros, who was walking beside him, nudged him with his elbow, a broad grin lighting his face.

'I hope they're all right,' Cenau added quietly.

'Gwynfor's no fool,' said Jeniche. 'He wouldn't put his family at risk. They'll be safe in Brocel.'

Cenau shrugged, obviously thinking of Caru. 'I hope so.' He tried to put on a smile; nearly succeeded. 'What about you, Cynfelyn?'

'Me?' He was silent a while and then shook his head. 'There's no going back there any more.' With a deep sigh he dropped back into thought. Jeniche saw that familiar sadness in his eyes again before his hand went up to his face to pummel the flesh. 'Anywhere green,' he said. 'With a flagon of good white wine, fresh bread, a mature cheese, sweet apples, and students courteous enough not to pester me while I doze.'

He looked at Jeniche with a rueful expression and she raised an eyebrow. His feet were as restless as hers. It would take more than a decent meal and somewhere to take a nap to keep him in one place for long. Although, she had to admit to herself, it did paint an attractive picture.

'And what about you, desert girl?'

She didn't have a place she thought of as home; a place she would most like to be. Makamba had once come close with its busy streets and hot nights, a certain baker's son with a shy smile, easy pickings in the merchants' quarter, Trag. But she was a different person now and she doubted if she would feel comfortable there any more. Or anywhere else, for that matter. It had been a good place to grow up, though, an excellent playground.

'Anywhere that's a very long way from the sea.'

Cynfelyn laughed.

That's when they reached the end of the road.

'It's moving,' said Cenau.

'What is?'

He pointed to the ground ahead. Some fifty or sixty paces in front of them the ground stepped up.

'And it's getting closer.' Without any shadow it was difficult to see, but as they stared, it quickly became apparent that it was sweeping toward them.

'Back! Back!'

'No need,' said Jeniche. 'Watch.'

They stepped back all the same.

Just as when they had first arrived high up on the spiral road, it was difficult to work out the perspectives, but there was an increase in the hum, a slight breeze, and the ground swept past in front of them at waist height and began to recede. A tiny whirlwind of dust followed in its wake.

'I need some height,' said Jeniche.

Bemused, Aros and Cynfelyn created a step with their hands and hoisted Jeniche up from the ground. She balanced there for a moment and then jumped down.

'It's a massive square, rotating. Like a millstone. The lake is in the centre.'

'How is that possible?'

'Seriously, Cenau? In this landscape?'

'Worry about it later, you two. We have to get up onto that if we want to get to the lake. I assume that's where we're going?' She turned to Cynfelyn.

'The Four-cornered Gate,' he said to himself. 'Yes. Yes. The island in the lake. It can't be anywhere else.' He watched the moving surface. 'How fast is this?'

Another corner swept past.

'Too fast here. It should be easier closer to the centre.'

'Half way along one of the sides,' said Cenau, eyes fixed on the receding edge.

'And only one chance to get it right.'

'I wish you hadn't said that, Jeniche.'

They tightened straps and belts, checked buckles, tied their swords up out of the way, made sure there was nothing else to trip over or get tangled, all the while watching as the square rotated, each corner sweeping past at breakneck speed.

'Jeniche first?' suggested Cynfelyn.

She nodded.

'Cenau next. And when you get up there, lad, stay on all fours and move away from the edge. Don't look at what's going past.'

He nodded, his mouth too dry to speak, and then flicked a piece of grit he had prised from the sole of his boot. They all watched as it hit the leading edge of the square, bounced forward to the ground and vanished beneath the slab. As the corner swept past, the trailing vortex of dust was just a little bit thicker.

With that image clear in their minds, they lined up as close as they dared.

'Next one,' said Jeniche.

The corner swept by and she ran, following the receding edge, picking her moment and throwing herself up onto the moving surface. Cynfelyn had kept Cenau back just long enough for Jeniche to roll, turn, brace herself, grabbing him as he passed, hauling him up. She heard him scuttling away as Aros leapt. He turned and shuffled up next to her, reaching out for Cynfelyn.

They should have waited. Cynfelyn found the edge sweeping toward him and forcing him out from the centre. He had to speed up to keep pace. The edge of the square clipped his foot and he tripped as hands grasped his clothing. Face down, he was swept along with the ground inches from his face and getting closer. The toe of one his boots began to bounce up and down.

He heard Jeniche shout and felt another pair of hands grab at his legs. The ground receded inch by inch until he was able to get a hand of his own on the upper surface and add to the leverage. The boot bounced once more and he rolled up onto the top of the square, face to face with Aros.

'That nap under the tree is looking all the more inviting,' Cynfelyn said as they pulled him away from the edge. He sat up and looked at his toes wiggling in the hole torn in his left boot. 'I was just getting those comfortable,' he added, trying not to think what the huge millstone would have done to him if he'd fallen.

One by one, they found their feet and learned the trick of leaning against the direction of rotation. It took Cenau three attempts.

'It's my ankle,' he said.

'The one with the bone in it?' asked Cynfelyn.

Cenau lifted his trouser leg and slipped off his boot without falling over.

'Good grief,' said Jeniche.

The shin was badly inflamed.

'I can walk all right, but it is tender.'

'I'm not surprised,' said Cynfelyn.

He took off his pack, found the remains of an undershirt and tore off some strips. He soaked them in water and bound them round Cenau's leg.

'First chance we get, that needs seeing to properly.'

Once they were all set again, they headed toward the lake. The rotation of the square made it difficult to keep in a straight line, but it didn't take long to reach the circular shore. There the movement was slow enough to step down without any trouble. It took a little longer for it to feel like the world had stopped spinning.

In front of them the milky green waters of the lake shimmered, a fine mist lying on the surface making it difficult to see the island in the centre. There seemed to be more light there, but there were still no shadows.

'Do we swim?' asked Aros.

'Perhaps there's a boat,' said Cenau. He looked at Jeniche. 'Or a bridge.'

'What do the legends say?' she asked.

'I don't know,' replied Cynfelyn. 'Nothing. This represents the sea. And we've already crossed the sea.'

'Do we actually know it is water? None of those gullies empty across the beach.'

She walked down the gentle slope and out onto the milky green surface. It gave slightly but held her weight. As she walked, she left footprints behind that slowly filled in and disappeared.

Cynfelyn shrugged. 'Come on, you two, while we can. But keep spaced out.'

The fine mist curled out of their way and twisted in whorls in the breeze of their passing before settling back. Likewise, the footprints stayed a while, marking their route before disappearing. Even though it held their weight, it still looked like cloudy water.

Not one of them breathed properly the whole way over, expecting the surface to give and drop them into the depths with heavy packs and swords dragging them under. When they reached the island, they stepped ashore as quickly as they could and stood engulfed in flames.

They had been invisible until they passed into them. Like the others, Jeniche had called out in surprise before realizing they were as much a mirage as everything else, thankfully less concrete than some of the other illusions they had encountered. Like the water, they were unnerving and they moved through them as quickly as they could.

Once they were inside the wall of fire, they could see a beautiful green garden; at its centre an ornamental fountain was faced by a throne.

'This is too exact,' said Cynfelyn. 'It can't be coincidence.'

'That's as maybe,' said Jeniche, 'but isn't there meant to be a cauldron here?'

'Crochan,' said Cenau. 'Yes.'

They went over the entire island, inch by weary inch. There were few places to hide anything and all the obvious ones had been searched straight away, starting with the throne. In desperation Aros scraped away some soil from one of the borders only to find that an inch down was a pale, smooth surface solid as rock. And as they watched, the soil seemed to grow back.

Cenau gave up first, his leg increasingly sore. He slumped on the high-backed wooden throne and rooted round in his pack for something to eat. Aros and Cynfelyn wandered around some more on the off-chance they had somehow missed a hiding place. Jeniche went to the fountain, hoping that the water there was real.

'There!'

Jeniche dropped the cupped handful of water she was about to sip. Cynfelyn and Aros came running.

'What is it?'

Cenau was almost bouncing up and down on the seat with excitement, pointing to the fountain. 'It's not a cauldron.'

'The fountain?' asked Aros.

'In the fountain. Look.'

They looked. Standing in the water in the bowl of the fountain, spray from the spout keeping it filled, was an exquisite chalice of white metal, the rim studded with pearls, enamelled decorations on the stem. Jeniche had seen those patterns before.

Cynfelyn wiped his face and heaved a great sigh, shaking his head. 'Your pack's open, Cenau. Will you carry it?'

'Me?'

'Yes, you.'

He lifted his pack from the ground.

Cynfelyn turned to Aros. 'Go on,' he said quietly. 'It's yours.'

Aros looked at the other three, uncertain. In this unreal world the burden he was about to take up seemed suddenly very real.

'You won't be alone,' Cynfelyn reminded him.

Aros reached into the bowl of the fountain. He lifted the chalice and as he poured the water in offering onto the ground, the blizzard hit them full force.

Chapter Twenty-Nine

Stunned by the sudden onslaught of cold and snow, they staggered into the lee of the stone gate. It offered precious little shelter from the blizzard, but it gave them time to gather their wits, pack away the chalice, struggle into their coats, and prepare themselves for the journey back to the ship. They had the Crochan, but the way ahead was still precarious.

Cynfelyn used the last of his undershirt to stuff the open toe of his boot; Cenau stripped off the still-damp strips from around his leg. By the time they were sorted, the storm seemed a little less harsh. Whether it was because they had recovered from the shock of being dumped into the middle of a howling gale or that the snow had lessened was a pointless speculation. Whatever the case, they were in the cold, half blind, and with no idea how things stood elsewhere.

It did occur to Jeniche to wonder whether they were still on the island, but she decided it was best to keep that thought to herself. Cenau already looked distressed, and standing where they were indulging in idle speculation was not going to improve matters.

Recalling the layout of the small valley as best she could, she led the way downhill, taking cautious steps in the fresh snow. Before very long they had dropped down out of the wind that streamed over the top of the island. It was still viciously cold, but the snow was no longer driving against their backs and rushing past them horizontally.

The further down they went, the straighter the flakes fell. They were large and drifted past in that idle way that can fool the unwary into thinking them benign. Shapes loomed out of the flickering grey flecks to become rocks and shrubs. The sound of their footfall was muted. Their breath blew out in clouds.

'It's not very deep,' said Cenau, trying to draw what comfort he could from the bleak scene.

'But we must have been in there for two or three days,' replied Aros.

Cynfelyn spoke from between the wings of his upturned collar. 'Time always runs at a different speed in the land of the fey.'

'Or when you dream,' added Jeniche quietly. She stopped, convinced for a moment she had seen several shapes struggling past them, headed up the slope.

Before she could call out, the snow swirled and left a temporary clearing in the air. It revealed that there was nobody there, but her heart was racing.

'We need to find those buildings to get our bearings,' she said out loud.

Just ahead of her, Cynfelyn had stopped and raised a hand.

The others stopped as well and listened. It was difficult

to hear anything in the snow but their own breathing. After a moment, Cynfelyn dropped his hand and knelt. Jeniche stepped up beside him and looked down to where he was brushing snow aside from something. A face appeared, eyes staring sightlessly into the cold sky. Snowflakes settled on them, making Jeniche blink. Cynfelyn pushed a hand into the clothing.

'Still a bit of warmth,' he said, looking up at Jeniche. 'Not been dead for long.'

'Gwerin?'

'He's not from the *Morfran*.'

He brushed more snow away from the clothing.

'Definitely a soldier,' said Aros, looking over Cynfelyn's shoulder.

'Keep close to me, Cenau,' said Jeniche as Cynfelyn stood and drew his sword.

Aros followed suit and they led the way on down the slope. At the bottom, they crossed the little gulley where the stream flowed, saw the dark shape of trees and found their way to the buildings. Jeniche took Cenau up to the tree line and skirted the ruins under their cover while the other two approached from the far side.

Cynfelyn scouted through the ruins while Aros watched his back. When they came to the building that was almost intact they hesitated a moment. Aros went first this time and in a moment came back out to wave to Jeniche and Cenau.

Within the shelter of the walls it felt a little less cold, but there was no shelter from the snow which covered the floor and had drifted into the corners. Cynfelyn repacked the piece of cloth over his toes; Cenau stood favouring his good leg.

'We eat,' said Cynfelyn, 'and then we make our way back to the boat. I don't suppose that book we found tells of an easy way down to the water?'

Jeniche shook her head.

The meal was cheerless. Stale bread. Stale cheese. There was no lack of water, but it was cold. By the time they finished, Cenau was shivering.

'Cold, lad?'

'Frightened,' he replied. 'And cold.'

'Me too,' said Aros.

'Well, for what it's worth, you're not alone.'

Packs secure, they set off again. The snow was falling less thickly as they crossed the little valley and began to climb up toward the cliff top. Cynfelyn let Aros lead.

The higher they climbed, the sharper the wind. It picked at the top layer of fallen snow and whipped it across the surface into small drifts, snatching at still-falling flakes and making them dance crazily in all directions. The one advantage was that it grew lighter, as if the cloud was passing. It was easier to see where they were going, but it was not lost on any of them that they too were becoming easier to see, crossing the white expanse in their dark clothes.

Close to the top of the slope, Aros caught his foot on something in the snow and fell forward. It was another body. A quick search through the snow revealed several more – three Gwerin, one Occassan, and the two members of the crew of the *Morfran* who had climbed up with them.

'That doesn't bode well,' said Cynfelyn.

He looked at the sky. 'We don't really want to risk that cliff stair when it's snowing. On the other hand—'

Firecracker sounds echoed in the cold air.

'I don't suppose we have much choice,' said Cenau.

273

The storm was passing as they reached the head of the stairs and the bay and tidal race appeared slowly out of the cold gloom. It was difficult to make sense of what they saw, given that there must have been running battles on land.

Anchored in the bay was the *Morfran*. She seemed untouched and they could see movement on board. Further out was a Gwerin ship that had clearly come off worst in its encounter with the maelstrom. Listing seriously, masts smashed, decks shrouded with torn canvas, rigging trailing in the water, it seemed dead.

'There must be another way onto the island,' said Aros. 'They didn't come up by this path. Perhaps they were trying to circle round.'

'And were dealt with,' said Cynfelyn. 'But why leave the dead lying?'

'Unless there is another threat.'

The retreating shroud of falling snow revealed it to them. Moving slowly through the slack water of the tidal race, another Gwerin ship approached, its decks lined with men.

'They must have waited for still water and hoped to sneak in.'

'So why give yourself away by firing your mosket?'

'There,' pointed Cenau.

Turning slowly in the water in the wake of the Gwerin ship was a small shore boat.

'That's from the *Morfran*. They must have posted a watch.'

'Well,' said Cynfelyn, 'I think the time for talk is past. Take care on the steps. Better we go slowly and die defending the *Morfran* than waste ourselves before getting there.'

'If that was meant to be a rousing speech...' said Jeniche.

'I'll work on it on the way down,' said Cynfelyn. His

face was set hard against the fear, but his left eye flickered in the hint of a wink.

Snow covered some of the steps, but the wind had kept most of them clear. Both wind and snow had gone now, sweeping along the channel and out to the east, but there was still the odd gust that sneaked along and tugged at their clothing.

It was probably the prospect of battle that kept their minds from the journey down, although the steps had been cut to make the trek as easy and as safe as possible. They snaked back and forth across the face of the cliff, one eye on the approaching Gwerin vessel, one eye on the steps. Even Cynfelyn managed to follow events without too much distress.

Half way down, someone on the Gwerin vessel spotted them and they heard the crack of moskets, saw puffs of smoke. One lucky shot kicked up chips of rock close by, but the new weapons were not accurate over a long distance. A good archer would have given them more cause for concern, but there were no longbow men on board. Before long the shooting stopped. It was when they got down to the *Morfran* they would need to worry.

Below, the Ynyswr did not wait for the battle to come to them. Unlike the Gwerin, they did have bowmen and they were not only finding targets already, they were sending arcs of flame across the closing gap. Sailors sent up with water to douse burning canvas were falling victim to other arrows. Cenau tried to close his ears to the screams and concentrate on the steps, keep his increasingly weak leg from giving out beneath him.

At the base of the stairs, sheltered from mosket fire by the bulk of the *Morfran*, they removed their packs and coats and tucked them into a large crack in the cliff face. They reached the sloping shelf of rock just as the Gwerin ship tried to ram the *Morfran*. The smaller hull and shallower draft of the *Morfran* protected it from the assault.

Seeing the marauder approaching, moskets firing, the captain of the Ynyswr vessel had ordered her pulled in as close to shore as possible. Before it could reach the hull of the *Morfran* with its reinforced prow, the Gwerin ship hit submerged rock. Most of the crew, though braced for ramming, had not expected an impact so soon or one against something so implacably immovable. Even a large vessel will give if rammed. An island will not.

Using an anchor rope, Cynfelyn climbed up onto the *Morfran* followed by Aros. Cenau went next, boosted all the way by Jeniche. They climbed up onto the deck to find noisy chaos.

'Stay close,' shouted Jeniche, drawing her swords and flinching as mosket shot splintered the rail beside her. Cenau drew his sword as well, but had no idea what to do. He need not have worried. The battle came to them.

Cenau had practised with his sword to the point where he could swing it in an open space without hurting himself. And he had read about battles in the Library. How this commander did one thing and another countered it with a different tactic, how armies were positioned and manoeuvred, how individuals fought. It had seemed well thought out and logical. He very quickly learned it was nothing but the hindsight of historians who had probably handled nothing more deadly than the knife with which they sharpened their pen. There, on deck, it was bloody mayhem and he was terrified out of his wits.

Jeniche kept beside him as long as she could, her swords

whirling and blocking, cutting and thrusting. Gwerin soldiers went down before her, wounded or dying. Cenau had the sense to remove weapons from the fallen while they were close to the rail and throw them into the sea. But they did not stay close to the rail.

As Jeniche fought forward, Cenau caught glimpses of the fighting around him. He kept expecting the sound of moskets, but they were useless at close quarters. Instead he saw people fighting for their lives and failing. At the far end of the boat, on the aft deck, he caught a glimpse of Awd. Moments later he saw Ruad close by. Of Cynfelyn and Aros he saw nothing.

He had made a few token thrusts at Gwerin soldiers who were otherwise engaged, but the sword still felt alien in his hand and the thought of deliberately pushing steel into another person's body filled him with horror.

Inevitably he became separated from Jeniche and found himself confronted by a large Gwerin with bloody hands. Perhaps he hadn't seen Cenau's small sword. Perhaps the sight of a scrawny, pale, terrified lad made him over-confident. He swung his sword back as if relishing the prospect only to find Cenau had, out of sheer terror, run him right through. The Gwerin fell forward, wrenching the sword from Cenau's hand and knocking him over.

Scrambling to his feet, he slipped and felt a sharp pain in his leg. Crawling to a capstan for support, he fetched up against a body, recoiled, saw it was Maiv. Dazed, he shook her, but she would not wake, would not move. And he realized, then, she was dead, a hole in the back of her tunic, a dark pool of blood around her breast and neck.

For a moment it seemed the world was silent. And everything in it was wrong. This was Maiv. A great warrior. And a gentle soul. She had helped him. Shared bread with him. Walked many miles with him. Died protecting him. He leaned forward, kissed her brow, and took her sword from her hand.

Ignoring the pain, he stood. Ignoring the weight of the unfamiliar sword, he went berserk.

Perhaps the spirit of Maiv guided his arm, or maybe anger lent him finer senses, but he carved his way through the Gwerin and Occassans without mercy. Swinging and hacking, ignoring each body as it fell to move on to the next one and rend the life from it.

He knew nothing of it, became aware of the voice that was screaming, became aware that it was his own. It died as the fire in him died and he let the sword fall, exhausted, finding himself face to face with an Occassan who held a mosket, aimed directly at him. He was so close he could see into the barrel.

The sounds of battle had gone. All that could be heard were the groans and pleas of the wounded and dying. Cenau trembled, felt weak, felt sick. He wanted to crawl away and curl up in a dark place. But he could not because death stared him in the face.

'Put it down!' someone called. 'You cannot win.'

Cenau risked a quick glance to either side. It was the crew of the *Morfran* that seemed to be in command.

Another voice spoke. Quieter. Familiar. 'Don't forget where your feet should be.'

At first it seemed nonsensical. He knew where they should be. At the end of his legs. And that was when the battle-fog cleared enough for him to recognize the voice and understand.

The Occassan didn't see what happened and he didn't

live long enough for anyone to have time to explain it. Cenau slipped his left foot forward, twisted at the hip and swayed. Before the Occassan could react, Cenau had grasped the barrel of the weapon and completed the turn. The Occassan was thrown over Cenau's shoulder, the mosket going off, and as he hit the deck next to where the lead ball had buried itself in the timbers, he died on Aros's sword.

Cenau, his leg blazing with pain, sword cuts to a shoulder and thigh, his hand and cheek burned by the mosket firing so close to his face, staggered and fainted.

Chapter Thirty

The shore boat appeared at last. It pulled out of the little harbour, turned to meet the swell, and made slow headway toward the anchored vessels. Wrapped well against the cold, Jeniche stood alone with her thoughts and watched.

Before long, the first mate joined her. 'Best tell the others in case we need to move quickly.'

She turned, her left shoulder still stiff. 'I don't think any of us will be managing that for a while.'

He replied with a grim smile and a nod. Swivelling on his good foot, he stumped off across the deck using a make-shift crutch, going up the steps to the aft deck on his backside. The bandage on his wounded leg was showing blood again.

Jeniche went in the opposite direction and through the door that led beneath the foredeck. She peeked in on Cenau, but he was still asleep. She hoped he wasn't dreaming. The others sat in the larger cabin where there was a vestige of warmth.

'The shore boat is returning,' she said. 'The first mate

wants us ready in case we need to move straight away.'

Cynfelyn put down the whetstone he had been using on his sword and sheathed the heavily notched blade. He put it on his bunk and stood.

'Come on Aros, lad. Duald. We're nearly there and we need to get ourselves ready.'

Aros groaned, but he got up. Duald waited until Aros had shuffled past before standing, his left arm still in a sling. They all had aches, pains, cuts, and bruises; the worst of them inside. The deaths of Maiv, Awd, and Ruad had been particularly hard to take, cut down as they had been by mosket fire.

But Cynfelyn had not let the living rest too much. Aside from pitching in to man the *Morfran*, they had helped on the captured Gwerin ship, the *Colgan*, and spent time trying to get fighting fit again. If nothing else, there were deaths to be answered.

'Did you look in on Cenau?' asked Duald.

'He's still asleep.'

'Best place.'

It was a sentiment they shared.

The cold embraced them as they went out onto deck. The *Colgan* was drawing alongside and ropes were being thrown. How the remnants of the Ynyswr crew had managed both ships on the voyage back from Inissgar was a wonder to Jeniche. They would probably all much rather have sailed the *Morfran* back, put into port, and taken their chances to make their way home. But from the moment the first mate took command, they had worked without complaint and seemed set to see things through.

The idea weighed heavily on Cynfelyn. He had not spoken much since the battle had ended. The Gwerin and Occassan survivors had been put on board the ship wrecked by the maelstrom and the first mate had commandeered the *Colgan*. His plan had been to fire it at sea, but Cynfelyn had persuaded him to bring it along. If the Gwerin had taken Ynysvron, a Gwerin ship might get them ashore where one from Ynysvron would not.

They had gathered their dead and sailed out on the next slack water. Even as they were leaving they could hear fighting break out on the crippled Gwerin ship, saw Occassan bodies being thrown overboard.

The Ynyswr tended their wounded as best their resources and skill allowed; their dead were buried at sea as their tales were told and their praises were sung. It had taken a long time. Each of their names had since been carved on a panel by the steps to the foredeck. Two more died on the journey back and others would never sail again. The only fate not decided was that of Cenau who slept below.

His physical wounds had been treated. The pus had been drained from the infected leg of which he had barely complained. The burns to his hand and cheek were healing. The cuts he had received as he had hewn his way through the Gwerin and Occassan attackers in a berserk fury were knitting. There would doubtless be torn and bruised muscles. None of this worried his companions.

It was the wounds in his mind for which they held a sombre vigil. He had slept most of the time since collapsing. The few moments he had been awake, he had barely been present; mindful enough to sip and swallow broth before collapsing back into sleep. There was no knowing if his mind was broken or whether he would wake without any memories of what happened. Either was possible.

Worse, perhaps, would be for him to wake with full

knowledge of what he had done. That might break him in other ways.

'No one should be a warrior against their calling,' Cynfelyn had said to Jeniche as they had carried Cenau from the surgeon's bloody table to his bed.

It had sounded like he was apologizing to her as much as he was to Cenau.

The shore boat came alongside and the crew climbed on deck. There was no joy in their faces and it was clear without a word being spoken that Ynysvron had fallen. They followed the men to the first mate's cabin and crowded into the small space.

'After Dunvran fell – it was a massacre they say – they took on the tribes one by one. There wasn't time to form alliances. They either fell or capitulated. Santach is expected in Gwydr if he's not already there.'

'What of the *Morgi* or the *Morlwch* or any of the others?'

The crewman shook his head. 'They've seen none of the sea fleet here. But it's a small port.'

'Are we too late, then?' asked Aros. 'Could we still raise an army?'

Cynfelyn shook his head. 'I wouldn't inflict more bloodshed on the people.'

'We give up then?' There was deep anger in Aros's quiet question.

Cynfelyn looked at him for a moment, although his eyes were clearly seeing something else a long way away. When they came back into focus, he smiled. It was a tired smile, but there was a spark there of something fierce and implacable. 'No,' he replied, his voice just as quiet. 'Never. But we take the fight directly to Santach. Remove the head from the body. Burn whatever remains to cleanse it of the parasites.'

They stood at the railing of the *Colgan*, watching as the *Morfran* was towed into harbour. The townsfolk had agreed to accept it for safekeeping, with its sails, ropes, and supplies in payment for looking after the wounded crew. They had not been bothered by the Gwerin, but they knew it was only a matter of time. There were even volunteers, young men from the fishing fleet who wanted to crew the *Colgan*.

There had been a long argument about whether Cenau should be put ashore. Cynfelyn wanted him out of harm's way. The local Derw was a good healer and would be able to look after the young scholar. Aros had not wanted to let him go. He argued that Cenau should not wake amongst strangers, that he was integral to the group and had earned the right to see the journey through to whatever end.

'And if that end is bloody?' Cynfelyn had asked. 'Are you prepared to take the responsibility?'

Jeniche had stayed out of it. She agreed with both of them. It was one of the reasons she had always worked alone, travelled alone. Fewer complications. And no one to blame but yourself.

In the end, the first mate had intervened and made them decide. He had talked with fisherman from the port and knew that if they wanted to catch the tide at the other end, they should leave now. So it was that as they watched the *Morfran* enter port, the sails were set and they got under way.

'That,' said a frail voice behind them, 'looks just like the *Morfran*.'

Standing by the cabin door was Cenau, wrapped in blankets. His feet were bare and his face was pale, cheeks hollow, hair a mess. And there was a shadow in his eyes.

Aros stepped across the deck. 'You should be in bed.'

'I'm hungry. Where are we? What's going on?'

Aros took a deep breath. 'Come on, back into the cabin. We'll get you fed first.'

Cynfelyn exchanged a worried look with Jeniche and followed them inside. Jeniche stayed on deck. It was just the four of them now. Duald had put ashore with letters and the book they had found on the island. The fight had gone out of him. He would travel north and east to Pengaver in the hope the island of the Derw was untouched. There were stories to be told, no matter what happened in the next few days, not least of Ruad and Maiv and Awd.

With the others inside, Jeniche lowered her weary body into a sheltered spot in the sun and listened to the sounds of the new ship. She had not been anything like as seasick on the return journey, although she longed for dry land. And as she drifted on the shores of sleep she wondered if the soil of Ynysvron would contain her grave. You can only put yourself in harm's way for so long.

The sky grew grey and the winds rose as the days passed. It did not get too stormy, but they had a rough time of it rounding the Tircantef Point and heading into the channel that would take them, eventually, to Gwydr. Gusty winds chased them all the way, teasing them with sudden hailstorms and flurries of snow.

Cenau didn't stop eating. The galley kept him supplied first with broth and then with thicker soups. In between he chewed on bread and cheese and strips of dried meat. Aros and Cynfelyn rubbed his sore muscles with liniment, all the time watching him warily.

A day out of Gwydr, as the sky darkened toward night, he lay in his bunk. Aros sat at the end, Cynfelyn was perched on a stool, and Jeniche was wedged into a corner sitting on a folded blanket on the floor. They had been talking softly of nothing in particular when Cenau sat up.

'What happened to Maiv's sword?'

The silence was absolute. Even Cenau stopped breathing for a moment.

'I remember what happened. I remember it all.'

'And?' prompted Cynfelyn.

'I regret every life taken.'

There was another long pause. It was clear he had more to say.

'It will haunt me until the light goes from my eyes. And I know I must meet them all in the Otherworld.'

He paused again, a frown on his face, a touch of fear.

Aros reached out and laid a hand on one of his shins. 'Maiv will meet you there as well. And the others.'

The frown cleared.

'The Gwerin brought the fight to me,' Cenau's voice shook. 'And I will defend the Land with whatever methods are used to despoil her; I will defend the people with whatever weapon comes to my hand.'

Nobody spoke. There was nothing to be said. Cenau wiped the tears from his eyes and stared at the cabin wall. Cynfelyn slipped through the door and returned soon afterwards with a long roll of cloth. He unwrapped it and laid Maiv's sword beside Cenau.

The young scholar sighed and laid a trembling hand on the hilt. 'And what of Cleddyf?'

'The Guardian's sword was found a long time ago. It is safe and will be there when it is needed.'

During the following day, it began to snow in earnest. They reduced sail and crawled up the channel to Gwydr against the tide, knowing it would turn to carry them in as night fell. With luck the gloom would keep prying eyes from seeing that the proper crew were not on board. It would be a close thing.

The channel alongside Gwydr was thick with ships at anchor, mostly from Gwerin. Shore boats plied back and forth to the port as the water there was too shallow for large vessels to tie up. It gave the seat of the Guardians access to the sea, but made an assault from that direction difficult.

Choosing a spot close to a small group of Ynyswr fishing boats, the first mate ordered the anchor dropped. No one approached the vessel, although curious eyes from the closest fishing boat watched them as they made secure and rigged for the night.

'I think a trip across might be of use,' said the first mate to Cynfelyn. 'We wouldn't want any rumours to get around about the crew of the *Colgan*.'

As one of the *Colgan*'s shore boats set out, Cynfelyn went to the opposite rail. Through the snow, he could just make out the shape of the hills on which Gwydr was built; see lanterns and torches flickering small in the winter darkness.

Chapter Thirty-One

It was cold inside the ramshackle hut, not least because the door was open. The frosty air was debilitating. Even when the door was closed, the fire struggled against the chill that found its way through cracks and gaps to plague them with a thousand sharp draughts.

Dwellings were not allowed outside the walls of the town and the structure was no doubt passed off as a store of some kind, but it had clearly once been lived in. Unless the fisherman who owned it kept his nets on bunks.

'Close the door, Aros. He won't get back any quicker.'

Cenau, shivering by the fire, didn't expect any response. He'd said it a dozen times already and knew what the answer was. And he knew it wouldn't get much warmer. The firewood was poor stuff scavenged from the shanty town and beach at night when it was easier to avoid the Gwerin patrols and no one would recognize them as strangers.

'Here he comes,' said Aros, stepping inside.

He took off the rag of a cloak he was wearing and draped it round Cenau. Cynfelyn came sweeping in and dumped the sack he was carrying by the fire. He held his hands over the sparse flame to try to warm them. The door scraped over the packed earth and rattled into the frame. Jeniche wedged it in place with a stone.

'No shortage of food yet,' Cenau said, peering into the sack.

'It was a good year,' said Cynfelyn, 'but with all these extra mouths to feed...'

He didn't need to say any more. They all knew who would get the food if there were shortages. Unless something was done.

Aros put more wood on the fire and Cynfelyn eventually settled, taking his share of the meal and eating in silence. It grew marginally warmer and Cenau began to relax. This was their second day ashore but he was still struggling to escape the bleak netherworld of a shattered conscience where principles and pragmatism fought to find common ground. Sitting around in a hovel whilst Cynfelyn sought a way into Gwydr, waiting all the while for Gwerin soldiers to burst in, had done nothing to ease his body or his spirit.

Aros was the same to a lesser degree although he did not carry the extra burdens of Cenau. The world beyond Pengaver had been hard, but he had at least been expecting what came his way.

'Well?' asked Jeniche.

Cynfelyn shook his head. 'I've been all round, now. The only way in is through the main gates down here. The inland gate is permanently closed.'

'I take it they're still searching everyone?'

'They are, Aros. They've got it down to a fine art.'

'And is Santach in there?'

Cynfelyn shrugged. 'Rumour says he is. Rumour says he

is still at Anclaer.' He laughed. 'I even heard one old fisherman claim he was skulking out on a Gwerin ship called the *Colgan* that slipped in two days ago. One thing is for certain. He wants a coronation on the winter solstice.'

'No,' said Cenau. 'We have the crown. If anyone is to wear it, it will be Aros.'

There was such conviction in his voice that just for a few moments they knew it would be so. And then the reality of their situation returned. The country was overrun with Gwerin soldiers. There were Occassans in the heart of Ynysvron. Cynfelyn's plan was reduced to four exhausted, haunted people sitting in a hovel around a fire that struggled against the cold.

'Have any of the crew had any better luck?' asked Jeniche, more to break the silence than in any expectation of good news.

'A couple of them got into the lower town. They said it's like everyone is preparing for a funeral.'

Unsurprisingly they lapsed back into silence. Cynfelyn, who had been on his feet all day, curled up on the floor and tried to sleep. The others stared gloomily into the fitful flames.

When they woke, Cenau had gone.

'How did he get through that door without waking anyone?' asked Aros, hefting the stone wedge in his hand.

'He's displaying a lot of talents no one suspected he had,' replied Cynfelyn.

'Let's hope they don't get him killed before he can put them to use,' added Jeniche.

'You'd better stay here,' said Cynfelyn as he crossed to the door. 'You're too obviously you. And someone should be here to slap the back of his legs if he gets back before we find him.'

He and Aros slipped out into the dark while Jeniche tried to coax life out of the fire. When she'd done what she could, she sat facing the door with one of her swords across her knees.

Outside, the odd flake of snow fell, pricking against their faces. A crescent moon played peekaboo between the broken clouds. They both wore old blankets as cloaks, their swords as much out of sight as possible. The Gwerin patrolled day and night, clearly wary of the possibility of an uprising even now.

Cynfelyn led the way down to the quays, keeping to the deep shadow of alleyways. It was soon clear there was no one there but Gwerin soldiers who stamped their feet and dreamed of warm beds. The waters were still and quiet with just the occasional flicker of a lantern on board one of the ships at anchor out in the channel.

From the waterfront, they made their way through the maze of sheds and warehouses, boatyards and fish stores, net lofts and subdued taverns to the main road to the south.

Gwydr was approached by two roads. The inland road that curved northward and went first to Anclaer was heavily guarded and closed to Ynyswr – hence the rumours of Santach's whereabouts. The road to the south remained open, although that was also closely watched.

Despite the weather and the presence of an occupying army, people still had to travel. Goods were brought to the town. People came to trade. The solstice was approaching and, the gloomy atmosphere notwithstanding, people would honour the turning of the year and the rebirth of the sun. At night, however, travel was pointless. Not only was it cold, but the gates of Gwydr were closed. Anyone arriving now would likely be found frozen to the road in the morning.

They went anyway, all the way to the last building on the town side of the river where the bridge keeper lived with his family. From there they could see more than a mile along the road before it curved behind a slight rise.

At risk of being seen, they flitted silently across the frost-pale road to the other side and followed the shadows, scouring every alley, compound, and pile of fishing gear along the way, right up to the main gates of the town.

Here there were more guards. They had commandeered a small barn, stripped it of the animal feed stored there, and turned it into a barracks. A low rumble of voices could be heard from within and a brazier could be seen glowing through the part-open door.

In the gloom, Aros and Cynfelyn looked at each other and shrugged. Unless they had missed him and he was now back with Jeniche, Cenau had vanished. Waiting for the guard to complete his token walk across the front of the gates before returning to the warmth of the hut's doorway, Aros heard a sound. He touched Cynfelyn's shoulder.

The guard had heard it as well. He stood listening, unaware of the presence of two Ynyswr warriors standing within sword reach. He had just shaken his head when the sound came again. A faint, dull scrabbling, something scraping against a substantial wooden structure.

Aros saw it first. A foot, high up on the wall beside the gate, searching for a toehold. He pointed it out to Cynfelyn and then disappeared into shadow. Cynfelyn held his breath. Even in the dark, he recognized the scruffy boot; crouched ready to tackle the guard if he should think to look upwards.

That was when there came another sound. A scrabbling

on wood. Not unlike the first, but from the direction of the next alley.

The guard turned away from the gate and peered in that direction. He didn't look worried as he passed Cynfelyn, more like someone glad of a bit of distraction from a boring task. Swivelling his head back, Cynfelyn saw another boot appear, held his breath, heard the faint mew of a cat.

The guard moved further away, squeaking between his lips. Cynfelyn shook his head. He was surrounded by fools.

Cenau dropped suddenly and hung the full length of his arms for a second before letting go and falling to the grassy bank at the base of the town wall. It was anything but elegant, or quiet, but he had the good sense to roll with the fall. He fetched up with a crash against the wall of the shack opposite the temporary guardhouse.

Cynfelyn grabbed the collar of his coat and hauled him off into the darkness as guards came bursting out into the cold. Eyes blinded by lamplight, it took them several seconds to get their bearings and organize themselves, by which time there was nothing there. Aros was lying on the roof of a nearby workshop and Cynfelyn was running as quickly and as quietly as he could with Cenau under one arm, his other hand clamped roughly over the young scholar's mouth.

Cynfelyn had been beyond angry. Shadowed by Aros, he had carried a struggling Cenau all the way back to their hut and dumped him by the fire. When Aros had come in moments later, he had gone to Cenau, checked over his grazes, made sure none of his older injures had opened up, and then sat beside Cynfelyn to add his own angry stare.

Cenau refused to be cowed. He stood, shook off some dust, sorted out his clothing, made himself comfortable, and

sat down again. Jeniche had to hide a smile as Cenau then
began searching through the food sack for something to eat.

'You do a very good cat, Aros,' he said when he'd finished
a piece of bread and washed it down with some thin wine.

Jeniche looked baffled. 'What's going on?'

'We caught this little toad climbing out of the town.'

'What?'

'Right by the guard post.'

Cenau's hand went up to his mouth. 'I didn't realize. I
thought I was further round. There's no one on guard on
the inside. And it was dark.'

'How in the name of all the gods and goddesses did you
get inside in the first place?' Cynfelyn hissed, trying to be
angry quietly.

'When you lot were snoring, I heard something.'

'Don't be cryptic. This isn't a seminar.'

'Someone singing.'

'Who?'

'I wasn't sure at first,' said Cenau, refusing to tell it in
any way but his own. 'That's why I went out to see.'

'I can guess,' said Aros. 'Look at the smile on his face.'

'Are you sure this is going to work?' She looked at her
hands, squinted into the mirror.

'It's only meant to be seen from a distance,' said Caru,
dusting make-up powder from her hands. 'You'll have to
stay in the wagon.'

Cynfelyn was staring in at her, trying not to laugh.

Gwynfor peered in as well. 'Excellent,' he said. 'Now let's
get all that ironmongery hidden.'

Inside the wagon, Caru lifted a mattress and set about
sliding several pieces of wood. A latch clicked and one of

the flooring planks came loose. When it was lifted a shallow compartment lined with fleece was revealed. The underside of the plank was also lined.

'Stops things rattling,' said Caru, placing Jeniche's swords into hiding.

'Simple players?' she asked.

Caru poked out the tip of her tongue. 'We sometimes need somewhere to hide our takings. Now let's get this looking like it was.'

While they were getting Jeniche settled into her role as Caru's grandmother, the others were outside helping Gwynfor with other hiding places. The wagon was parked outside a wheelwright's workshop and the bed had been stripped of its barrels, pieces of stage, and other boxes and attachments. Whilst the wheels were being removed and axles greased, swords were being slid into convenient hiding places.

Once they were safely hidden, the crown and the chalice were put into the props basket and Gwyan was fitted with a lantern that hid the spearhead. Costumes were produced and Aros and Cenau were kitted out as fools, whilst Cynfelyn was given the traditional garb of a villain.

As they were dressing, Cenau whispered to Cynfelyn: 'What of Cleddyf?'

'Don't worry, lad. The sword will be waiting, just as I promised. Has been waiting. For a long time.'

The anger of the previous evening had been forgotten. They had spent a restless night waiting for the dawn, eager to see their friends again, gather the news. Cenau had told them some of it. Of how he had heard Caru singing and gone out to see whether or not it was a dream. Of how he had ridden into the town with the players just as the gates were being closed.

295

Rumbling along to the wheelwright, Gwynfor had explained: 'We travelled safely all the way to Porthmawr. More and more people were heading for whatever boats were available. Prices were scandalous. And the longer we stayed there, waiting for safe passage, the better seemed the news. I have no love for the Gwerin or what they have done, but Ynysvron seemed to have rolled over and accepted its fate. Apart from one or two places where fighting persisted, the countryside seemed safe. We talked it over for two days and then decided to go back and get the wagons. It is our country, after all, and we did not see why we should flee.'

'But what made you come here?' Aros had asked.

Gwynfor had shrugged. 'We have spent the winter solstice at Gwydr every year since Caru was born. Besides, if anything was going to happen, it was going to happen here. And Caru insisted.'

They had looked down then at Caru and Cenau walking side by side.

Now they were dressed up and ready to go.

'There's still time to change your mind,' said Cynfelyn. 'If they discover what is going on, your lives will be as forfeit as ours.'

'We might just be players, but this is our land and we have made our choice.'

Gwynfor pulled the gold piece and the token from his purse and handed them back to Cynfelyn. With that, they rode along the main road through the shanty town to the main gate of Gwydr, calling out the entertainments they would be putting on during the solstice festival. The guards searched the wagon thoroughly, laughing at the sharp tongue of the old woman who would not be moved. They took off everything that was not fixed and looked inside, tapped everything that wouldn't move to sound for hiding places, just as they had the day before. And when they had finished, the whole merry troupe rode slowly up into the heart of Ynysvron, a heart held firmly in the grasp of the Gwerin warlord, Santach.

Chapter Thirty-Two

Jeniche was going mad. Slowly. Surely.

She had been stuck in the wagon for several days now, creeping out only in the dead of night to wash and to exercise. Everyone else had been busy. The players sang, juggled, and put on shows. Cynfelyn disappeared on mysterious errands or huddled in a corner by the brazier talking to people as he pretended to read their fortunes. Goodness knows what he told genuine customers.

Aros and Cenau had vanished altogether. Cynfelyn had them hidden somewhere out of harm's way. She hoped for their sake it was warmer than the wagon.

In the end, she took to sleeping.

The days passed and despite the reluctance of the native population to accept the invaders as new rulers, Gwydr filled with people. It soon became clear that surrounding villages had been visited by troops of Gwerin soldiers, each with its complement of Occassans, who had offered a stark choice. Join the celebrations for the winter solstice coronation of Santach as Guardian of Ynysvron or watch their village burn.

The day before the solstice, Jeniche was woken from a doze by someone banging on the side of the wagon. Heart thumping, she pushed aside her blanket, ready to spring.

'What is it?' called Gwynfor. Jeniche guessed he must have been doing a bit of fortune telling in place of Cynfelyn.

An unfamiliar voice said: 'You in charge here?'

'I am.'

'You're wanted.'

Peering through a gap in the canvas, Jeniche saw Gwynfor following a Gwerin soldier. Gwynfor turned and waved someone back. He did not look too worried and the soldier had his sword firmly sheathed.

Cynfelyn appeared shortly afterwards and poked his head through the canvas.

'Time to get ready,' he said.

'What's going on?' asked Jeniche. 'What have you been up to?'

'If the right strings have been pulled, tomorrow's solstice feast will have a traditional entertainment provided by Gwynfor's Players.'

'We're going up to the Great Hall?'

Cynfelyn nodded. Since they had arrived in Gwydr there had been talk and planning and trying to find ways to strike at Santach. Now, one of those plans was falling into place and the strain showed on Cynfelyn's face. They were going to take the wagons up into the heavily fortified inner sanctum, take their costumes and props into the Great Hall and there perform in front of Santach and the massed ranks of the Gwerin commanders. And then the four of them would try to topple an entire army.

'And Gwynfor knows? He's agreed?'

'They all have. They crossed the line just by bringing us

299

into Gwydr.' Cynfelyn looked at her, his eyes searching. 'It's not your fight—'

'Don't even dare suggest it,' she said. 'I have friends to stand by and scores to settle. And this seems as good a land as any to die for. If I must die.'

Cynfelyn reached a hand into the wagon and touched her cheek with his fingertips. 'Thank you,' he said.

'But the Occassans are not getting their hands on this.' She pulled the pendant out from under her clothing and slipped it over her head. Her hands trembled slightly.

Gwydr was built on three hills. The main part of the town sprawled across the largest of the three and was enclosed by a ditch and mound topped by a wooden palisade. Around the southern end of this on a low rise that many would not honour with the name of 'hill' was the shanty town that had grown alongside the waterfront. The third and highest hill, to the north, stood with its feet in water and marsh and was topped by the citadel, traditional seat of the Guardian of Ynysvron.

The town was the nearest thing Ynysvron had to a capital; the citadel, the nearest it had to a palace. Ditches and mounds. Another wooden palisade. Watchtowers. All this enclosed a space that housed stables and sleeping quarters for the Guardian's bodyguard; workshops; smithies; armouries; kitchens; and in the centre, the huge Great Hall. It had all been empty for a long time, half-heartedly maintained against a day few thought would ever come again and certainly never under the present circumstances.

In recent weeks, the Gwerin had pressed locals into refurbishing the hall ready for the coronation of their leader. A steady stream of artisans and skivvies had travelled in and out of the citadel. Repairing, sweeping, tidying, grooming horses, carrying in supplies, cooking, they had worked under the increasingly bored eyes of the guards. Had they been more alert, the guards might have noticed that some of the artisans were making lantern poles from yew that looked remarkably like bows, whilst others were sifting through the bundles of kindling to choose the straightest shafts; that workers' tools were being transformed into weapons; that more people were coming into the citadel than were leaving.

The players' wagons were driven in under guard and they were immediately conscious of the overwhelming number of Gwerin soldiers. The workshops were busy, the stables lit with lanterns, the kitchens gave off heat and filled the air with delicious smells. And everywhere they looked were Gwerin uniforms.

Under the direction of an ostler, they parked the wagons in a corner to one side of the gates. Everything they needed to take in for their entertainment was carefully inspected: the lantern they would use to represent the sun was checked to make sure it contained nothing of danger; the wooden swords had each blade tapped and tested for bluntness; and their costumes were gone through in search of secret pockets.

They changed there under the eyes of the guards who were blissfully unaware of how easy a stage magician finds it to misdirect the eye and swap things in plain view. All the same, they were each of them stretched to the limit of their nerves as they were led up the steps to the doors of the hall.

If the courtyard had tested their resolve, walking into the brightly lit hall weakened many a knee. The heat was stifling and the noise, already heard from outside, was tremendous. Everyone seated at a table toward the far end was talking loudly. Everyone seated near the doors was muted or silent. Everyone dashing hither and yon with platters and flagons was keeping their mouths shut and heads down.

It took a moment to work it all out, by which time it was far too late to back out. They passed between the tables where subdued Ynyswr chieftains and tribal elders were crammed in with their Derw. A silent insult. Behind them in the shadows stood Gwerin soldiers to make sure they did nothing but sit and eat.

A perceptible gap separated them from the ranks of Gwerin commanders and warriors who had earned their place before their warlord. They had more room and were enjoying themselves mightily. The drink was already flowing freely and the feast had barely begun.

It was between these tables that a space had been cleared for the entertainers. As Gwynfor and his troupe approached, a group of acrobats went cartwheeling through them to the door, sporadic table banging showing at least some approval.

Beyond the empty space was the dais. Behind his own table, Santach sat in the centre. He was flanked solely by a dozen senior Occassans who sat at long, upper tables. Behind them stood a formidable-looking bodyguard armed with moskets. Jeniche looked at Cynfelyn. His face was bleak, but he managed a wink.

Santach surprised Jeniche. In those last few moments she wasn't sure what she had expected, but this mild-featured man was not it. But he did not need to be a monster. Ordinary men were capable of the worst. Her hands were cold and she shivered. Cenau beside her looked as if he might be sick.

Gwynfor gave a perfunctory bow in the direction of the dais and turned to the players. 'Positions,' he said.

302

They spread out into an arc, with the players at either end flanking Aros who carried the lantern, Cenau and Jeniche who were both cloaked and hooded, and finally Cynfelyn, dressed in the old clothes that represented the dying year.

Nobody paid them any attention until Santach leaned forward a fraction. Silence was almost immediate and that alone was enough to convince anyone who doubted just how powerful the Gwerin Warlord was.

When every eye was on him, Santach stood and made his way round the table to stand on the edge of the dais where everyone could see him clearly. He smiled but there was no warmth there.

'For too long,' he said quietly, 'Ynysvron has been divided. Tribe against tribe. Bandits roaming unchecked.'

Jeniche could feel Cenau shaking with anger.

'It grieved us to hear of such strife. Almost daily Ynyswr came to our shores to plead for help. What could I do? It was not my land.'

Santach put on a pose as if thinking what he could do to help the poor, disorganized Ynyswr.

'I took counsel.' One of the Occassans leered. 'In the end I could not see the people suffer any longer at the hands of those who would not act.'

Jeniche struggled to make sense of that, decided it was pointless trying.

'At the invitation of the people and with the aid of our good friends the Occassans, we came to bring peace. The fighting is done. Now we must stay to rebuild the land and see it whole.'

Cenau could take no more. He stepped forward.

'Don't try to think like a soldier,' whispered Jeniche, and she heard Cynfelyn say the same.

The silence became absolute as people realized someone was daring to interrupt the Warlord.

Casting back his hood, Cenau took a deep breath to calm himself.

'This land will reject you and yours,' he said, for all the world as if he were passing the time of day with a friend. 'And if you try to force her, she will wither and drag you and yours down into disease and starvation. This curse I lay.'

The gathering was too stunned to say or do anything.

Cenau undid the clasp of his cloak and let it fall, revealing Maiv's sword on his hip. One or two of the Occassans smirked at the sight of such a pale, skinny lad with a warrior's sword.

'The people of this land,' continued Cenau, 'will reject you and yours, for they have a Guardian who has come here this day to take his place.'

Santach laughed. There was no warmth there, either. 'This is a dangerous joke, boy.'

Aros stepped up beside Cenau.

'It is no joke,' said Cynfelyn.

Moskets were raised and aimed. They could hear Gwerin soldiers behind them fidgeting to get out of the line of fire.

Cynfelyn stepped up behind Aros. 'I, Cynfelyn ap Emrys, Pen Derw of Ynysvron, stand before this assembly with the Four Hallows—'

'It will only take a word,' interrupted Santach, the cold smile still on his face, eyes flicking with contempt over Cynfelyn's dirty, torn clothing and the hole in the toe of his boot.

'Then we will all die.'

The smile faded, eyes flicking uncertainly. Jeniche wanted to turn and stare up into the deep shadows in the rafters of the building where a company of Ynyswr archers had hidden and from whence came the faint but distinctive creak of many bow strings.

'Show us these baubles then from your actor's basket,' he said, looking from Cenau to Aros. 'And dress up these two children you have been preparing.'

Cynfelyn did not need to go to the basket. He raised high the crown that was already in his hands and lowered it towards Aros's head. From the back of the hall came a whispered wave of sound: 'Carreg', as the Ynyswr seated there saw the dark circlet.

With the crown in place, Cynfelyn reached up and flicked the lantern from the top of its pole to reveal Gwyan. And with a quickness of hand that impressed the petrified Gwynfor, he produced Crochan and stood with it held high.

'A king without a sword,' mocked Santach. 'And crowned in front of his well-armed enemies.'

Santach raised his hand and the air was filled with arrows. By the time he turned to look for cover, not a single Occassan was left alive. A great roar went up by the main doors and Santach turned back in time to see Cynfelyn hold aloft Cleddyf before handing it to Aros.

The players leapt into action. In a matter of seconds, three of the Hallows had disappeared, along with cloaks and anything else that might encumber Aros, Cenau, and Jeniche, who drew both her swords.

Gwerin soldiers were trying to get up from their tables and defend their Warlord, only to find their legs tangled in rope. Someone threw a sword to Santach that clattered on the dais. He scooped it up and jumped down to meet Aros, anger and desperation channelled by skill beating back the newly crowned Guardian.

Aros was taken by surprise. The idea had been for Cynfelyn, Jeniche, and Cenau to keep a space clear for the two to fight it out. The Hallows were all very well, but the new Guardian had to prove his worth. But it began to go wrong very quickly.

A staggering Gwerin threw himself at Aros's feet and brought him down. Jeniche was closest, but before she could block Santach's path he was on Aros, swinging his sword down in a killing blow. Aros, remembering the lessons he had learned from Jeniche, kicked and rolled. Santach's blade bit deep into the back of the Gwerin's neck, killing him instantly.

As Aros struggled to get out from under the dead weight, Cenau and Jeniche put themselves in Santach's way. Cenau went down almost immediately, Maiv's sword clattering on the floor, blood pouring from a wound as he lay still on the boards amongst piles of fruit, half-eaten loaves, and fragments of pie.

Jeniche was not such an easy prospect and her two swords began nicking Santach's flesh, keeping him at bay until Aros climbed back to his feet. He managed to say: 'See to Cenau,' before blocking a swing at his legs.

Turning, Jeniche saw the entire Great Hall had erupted. The archers had gone from the roof beams and she saw several in the doorway loosing arrows into the courtyard. Hand-to-hand combat was taking place around, over and possibly under the tables. Cenau was no longer where he had fallen, a smeared trail of blood leading to one side of the Hall. There, behind an overturned table, she found Caru desperately trying to staunch the flow of blood from a thrust to his side.

Cynfelyn arrived just afterwards and between them they stripped off Cenau's tunic and wadded it against the wound.

'Go watch Aros's back,' said Cynfelyn.

Wiping blood from her hands, Jeniche picked up her swords, leapt a low sweep from a sword, to which she replied with a fatal thrust, and made her way back to where Aros fought. Arrows sticking from his chest, a badly wounded Occassan lurched in front of her. He was big, in a frenzy of pain, swinging an axe he had found somewhere.

She slipped beneath a swing of the deadly axe and found the back of his left knee with the points of both blades. With a cry he went down, just as Santach did a neat twist with his sword to wrench Aros's blade from his hand. She heard Aros's wrist snap and saw the pain in his face as he fell.

Santach turned as if he expected applause, the cold smile back on his face, so he did not see Aros roll and come back to his feet with Maiv's blade in his left hand.

The smile on Santach's face became an 'O' of surprise and then a grimace of pain as hard, sharp steel pierced a kidney and pushed on through the stomach to emerge in front of his horrified eyes. He looked down at the bloody blade for a moment and then fell forwards. Dead.

Chapter Thirty-Three

The late afternoon sunshine was warm on her legs as she admired her new boots again. Honest boots; a gift from Aros. They had been specially made. Robust, yet supple. Thick-soled. Perhaps that should have been a clue.

A sweet breeze blew along the shingles on the stable roof where she lazed. The cuts and bruises had long since healed and she was beginning to feel once more that she was getting soft. Just for the moment, though, she didn't care.

From her vantage point she looked down onto the courtyard. It was amazing how much had changed since the solstice. All sign of the Gwerin and the Occassans had gone from Gwydr and the whole place was alive with a relaxed optimism that was matched perfectly by the early spring weather.

Cynfelyn appeared on the steps of the new Great Hall with Annys, the Derw he had slapped all those years ago so that he might be sent into exile. They talked a while, enjoying the sunshine as well. When they had finished, she kissed his cheek and went back inside. Cynfelyn remained basking in the glow, looking as if he owned the place and half the world as well.

Not long afterwards, Aros came riding through the gates followed by a small bodyguard. He dismounted and went up the steps. He still favoured his left hand, she noticed, even though his right wrist had healed. Annys would make sure he kept up his exercises to strengthen it.

The others dismounted as well and when Aros rejoined them, the horses were led in beneath where she lazed. She could hear the soldiers talking quietly, knew exactly what they were doing, where the harness was being hung. She thought of Trag. He would have loved it here. The Ynyswr were a people that venerated their horses.

It had been a long road since then. Friends made and altogether too many lost again. This journey had come to an end and as those below set out on new ones, she was left up here.

Someone laughed and she smiled. Caru stepped out from one of the small dwellings built up against the citadel wall. Cenau, holding onto her arm, walked slowly beside her. Of them all, he had given most worry and even now he was weak, but he was in good hands. She watched as they crossed the courtyard and sat on a bench beside an older couple, Cenau's parents. Jeniche rested her head back on her folded jacket and, content that all was well with her world, closed her eyes and dozed.

She woke with a start and sat up. The sun had set and the bleached blue sky carried the first stars of the coming night. The breeze now carried a reminder that there was still snow on the hilltops. She put on her jacket and climbed down, crossing the yard to where she could hear laughter, to where wonderful smells of cooking filled the air.

They had taken to eating their evening meal together in one of the kitchens, just as they had in those first days after the battle. Jeniche treasured those times. Laughter. Good food. Friends. And somewhere safe to sleep afterwards. That night she drank it in just as the camels she had once ridden stored water before a long trek across the desert.

Like a shadow she slipped out of her small room above the stables and across the courtyard. The gates of the citadel always stood open now and she went out into the main part of the town. From a barrel painted with the mark of the Derw that stood beside a pile of building materials, she retrieved her swords and pack. The smell of fresh sawn timber filled the air where rebuilding was still going on. The battle in the Great Hall had spilled out onto the streets and down to the harbour. Houses and workshops had burned and most of the Gwerin fleet had been set ablaze where it was anchored, pitch daubed on the hulls from small boats in the dark and set alight at a signal from the shore. The Great Hall, fouled with the blood of invaders, had been torn down and rebuilt from the foundations.

The dead had been buried and honoured; prisoners shipped off across the Gwerin Sea and allowed to swim ashore. Occasionally word would come of an Occassan, but those that had survived the slaughter were few and far between. Where fighting men could be spared the Occassans were hunted without mercy for the memory of the thousands they had massacred at Dunvran.

'Slipping off again?'

She stopped and turned, searching the shadow between buildings. Cynfelyn stepped forward.

'Nothing much here for me, now.'

'Not even Aros?'

She knew Cynfelyn was teasing. That was one of the things she would miss.

'No,' she said and turned to look back up the hill to the citadel and the nearly completed new Great Hall. 'He has another and she will keep him busy. And happy.'

'That is true. It will be years, if ever, before he can relax. Same as Cenau. They have done so well, beyond anything I could have hoped for.'

'Do you think it was all worth it?'

'We did what we thought was best. It was this or generations of servitude ending in...' He shrugged. 'Who knows? There's still a lot to do.' He paused and sighed. 'All the same, I still worry about inflicting all that on them.'

'At least they'll have you to keep an eye on them.'

Cynfelyn said nothing, looked up at the sky where stars burned. Jeniche, out of habit, touched the pendant where it lay beneath her clothing.

'You dug that up again?'

'Are you changing the subject?'

He laughed softly and stepped back into the shadows. When he reappeared, his sword was hanging from his belt and he was struggling to get his pack comfortable on his back.

'I've done what I set out to do all those years ago. It's their world now. They won't be alone,' he said. 'I stepped down from the Council today. Annys was elected Pen Derw in my place. She will see them right.'

Jeniche set off down the main street, her sadness at leaving now much muted as Cynfelyn fell in beside her.

'Does she know?'

'That my feet won't keep still? Yes. Have you told anyone?'

'I've left letters.'

No one paid them any attention as they strolled through the south gate and past the waterfront.

'They'll say you've run off with that good-looking young woman from foreign parts,' she said.

'Two out of three,' he replied.

She threw a punch, the knuckles making contact.

'Where were you thinking of going?' he asked, still rubbing his arm as they crossed the bridge and headed south.

'Somewhere warm,' she said. 'And dry.'

A Guide To Pronunciation

The Ynyswr have an ancient and complex language known as Ketic in which the pronunciation is not always obvious from the spelling. Here is a handy guide to help you pronounce the names in the text correctly.

Addas – *Ath-as*
Aderyn – *Add-erin*
Anclaer – *An-clare*
Annys – *Ann-ees*
Aros – *A-ross*
Awd – *Ord*
Banadd Corrach – *Ban-ath Core-ack*
Bradan – *Brath-an*
Brocel – *Bro-kell*
Bron – *Brown*
Carreg – *Kar-reg*
Caru – *Ka-roo*
Celydon – *Kelly-don*
Cenau – *Ken-awe*
Cleddyf – *Cleth-iv*
Colgan – *Coal-can*
Comyn – *Kom-in*
Crochan – *Krok-an*
Cumran – *Coom-ran*

Cynfelyn ap Emrys – *Kine-vellin ab Em-reece*
Cysgodion – *Kis-god-eeon*
Daearyddiaeth – *Day-are-ith-ee-aye-eth*
Dun – *Doon*
Dunvran – *Doon-fran*
Durm – *Derm*
Derw – *Deroo*
Derw Hyn – *Deroo Hin*
Eithrig – *Aye-thrig*
Enfys – *En-viss*
Eog – *Ee-og*
Feoras – *Vay-o-rass*
Fidchell – *Fee-kull*
Greftwr – *Grev-toor*
Gwerin – *Gwe-rin*
Gwyan – *Gwee-an*
Gwydr – *Gwid-er*
Gwynfor – *Gwin-vor*
Ilar – *Eye-lar*
Inissgar – *In-ish-car*
Ketic – *Key-tic*
Madval – *Mad-fal*
Maelduin – *Male-dwin*
Maenmawr – *My-en-more*
Maiv – *Mave*
Maura – *Maw-ra*
Morfran – *More-vran*
Morgi – *More-guy*
Morlwch – *More-luke*
Morwyn – *More-win*
Nuala – *Noo-arla*
Pen Derw – *Pen Deroo*

Pengaver – *Pen-gaver*
Porthmawr – *Port-more*
Rhan – *Ran*
Rhonwen merch Sioned – *Ron-wen mark Shon-ed*
Santach – *Sarn-tack*
Savain – *Sar-fane*
Taid (grandfather) – *tayed*
Talfryn – *Tal-vrin*
Teague – *Tayg-ewe*
Tircantef – *Teer-can-tev*
Tirmawr – *Teer-more*
Trevisgol – *Tre-fis-koll*
Tymestl – *Tie-mestal*
Vran – *Fran*
Waltarian – *Wall-tarian*
Ynysvron – *Innis-fron*
Ynyswr – *Innis-oor*

Acknowledgements

It is important to recognise that no matter how reclusive (or grumpy) a writer might be, they do not work in a vacuum. A lot of people have intersected with my writing life and I am grateful for all the encouragement and wise words they have given so freely. Some, however, deserve especial thanks. Barbara, who keeps this world in order whilst I commit acts of mayhem in others; our cats, who commit mayhem in this world to ensure I sometimes take a break; Leslie Gardner, *agent extraordinaire*, who has faith in me, which is a commodity to be much treasured; Natasha, Rachel and Cherie, the Harper *Voyager* triumvirate who have turned my words into beautiful books; Michael Moorcock, who inspired the whole journey; Joanna Russ, who taught me a different perspective; and my good friend Susan Murray, who read early drafts of this and other Shadow in the Storm books with an ever astute eye.